JENNY'S DREAMS

A NOVEL

BY

Sylvia Ann McLain

BOOK THREE OF THE SPINNING JENNY SERIES

SPINNING JENNY:

(Noun)—A spinning machine of the nineteenth century, with multiple spindles, so that a spinner may spin several different yarns at the same time.

CHAPTER ONE

November 1843

THE DISTANCE FROM NATCHEZ to Vicksburg is seventy-two miles, a three-day trip; a long time for free people to be out on the road, especially since the rain that passed through earlier left glassy reflections of the late afternoon sky in all the ruts and gullies, and the road is soft as pudding. It's a hard pull for the horse, Dun; the buggy teeters and its wheels wobble, but Walker holds the reins tight. Sitting next to him, Jenny wonders if Dun can make the trip. She swaddles Rosabel in a shawl and holds her securely as the buggy tips and bounces over the ruts.

The road is busy with traffic: lone riders, young men with ambition in their faces; families in buggies much finer than theirs; farmers in overalls driving wagons with kids or slaves sitting in the back. Occasionally a slave raises a hand silently to acknowledge Jenny as their wagon passes; otherwise the travellers take little notice of her and Walker. She can almost make herself think that she, Walker, and Rosabel are just one more speck in the flow of humanity, a small black family in a dilapidated buggy missing its doors, its iron wheels rusty, pulled by a gimpy horse.

"Slavers might be out here," Jenny says, but the buggy lurches into a deep rut as soon as she says it and Walker pulls hard at the reins, so the comment is lost.

Rosabel sucks her thumb and watches the road with big eyes. The log cabins they pass look forlorn, wispy smoke drifting over the wet roofs and dim lamps burning in the windows. The air smells loamy and rich. They hear noises which Rosabel, a city child, isn't used to: a panther screeching in the swamp somewhere, an alligator hissing and clicking as it glides across some black bayou. Jenny knows these sounds; when she lived on Bayou Cocodrie with Cornelius and Malachi she heard them every night. She's glad she remembered to bring a sock doll for Rosabel; the child clasps it to her chest without looking at it, but Jenny knows it's a comfort to her when the animal sounds grow loud.

As the sun sets and the scene turns purple, the road gets narrower and vines and brambles reach out to scratch at the buggy. Walker drives the horse along the drier ridges in the road. Jenny watches the woods.

"I don't like bein' out on country roads in the dark," Jenny says as Rosabel whimpers.

"We got no choice if we gonna get to Vicksburg," he says. Without taking his eyes from the road he reaches over and takes her hand. "You okay?"

"I'm all right," she says.

"What you scared of?"

"Slave catchers could be out here. We got no business bein' on the road."

"We got as much business as anybody else," he says, but right then a white man with a wagon full of slaves drives past them. "Well, maybe we ain't got the right but we do have the business. There ain't no law says we got to hang 'round Carefree and wait for some ignorant sheriff to come for us."

"The only place I ever feel safe is Carefree," Jenny says, shifting Rosabel around.

"That right?" He frowns. "Why would that be?"

Because you don't know the things I've seen, she thinks. Walker's so much older than she is, and while he's seen a lot in his long life, she could tell him some things: how she sat in the Vidalia jail one night, thinking it was her last night on earth, until Cornelius burst in and freed her and set the sheriff on her tail. How she lived in New Orleans after her husband Adrien died, and took a chance on a sharp-faced woman, Margot, who moved in with her to be her midwife, her *sagefemme*; and then how Margot wasn't there when the baby came, so her friend Rosie delivered Rosabel, Rosie not knowing the first thing about bringing a baby into the world. How she rescued an Irish child, May, from the dock in New Orleans when no one came to meet the girl, and then brought May and Rosabel to Natchez because she knew Cornelius wouldn't turn them away. For a woman just twenty years old, she's done some big things.

Walker must be about forty, she guesses, and a man that old is bound to know way more things than Adrien knew, because Adrien was only eighteen and only knew enough to get himself killed in New Orleans. Walker's even older than Cornelius, so he probably knows more. Cornelius knows things too, she thinks, as much as she can understand a white man; but she doesn't think about him too much. Right now he's gone to Mrs. Landerson's funeral at Saint Mary's Church; he'll be surprised when he gets home and finds out she's gone.

Three hours ago Walker burst into the kitchen and said, "The new sheriff at Vidalia has your picture stuck up on his office wall, and he's gonna come for you. We gotta run." It was the first time she'd ever seen fear on Walker's face; he looked around the kitchen as if the sheriff's face might be at any window. So they left without even a goodbye to Cornelius.

Two years ago she came down this same road with Walker, going the other way, but he doesn't mention it. It was the day Cornelius freed her and bought her a steamer passage to Cincinnati, free soil. But Walker was on the boat and he talked her into getting off, because Cincinnati was full of slave-catchers, and she wouldn't be safe there. She's not feeling all that safe right now. Walker's warned her often enough about the country roads. If they had money, they could've bought tickets on a steamboat and made the trip to Vicksburg in a few hours, but between them they had only four dollars.

Walker keeps looking at the woods, jerking his head back and forth when he can take his eyes off the road, so Jenny looks too when she's not busy hanging onto Rosabel, who's restless and unhappy. Well, what child likes to be grabbed up and packed away from all that's familiar? And they're all tired.

When they pass Cemetery Town, it's the same shabby place Walker pointed out to her the last time they travelled this road: houses backing up to the cemetery fence, their saggy porches lining the road. Walker warned her about the boys who lived there and used to pelt him with slingshots whenever he passed this way. But there aren't any boys out right now, which she's glad to see. Dun trots as fast as an old horse can. Walker knows the road because his mammy and his brothers and sisters all live in Vicksburg, and he used to go visit them pretty often.

A final ray of sunlight slants from under a long flat gray cloud and then just as quickly disappears. Night comes fast, and shapes big as boulders move slowly across the dark fields, but those are just cows looking for a place to bed down.

"It's gettin' too dark to go on," Jenny says.

"We got a late start," Walker says. "We better put as much distance as we can between us and that sheriff." He pulls the horse to a stop and gets down to hook a light'ard torch to the side of the buggy. As they drive along the flare jumps against the trees. Now they have the road to themselves. They haven't passed a cabin for a while, and the woods are dark. Now and then a shadowy shape slinks across the road, fox or coyote, probably.

Weariness washes over her. Rosabel dozes against her chest. Finally Walker turns the buggy off the road into an unfenced field. He pulls Dun to a stop and looks around.

"I don't see any bulls out here," he says.

He drives the buggy deep into the field past a skeletal splayed tree that stands alone, its unbarked trunk and branches reaching out of the ground like a ghostly hand. "I remember that tree," he says. "I guess lightnin' got it."

Beyond the tree is a building that must have been a barn, but the roof is caved in and sagging to the ground.

"I remember this barn too," he says. "Lightnin' must 'a got it too. You tired, ain't ya? Let's just stop here."

Jenny hands Rosabel to him and gets down to spread a quilt on the ground under what remains of the roof. Walker lights a lantern and sets it on the ground, and odd-shaped shadows leap through the ruined barn. While the baby whimpers, Jenny gets a sack out of the back of the buggy; it has the biscuits Dancy gave them on their way out the door and some slices of the roast they had for dinner earlier. Jenny breaks off part of a biscuit and hands it to Rosabel, who gums it. Then she nurses Rosabel, who falls asleep, and then she and Walker eat.

Jenny sits beside Rosabel, her knees pulled up. Beyond the little circle of light, darkness hovers like a shroud. But it's not silent darkness; critters snuffle not far away.

She looks up at the moonless sky and thinks about Carefree. At this moment Esther's probably out in the kitchen, her day's work nearly finished. May's probably sitting in the kitchen eating whatever sweet Esther saved up for her. A pang of homesickness tugs at Jenny's heart. She'll miss Esther and May.

She looks over at Walker, who sits on a fallen log a few feet away. She can just make out his dark face in the lamp light. For once he doesn't have much to say, so he must be as tired as she is. Walker's always been good to her, but she's never thought too much about him. She should have paid him more attention, she thinks now; but once she got to Natchez her whole mind was taken up with Adrien Jean-Pierre. Walker just shrank into the background along with everyone else.

They'll miss Walker at Carefree. He seemed to be everywhere there, bustling about repairing a loose board here, a hanging shingle there. He earned his keep that way, and in his spare time he was the Mayor of Natchez for the freed slaves. He got them jobs, took them some of the leftover food Esther cooked, and gave them plenty of advice about their problems. Esther thinks Walker's a busybody, but it's a good thing he knows what's going on around town. If he hadn't learned about the new sheriff in Vidalia, they wouldn't be on this run right now. But as important a man as he is in Natchez, Walker has a smile as wide as the Mississippi, and he always fills Jenny in on what's going on: which free person is in trouble, and which ones are prospering. Sometimes he brings home sweets that some white lady's shared with him; spice cookies sprinkled with sugar, or even better, some Whiskey Lizzies. He's smart, she thinks; it's easy for people to overlook that, him being such a small man. He dresses sharp, because rich ladies around Natchez give him clothes their boys outgrew. She's never seen him wear coveralls or a ragged shirt. He's doing a good job driving Old Dun, which isn't much of a horse, and the buggy's the old rusted one they kept behind the barn, but Walker's got on nice green pants and a tweed jacket. He's tidier than she is, but then he doesn't have Rosabel smearing chewed-up crackers all over his clothes like she does.

They both have their freeing papers. His is folded in the inside pocket of his jacket, and hers is stuffed into her satchel. She used to carry hers in the bodice of her dress, but with Rosabel having to be nursed, it's been more convenient to keep it close by, tucked under her tignon or in a dresser drawer. When they fled Natchez, it was the first thing she put in her satchel.

Jenny Cornelius is forever free, the same as if she was born free. Rosabel, born a free child in New Orleans, is free, too. Being free keeps you out of slavery, but it won't keep you out of trouble. Adrien was a free Creole, but he was dead in an alley the day after they moved to New Orleans. He never even knew he had a child coming. But after all this time, her memory of Adrien is growing dim.

Jenny changes the baby and lies down on the quilt, pulling up a blanket to cover them. Rosabel's light breaths are like sighs. Walker stands by the barn, watching the fields. Jenny dozes.

After a while, hours probably, Walker turns down the lantern and slips in beside her. She moves over to make room for him on the quilt. When he reaches for her under the blanket, she isn't surprised, but she considers: Rosabel is still a nursing baby, and she hasn't started having her monthlies again; and it's been so long since Adrien died. But is Walker what she wants? She rolls away, turning her back to him, and she senses the disappointed tension in the way he breathes. So she turns back over and reaches for him. She won't refuse him.

Later, the night grows inkier, and Jenny lies awake, her arms folded under her head. She's glad the clouds have moved out. She sees the big wheel of stars reaching far into the depths of the heavens, brilliant and sparkling. *They're telling me something,* she thinks; if Rosabel were awake, she'd point them out to her, because when the girl's older, the stars might tell her something, too. Some glory is out there, in that deep ocean of blackness. It makes Jenny dizzy to look at them. She feels she could fall up and off the earth in this cold Mississippi night, and drown in that glittering whirlpool of stars.

The cold breeze that touched Jenny's neck as they drove away from Carefree almost made her turn around to look back at the big house, but at that moment Rosabel started to whimper, so she shifted the girl around on her lap, and then the breeze was gone. But eye sockets empty of eyes were watching them go from the silent upstairs bedroom. Spectral, the shades of Carefree's long past huddled at the window, floating against one another like motes of dust. The limbs of the hickory trees were scratching against the house, so their words were unheard. They were all there: Josephine Coqterre in her old-fashioned lace cap, and her daughter Stephanie, the prettiest of the group; even old Emile Coqterre himself, whose mind was clouded before he died. And the slave Lucy Ida, tiny and ancient; and Esther's boys, August and Littleton, who died of malaria when they weren't yet two years old. Now they're big strapping young men, and the biggest talkers in the group.

What the ghosts want is to have the house to themselves, and a couple of years ago they almost did, but then Cornelius inherited the place and all these people moved in. So they exist in a state of suspended animation, waiting for that day to come back.

"There they go," August said as the buggy made the turn at the gate. He's the newest arrival here, and he's settled in to become a permanent resident. For a long time he wasn't sure he belonged here, even though he hovered around Esther when she lived out in the slave house by herself. The big house was empty then, but she came in every day to wind the clocks, and August roamed the halls alongside her, a flutter in the still air. The other ghosts will never go anywhere else, but August always imagined that he really belonged down by the river, floating out to greet the steamers and flatboats that pulled into the dock at Natchez. He enjoyed the talk and hustle of the riverfront. If he'd lived, he would have liked to be a businessman, he thought; a cotton merchant, or a dealer in cattle. But after he found out that others like him were living in the attic at Carefree, he moved back into the familiar old house, and his brother Littleton did too, because it's always good to be part of a colony.

"Where they goin'?" Littleton asked, crowding his brother away from the window. August pushed back and then they both rose and chattered, transparent as glass.

"I don't know," August said. "But they left in a hurry. I bet Cornelius don't know nothin' about them goin'."

"Mind your own business," Littleton said.

August said, "I always try to keep up with Jenny."

"When are Cornelius and Euphonia comin' back from that funeral?" Littleton asked. "There ain't no reason for a funeral to take that long."

"I never liked that Euphonia," August said as another cloud passed over, coloring the windowpane.

"Cornelius is all right, though," Littleton said. "He's always been good to our ma."

"But he coulda married so much better," August said. "He coulda married into society, fine looking man as he is, and with this big house.

I don't know why he went for her. What was he thinkin'?"

Behind them the other shades rose and settled, chattering their agreement. August decided to let it go; their opinions didn't mean much. And anyway, it was Cornelius they all favored, no matter whom he married. That was no big secret.

When the others quieted down, August said, "I'm goin' out."

"To where?" Littleton asked.

"I'm gonna go help Cornelius, of course. He needs help." He slipped through the window.

"He looks to me like he's doin' all right," Littleton said, but August was already gone, floating out over the lawn and the road, heading down toward the river.

CHAPTER TWO

THE OLD OAK TREES BEHIND SAINT MARY'S CHURCH are still dripping from the morning's rain when Elenora Landerson's casket is carried out to the graveyard there. Every little breeze brings fat drops of cold water cascading down onto the gleaming coffin with its sad spray of white carnations. Cornelius and Euphonia stand a little apart from the mourners, but all Natchez, seemingly, is watching them; the Carsons are well known. The locals may not see much of them, but Cornelius is John Landerson's business partner, so of course they'd be here at Mrs. Landerson's funeral. Cornelius is a tall man in a black suit with a string tie, and he carries a wide Spanish hat. Euphonia is wearing a silky black dress with a necklace of creamy pearls and a feathered hat.

John Landerson stands at the graveside and the mourners glance at him to see how the young widower with many children is bearing up.

When the final prayers are said and the pallbearers start to lower the coffin with ropes, Cornelius takes his wife's arm and they walk over to John to speak their final condolences. John's two oldest boys, nine-year-old Freddy and seven-year-old Tim, stand like bereft relics beside him. The younger children are not here.

Euphonia takes John's hand in both her own. She says, "We're here for you, John. You know that." When Cornelius shakes his partner's hand, he feels the weakness in it. This is a change; Cornelius has never seen John exhibit anything but the energy and enthusiasm of a successful businessman.

As they move away from the crowd of mourners and head down the brick path to where their carriage waits, Cornelius looks back at John, who stands slumped at the graveside. His partner at this moment is a small defeated figure, even though he's actually a tall man. Cornelius hopes John won't fall into despondency. Surely with his wealth and his many slaves, he'll be able to steady himself. But with six children, none over nine years old and one a mewing newborn, any man could be overwhelmed. Cornelius hopes the slaves at the Elenora House are competent enough to manage the household without a strong-minded mistress, which Elenora undoubtedly was.

Daniel, the Carsons' fourteen-year-old driver, is sitting on the barouche with the reins slack in his hands, his black cape shiny with raindrops. When he sees them coming down the sidewalk, he sits up and grins. The barouche requires two horses, and Cornelius knows Daniel is eager to get the team going.

But after he helps Euphonia up into the carriage, Cornelius signals the boy to wait. He walks back along the sidewalk and ducks through an iron gate that's almost swallowed in red Virginia Creeper vines, where a flat stone marks Stephanie's grave. Green moss has eaten across the stone, which has sunk an inch into the ground. Cornelius takes off his hat and stands staring at the inscription: *Stephanie Coqterre Carson. 1816-1835*.

It's getting hard for him to remember Stephanie as a living woman, but she walked these Natchez streets as a schoolgirl and then as a young woman, and for two years she lived with him on Bayou Cocodrie. Those days sometimes seem like they belong in some other man's life.

After a moment he turns and walks back down the sidewalk, looking up at the clearing sky. Patches of blue are appearing between the gray clouds. With luck they'll get home without getting wet. There's no reason to put the top up. He climbs up onto the carriage and sits facing Euphonia, in their usual seats.

"We're on," he signals to Daniel, and they drive away down the street.

It's a rough ride home; Cornelius notices how restless the horses are. Chico's always been spirited, but Eagle's normally a steady stallion. But today they're both pulling at the reins and lifting their hooves high. Daniel's spooked them with his erratic driving, Cornelius thinks. And the boy shouts at the horses as they turn the corner, so it's a noisier trip than it should be.

Daniel's been itching to drive the barouche ever since he came here from Cornelius's Louisiana plantation, but the boy doesn't yet have a sense of horsemanship. Their foreman Elliott Badeau would normally be their driver, but today, as Cornelius and Euphonia were getting ready to leave for the funeral, Daniel came to the back door and asked for the umpteenth time if he could drive; and on an impulse Cornelius said he could, which made Euphonia's mouth pinch unpleasantly.

The barouche rumbles down Main Street. When it turns the corner where the brick pavement ends, the carriage lists to one side and then the other, the wheels flinging up curlicues of mud. Euphonia throws Cornelius a look of exasperation, which he ignores. He'll let Daniel handle the horses however he wishes; it's the only way a boy can learn. Fortunately Daniel knows to slow the horses after they make the turn, so the barouche won't end up a mud-splattered mess, and the passengers won't either.

As Carefree comes into view, Cornelius looks up. It always lifts his spirit to see his house from the road. The four columns on the red brick house welcomed him the first time he came here, over ten years ago, to visit Stephanie, and he still feels that glow. Now the house is his, and he takes pride in its upkeep. Today he notices that a black shutter on an upstairs bedroom window is hanging slightly askew, probably because of the strong wind that came with this morning's rain. He'll mention that to Elliot and tomorrow it'll be hanging straight again.

As Cornelius gazes at the house, the light changes; clouds are covering the low sun again. The thought comes to him that someone is inside that upstairs room watching them drive up. He starts to point it out to Euphonia, but she's rummaging in her beaded purse for something and not looking up at the house. She snaps her purse closed and pulls off her black gloves and lays them across her lap. Then she leans back and closes her eyes. Her complexion is pale, her long nose and strong jawline clearly defined as one last beam of light illuminates her face.

If he mentioned what he saw to Euphonia, she'd say it was ghosts. She believes in such things. He doesn't. Then he thinks it was probably the housekeeper Esther he saw in the window; she goes in to wind the clocks every evening. And of course the window panes are reflecting the scudding brown clouds.

He says, "Sad about Elenora." Euphonia opens her eyes and nods, looking away from him; she's not one to dwell on sad news. But Elenora wasn't even thirty years old, and with her sixth child she died in childbirth. Cornelius didn't know her all that well, but he certainly saw her at parties and around town. Euphonia knew her better than he did, because Elenora and Euphonia were in the same circle of wives. One thing is certain: her death will upend many lives.

When they reach Carefree, Daniel drives the barouche up to the front of the house and Cornelius helps Euphonia down. Holding her skirt to one side to keep the hem off the wet grass, she goes up the steps without looking back.

Cornelius turns to Daniel and says "Good job." The boy beams.

When you're older, you'll be able to spot sarcasm, Cornelius thinks, chuckling. Well, the boy will learn to drive a team, but learning takes time. It'll be handy to have someone besides Elliot who can drive the barouche.

He goes into the house. He wants to talk to Euphonia about some things that are weighing on his mind, but she's already heading up the stairs. So he goes into his office at the back of the house, where the work he spent the morning on is spread out on his desk, waiting.

CHAPTER THREE

BY NOON ESTON FERRIS, THE NEW SHERIFF of Concordia Parish, figured he'd already put in a day's work, since he spent the morning in Vidalia getting Sheriff Willie Haynes buried. Right after Willie was buried, Eston let himself into the sheriff's office, and just as he feared, the place was a jumble of files and newspaper clippings, all of it piled on top of cabinets and crammed into overflowing drawers. He could see it would take months to sort through it all.

But when he spied the two daguerreotypes that Willie left tacked up on the wall, he figured they represented a clue relating to some old case Willie couldn't solve. He walked over and yanked the pictures down so he could study them. One image was of a white man in a big hat; in the other photograph, a black girl was holding a small boy on her lap—the white man's son, he guessed. As luck would have it, a few minutes of determined searching through the papers on Willie's desk told him who they were and what their crimes were: the slave girl holding the kid was Jenny, charged with assaulting a white woman; and the white man was her owner, Cornelius Carson, who broke into the jail and took her right out from under the nose of the deputy who still works in the office, Cotton Ferguson. Eston has already decided he might have to sack Ferguson for general laxness and laziness, but for the moment he needs somebody to cover the office when he's not there. Willie pencilled the word "Natchez" on the file, so Eston figured that's where he'd find Carson, and probably the girl too.

After the rain cleared out, Eston walked out to the stable behind the office and saddled his big mare Dixie. He rode down to the ferry landing and got there just as the ferry was pulling out, so he rode over to the hotel. He tied the horse to the railing and sat on the bench watching the ferry get smaller and smaller until it looked like a toy boat out on the wide river, its puny engine rumbling and its smokestack giving off little puffs of smoke.

Other travellers were waiting too, and they gave him some space, he noticed. The bench was long enough for several people, but he had it to himself. He was wearing his black funeral suit, but the only thing people really noticed was the badge pinned to the lapel. Once they saw it, they moved away from him, preferring to stand. Well, he's a newcomer to Vidalia, but it won't be long before his face is familiar in these parts. Sheriff Haynes was well-known because he'd been here forever, but he was slow-moving, happy to let things slide. In his twenty-six years of life, Eston's never been willing to let things slide.

When the ferry returned, he led Dixie up the gangplank and then stood to one side watching other passengers get on. This must be the usual wash of traffic on the river, he thought: tired women in crocheted shawls and sun-burned farmers in threadbare suits, kids sticking their bare feet through the railing; some slave women and their master standing in the center of the deck. And there were haltered yearlings, squawking chickens in coops, and boxes and barrels of who knows what stacked around the deck. Eston wouldn't have thought that much cargo had to be transported between Vidalia and Natchez.

By the time all the passengers and freight and livestock were loaded on, Eston was crowded next to the railing. Dixie stepped forward as the ferry swung out into the current, so he tied the reins to the rail to steady her.

A pretty blond-haired woman in a green gingham dress stood next to him. She glanced at his badge.

"You the police?"

"I'm the sheriff of Concordia Parish."

She raised her eyebrows to show her surprise, and then she moved away from him, which he'd rather she didn't; but he knows that's how people react to the authorities, giving them space. A young woman shouldn't be travelling alone; it's dangerous out in the world.

He studied the approaching shore. *So that's Mississippi,* he thought; he's never been there before. It's higher land than Louisiana; he could tell that from the hotel porch. It might even be more hilly than Alexandria, his hometown which he left just a week ago, and they certainly have hills there, gently mounding hills like soft breasts, covered with pines. With hills you can get deep dark valleys, so Mississippi might be generally a wilder kind of place than Louisiana.

When they docked at Natchez-Under-the-Hill, he led Dixie off the ferry. The area behind the dock was crowded and noisy, a jumble of buildings. He'd heard of the notorious Under-the-Hill; it's not a place decent people would frequent. Off to the left he saw Silver Street running up the bluff to Natchez proper. Most of the ferry passengers were straggling off in that direction, but some of the men were ducking into one of the establishments in Under-the-Hill. He looked around for the girl who spoke to him on the ferry, and he saw her slip into a building with the word "Hotel" on a sign over the door.

It was a steep, muddy ride to the top of the bluff, but Dixie took it well. His first stop in Natchez was the Adams County Sheriff's office. He needed to find out what he could about Carson and his slave girl Jenny. He expected a cordial reception; the two sheriffs are colleagues, after all, brothers in law enforcement, their offices scarcely two miles apart, separated only by the wide Mississippi.

The sheriff's office was easy to find; the address, which he'd gleaned from a note on Willie's desk, was posted right on the door, not far from where Silver Street spilled its travellers at the top of the slope. It was a small frame building practically swallowed by the biggest magnolia tree Eston ever saw. He ducked beneath the branches and knocked on the door. When he heard a noise from inside, he pushed the door open. A burly deputy sitting behind a desk looked up at him. Eston took off his hat and introduced himself.

He saw the deputy appraising him. For the first time he felt self-conscious about his own slight form, his narrow neck rising above the too-large white collar, his pencil-thin legs. His church suit did him no favors, but he was glad he had the badge pinned to his lapel.

"You the one took Willie Haynes's place?" the deputy asked.

"Yes sir. He was buried this morning."

"Yeah, we heard about that. I'm Deputy McKenna. Somethin' I can help you with?"

"I was hopin' to introduce myself to Sheriff Williams. Is he here?"

"Nope."

"He be back this afternoon?"

"I couldn't say."

Eston glanced around the office. Now, this is what a sheriff's office should look like, he thought; a person entering this office gets an impression of orderliness and authority. Through an open door behind the deputy's desk he could see the bars of the cell block. Given the scene at Under-The-Hill, he guessed that most of the arrests came from that part of town.

"I'm lookin' for a man named Cornelius Carson. You know him?"

The deputy scraped his chair back and stood up, moving his cigar around in his mouth. "Yep."

"Where would I find him?"

"Well, ordinarily I'd say you could just go up to his house, a place named Carefree. They got that wrote on the post as you go in. It's out on the Woodville road, out east. But if I was guessin' I'd say he ain't home right now." He looked at the clock on the wall. "He's probably still at Saint Mary's Church. They're havin' the funeral for Miz Landerson. That's where Sheriff Williams is too."

"How would I find that church?"

"It's right down the street, the white church with a tall steeple." He pointed toward the door. "Go out here to the corner and turn right on Main Street. Can't miss it."

Eston went back outside, glancing up at the shovel-like green leaves of the magnolia tree, which if they trembled would soak his black suit. Dixie was still quivering from the long pull up Silver Street. He swung up into the saddle and rode north toward the church.

So this is Natchez, he thought, eying the shops that lined the street. The windows displayed all kinds of merchandise for a city full of customers: hats, trimmed and untrimmed; cooking pots; glassware; bolts of fabric. There was a hardware store, a feed and seed, and a cobbler with racks of shoes obscuring his window. Vidalia could use a cobbler, he thought; a pair of good used shoes with new soles could last for years, as Eston well knew, having never had a brand new pair in his life. Even though the rain had just stopped, shoppers were making their way along the sidewalks, their upside-down reflections shining on the wet bricks. By comparison, Vidalia streets would be dead quiet at this hour.

When he came to the church, a line of black buggies at the curb told him the funeral wasn't over yet. He tied Dixie to the fence and went up to the church just as the doors opened and the priests came out, followed by pallbearers carrying the casket. He stepped to the side and watched as the mourners emerged.

A tall man carrying a large hat came out with a woman in a silky black dress. Eston saw his profile and thought, *Carson.*

Eston followed the crowd to the cemetery and stood behind the mourners, watching Carson and his wife out of the corner of his eye. When they left he followed them out to the sidewalk and watched Mrs. Carson climb up into a large barouche. He stood at a decent distance as Carson went back into the graveyard for a few minutes before returning to sit opposite his wife. As they drove away they seemed to float above the street. Eston had never seen such a carriage before; he was sure there weren't any like it in Vidalia.

Carson is rich.

This changed his plan. Going after a rich man was different from running after a bayou rat. Willie's notes on the case said Carson had a hundred arpents and two cabins, but this man's dress, his bearing, and his carriage reflected a different world than that. Eston knew he'd have to tread carefully. He'd better talk to Sheriff Williams first and see what the situation is. But if the sheriff was here at the funeral, Eston couldn't pick him out.

As mourners swarmed past him on the sidewalk, Eston untied his horse and swung into the saddle, shaking the reins. He said "Hut!" but Dixie wouldn't move. He looked around, wondering what made Dixie uncooperative. He dismounted, his shoes slipping in the mud, and spoke gently to the horse. He lifted her front hooves one at a time, examining them. Neither hoof had cast a shoe.

In the cemetery behind him the two gravediggers finished their work and walked toward the gate. Eston mounted Dixie again and shook the reins, but the horse didn't move. As the gravediggers walked past him with shovels on their shoulders, rain began to spit down. One of the men glanced at Eston's badge and nodded, "Sheriff."

He said to no one, "Well, I ain't walkin' back to Vidalia in the rain! Giddyap!"

But no matter how hard he spurred the horse and how powerfully he jerked the reins, Dixie stood unmoving, watching the street, placid as a cow surveying a country meadow.

Maddeningly, inexplicably, lame.

CHAPTER FOUR

CORNELIUS SITS AT HIS DESK with his head in his hands. It's been a tiring day. He was at his desk just after dawn, preoccupied because he has much to do and knowing the afternoon would be taken up with Elenora's funeral. Now, in the late afternoon, he has to pick up where he left off. He gets up and pours himself a glass of whiskey.

The house seems too quiet. At this time of day it's usually a noisy place, Dancy and Esther setting the table in the dining room and three-year-old Thomas jabbering somewhere in his loud voice; Jenny prattling with her baby Rosabel in her room across the hall. Daniel, just learning to be a man, would be everywhere, tailing Walker Jackson or Elliot Badeau or Cornelius himself, talking up a storm and soaking up everything he can; and there are always doors opening and closing and clothes billowing and thumping on the clotheslines. Dogs bark, horses nicker. Euphonia complains, but to Cornelius it's all just the sounds and smells of life. He doesn't mind it.

He takes out his atlas and lays it open on the desk. He has a long trip facing him. He's promised Malachi he'll take him to Albemarle County in Virginia, where the old man was born. Mal's hoping his brother and maybe even his mother are still alive, but he hasn't seen either of them since he was twelve years old, so Cornelius isn't sure they'll be able to find them. After that, Cornelius wants to come back by way of Georgia so he can visit his own mother's grave behind the little church he remembers.

To undertake such a long trip with an illiterate companion, to visit Virginia, a place he's never been, is a sobering responsibility, and he almost regrets promising Mal he'd do it. But Mal's over sixty, so time is short. It doesn't feel right to put him off any longer.

He turns the pages of the atlas until he comes to the map of the entire country. He traces out a route with his finger, figuring he and Mal can take a steamer to New Orleans, then catch an oceangoing vessel around Florida and up the east coast to Norfolk or the Chesapeake Bay. That will put them within striking distance of Albemarle County, which is deep in Virginia. He estimates it'll be a five-month trip.

Such a long trip will mean leaving Carefree in the hands of Elliot Badeau, who after all could resign at any time. If he does, Euphonia will have to take over and supervise the household.

While he was at the funeral it occurred to him that he should make a will. A will is powerful; it can change the course of a family's life for generations. It was Emile Coqterre's will that put Cornelius in this fine house at this moment. Emile amassed a fortune and built the house, and when he passed, the house and fortune came to Cornelius along with a thousand-acre plantation in Louisiana. Emile certainly felt no love for the cotton farmer who eloped with his stepdaughter, but the flinty old Frenchman did love Stephanie. By Emile's will Cornelius rose in the world.

A will would protect the family he has now. He'll get John Landerson to prepare one, once John's steadied himself and reopened his law office.

Thunder growls across the sky. Maybe the rain's not done with us, he thinks. He takes out a sheet of paper from his desk drawer and dips his pen into the inkwell. He writes:

HOUSEHOLD OF CORNELIUS CARSON
Natchez, Adams County, Mississippi
November 30, 1843

To wit:
Cornelius Carson, age 34, Proprietor
Euphonia McKee Carson, his wife, age 42
Thomas Carson, age 3, his son
May Carson, age 8, his ward

He pauses and taps his finger on the paper. Then he puts a question mark after the last entry; no one really knows how old May is.

EMPLOYEES:
Coella Taylor, nursemaid to Thomas and May
Elliot Badeau, foreman and manager of the grounds

FREE PERSONS RESIDING AT CAREFREE:
Jenny Cornelius; her daughter Rosabel, age nearing 2
Esther Coqterre, cook and head housekeeper
Malachi Carson, helper
Walker Jackson, handyman
Dancy Carson, housemaid; her baby Henry, age 2
Bo Carson, laundress; her son Daniel, age 14
Felisa Carson, helper
Cassie Carson, helper
Traysa Carson; her baby George, age 2
Virginia Carson, elderly

Jane Carson, elderly
Margaret Carson, elderly

ASSETS:
House: Carefree, Natchez, Adams County, Mississippi, with
dependency and appropriate outbuildings, privies, stables, etc.
Plantation, suitable for cane or cotton, located on Bayou Boeuf,
Rapides Parish, Louisiana. 1000 acres more or less, with two
houses, cabins, privies, barns, etc. Not under cultivation. For sale.

He wonders what he needs to add. He starts to write *Slaves: none,* but then he draws a line through it. There are no slaves at Carefree, but he properly still owns the hundred fieldhands who came with his plantation. But they were stolen from him and sold off into Texas before he even knew about them, so his chances of ever recovering them are slim. He also has the money Emile left him: two accounts at the Planters' Bank totalling over $100,000, a city fortune. And as soon as the cane plantation is sold, which he hopes will be by spring, he'll add the proceeds from the sale to his bank account.

If he should die, all of it—the fortune, the real estate, the responsibilities—will go to Euphonia. He knows he's healthy, but a young man can die as easily as any other—a skittish horse, a falling tree in a storm, a thief lurking in the dark with a knife—any mishap will do. The *Natchez Gazette* reports it all the time. It would be hard for Euphonia if anything happened to him, but she's a strong woman. He's seen how well she adapted herself to city life here. She'd need some time to get her bearings though, as any widow would. He himself's been made a widower twice, and he knows the shock that brings.

He studies the page. Here is his life laid out before him on this sheet of cream-colored paper: his family, his employees, his property. Listing his holdings will help him keep an orderly record in his head, as well as on this paper. But Carefree is an unusual estate, an abolitionist island in the midst of slave-land. And the people here didn't arrive in the traditional way, by a couple marrying and then surrounding themselves with many children, a household growing with every new infant and the complications each brings. Everyone at Carefree arrived by a circuitous route. Malachi he'd bought from a trader near New Orleans many years ago. And Jenny was a child cast to the winds herself; she was about ten when Cornelius bought her out of a slave coffle right here in Natchez. Now she's a grown woman with a child of her own, and she's free, because Cornelius won't be a slave owner if he doesn't have to be. She was the first slave he freed.

Jenny rescued May and brought the little girl here as a surprise guest. To Jenny, Carefree is home; Cornelius takes some pride in that. She's had other homes, including Cornelius's cotton farm on Bayou Cocodrie; and she lived somewhere in New Orleans, obviously. And she must have had a home before he bought her, but she's never spoken of it.

The two-story building behind the big house used to be called the slave house, but now they all try to remember to call it the Dependency. It's crowded with Cornelius's former slaves. Malachi, Esther, and Walker Jackson each have their own rooms, and the twelve women and three kids he brought from his plantation live two to a room out there. When he went to Rapides Parish to inspect the plantation, they were the only people left there. A hundred other fieldhands were specified in the will, but Bernard Ratout, the overseer, had sold them off before Cornelius even knew about them. He wonders where they are; the only thing the slave auctioneer in Pineville would tell him was Texas. Can he ever recoup his loss? Should he even try to, given his principles?

The room grows darker. He looks out the window; heavy clouds ready to burst are obscuring the sun. He watches the play of light across his desk, and the ink on the paper in front of him suddenly fades until all he can see is the pale rectanglar sheet, as blank as if he'd written nothing at all. It occurs to him that even a household as large as his could vanish like the writing on this paper. It vanished for Emile Coqterre, even though Emile thought he'd made himself into a grandee; but within a few short years he was in his grave.

A flash of lightning crackles outside the window, and he reaches over to strike a match to the lamp. The room brightens and the writing on the page comes back into view.

There's a certain grimness to making a will, even though it's a necessary thing. Thoughts of death are unusual for him, but seeing the mahogany casket today was a shock, no question about it. Poor Elenora. She was a nice woman, as far as Cornelius knew her, and attractive too, in her plain way.

He writes, *In the name of God Amen,* at the bottom of the page. He opens his desk drawer and slides the paper into it. Then he turns to the other matter pressing him.

Ever since John Landerson proposed the steamboat venture some months ago, Cornelius has enjoyed analyzing the construction of the wooden vessel, picturing the great salon, the twenty staterooms, the white painted deck railings carved in elaborate whorls, the fan stacks. The *Euphonia* will be both a splendid large boat and a profitable investment.

Cornelius has a connection to the river, after all, so the steamer project is close to his heart. He still nurses memories, mainly good ones, of the days when he worked on the riverboat *Abigail*. It was back before he owned his farm, or a single slave; before he married and became a father; before Malachi or Stephanie or Jenny came into his life. He was twenty years old and he loved the freedom of the river, the constantly changing vista of riverbanks and river towns, the thump of the stern-wheel thrashing the water. He was fascinated by the variety of flatboats that floated the river and by the hat-waving frontiersmen who manned them. The *Abigail* wasn't much of a boat, but to the men on the flatboats any steamer was a haughty river queen. Whenever the *Abigail* raced past a flatboat, the flatboatmen would jump to their feet hooting and holler-ing, and often as not they'd dance a jig. The flatboats came from Ohio or Indiana; farm boys hammered them together and loaded them with whatever cargo they thought would sell in New Orleans, more than a thousand miles away. When they reached New Orleans they'd sell the cargo there and then sell the boats too, because nothing's better for building houses than northern hardwood, and there's always a buyer. Many a proud house in New Orleans is framed with timbers that came down the river as a flatboat.

With money jingling in their pockets, the boatmen would whistle off into New Orleans; the city has so many attractions for vagabond young men, the same attractions it held for Cornelius when he was young—honky-tonks and bawdy houses, minstrel shows, gaming tables. Eventually the boatmen would get themselves back where they came from, poorer in dollars but richer in experience.

But it wasn't a life without danger. When the *Abigail* exploded south of Baton Rouge on a summer day in 1830, Cornelius and most of the crew made it to the riverbank just in time to look back and watch the steamer fold in on itself and disappear beneath the gray-brown water. The sound of the explosion deafened him for a month. After that, with the *Abigail* at the bottom of the river and his mother's old Georgia farm worn out, Cornelius figured he had no home to return to and he liked Louisiana, so he stayed. Even something as insignificant as taking a job on a broken-down steamer can change the course of a life.

He brushes the memories from his mind and focuses on the boat plans before him. The *Euphonia* will primarily be a passenger boat, the finest on the river. It exists only as a drawing now; but in a few months, after he returns from Virginia, it will rise at a boatyard in Pittsburgh, Pennsylvania. John located a builder, a Scotsman named McCann, and he and Cornelius studied the specifications and signed the contract. Cornelius thought it would be better to have the boat built closer to Natchez, but John said the boats built in Pittsburgh are the best on the river. Cornelius can picture the construction; after the keel is laid, the boat will rest like a beached whale, its framework a skeleton of wooden ribs and uprights. After many more months the interior will be finished; artisans in New York will craft the brass fittings and then the furnishings will be brought on board: four-poster beds with thick mattresses, carved French chests, tasseled silk curtains the color of whiskey.

The *Euphonia* will be an enormous first-class hotel cruising the river, dwarfing other steamers. Cornelius likes to picture her coming into the riverfront at Saint Louis or Cincinnati or Memphis, her whistle hooting one long and two short high-pitched blasts. The sound will carry for miles into the woods, and everyone will learn to recognize the distinctive signal that means the finest passenger steamer on the river is arriving. And then with the constant roar of the engines—

—*the constant roar of the engines*—

He taps the paper. Ever since he got the plans, a half-formed worry has gnawed at him like a mouse chewing at the cardboard of an old portrait. Every day he unrolls the plans and spreads them out on his desk. The boat designer is obviously a skillful man. Looking at the drawings,

Cornelius can envision what the ship will look like; the plans provide not just a floor plan but elevations, with views of the sides, stern and prow.

He and John have worked well together on the project, he thinks, considering they were strangers to each other a couple of years ago. The men agreed they'd call the boat the *Elenora and Euphonia,* and they began to refer to it as the *Double E.* But sadly, now Elenora's dead, and Cornelius figures it'll have to be just the *Euphonia.* Seeing Elenora's name emblazoned on the boat would conjure up sadness for John and for the children too, when they're older.

The boat that existed only on paper grew larger over the summer, because he and John agreed to add more staterooms, which will add to the profits. John calculated the cost of the added deck space and the ten additional cabins, and what they'll add in revenue. Cornelius could see the advantages of an extension to the back deck that added twenty feet to the stern deck. Now the *Euphonia* as planned will be a boat over two hundred feet long, with a beam of forty feet. Huge.

But the boiler, encased in its framework belowdecks, stayed the same size. Only the size of the boat and the expectations changed. Cornelius taps his pencil.

All of a sudden the house becomes noisy again. He chuckles as he hears Thomas running out the back door with Coella, scolding, right behind him. Then the back door slams; the boy has escaped Coella's grasp, as he often does.

Deciding there's no answer to the questions gnawing at him, he slides the plans into a yellow folder. He'll confer with John about the boiler, and he'll see about getting a will made up. But those things will have to wait until John opens his law office again.

CHAPTER FIVE

EUPHONIA STILL HASN'T COME DOWNSTAIRS, so Cornelius locks the desk and walks down the hall to the parlor. He sits on the sofa and leans back and closes his eyes. When Euphonia comes down, they'll have a quiet dinner and retire early, he hopes.

A few minutes later, the sound of a dog barking outside rouses him. Through the window he can see the kitchen behind the big house. As he watches, half-asleep, the kitchen door opens and Esther comes out. The clouds have moved away and the sun's last rays strike the white-washed bricks of the wall behind her, so Esther is a dark silhouette: dark face, dark dress. She walks toward the house. The white tignon she wears when she cooks is tied around her head, and her limp skirt flutters about her legs. Lately he's noticed that the lines and creases of her face are pulled deeper than usual, although from here he can't really make out her features. She's probably coming in to wind the clocks, he thinks, as she does every evening. A moment later he hears the back door open and then close with a little click.

She taps lightly at the parlor door. "Excuse me, sir."

"Yes?"

She steps into the room and stands near the door. He sees that what he thought earlier is true; the wrinkles on her face are looking more and more like the crazing on an old china plate.

"I come to tell you somethin', and sorry for disturbin' you," she says in a low voice. "But I need to let you know Jenny's gone away with Walker Jackson. They left while y'all was at the funeral."

Cornelius reaches over and turns up the lamp. "Jenny's gone? Gone where?"

"Well, I guess they went up to Vicksburg, 'cause that's where Walker's fambly is. That's what Walker was talkin' about."

"So when are they comin' back?"

"I don't know 'bout that, sir." Esther folds her hands together. "The thing is, Walker said the sheriff from Vidalia's comin' after Jenny, and he's comin' after you, too. I don't know if I understand all he said, 'cause he didn't take time to explain it all. But he said you was on your own, and you'd be all right. He wasn't worried 'bout you. But he said Jenny had to scamper on out of here, and he'd go with her."

Cornelius frowns. "The sheriff from Vidalia?"

"Yes sir. He said that sheriff was at Miz Landerson's funeral. Walker told me to tell everybody here that if the sheriff comes askin', we to say there ain't nobody here named Jenny. That there used to be a Jenny, but she left a long time ago, and nobody's seen her since. Walker says the sheriff's got your picture hangin' on his office wall, and he knows what you look like. He's got a picture of Jenny too."

Cornellius looks out through the window, where the lawn is turning from purple to black.

So the sheriff's got hold of the daguerreotype portraits they made back when they lived in the Cocodrie. He remembers when they sat for the photographer in that little makeshift studio. Cornelius was intrigued by the novelty of a device that would make an image of a face that wasn't painted, but real, a face that would look exactly as a person looked on that day. Jenny didn't want to get her picture made; she said it seemed like witchery to her, the way the people in the pictures were stuck in those little frames. *As if you know anything about witchery*, he'd thought then; and he insisted they do it. He paid twenty-five cents for three images: a portrait of himself, and one of Malachi, and one of Jenny holding Thomas.

He left the pictures in his cabin when he high-tailed it for Texas. But the sheriff must've come poking around his cabin and took the two photographs he wanted, leaving the one of Malachi.

And that sheriff invited himself to the funeral today. Cornelius hadn't paid much attention to the people at Saint Mary's; when he looked around, he noticed that the church was full and the crowd was about what he expected: society people, the women dabbing at their eyes with lace handkerchiefs. But he didn't see anyone who looked like a sheriff there.

"Well, I just figured you best know what Walker said," Esther says. She walks out and goes up the stairs. In a moment Cornelius hears a soft creak as the clock-face opens in the upstairs hall.

So the sheriff in Vidalia knows him, knows where he lives. The curtains rustle at the window and cool air touches his neck.

What Jenny did wouldn't be a crime in any other society, he thinks. A woman stole her money, and Jenny took after her. Adelaide Halloran got the worst of it, a black eye and a broken nose, and she was probably missing some hair when Jenny got done with her. But Adelaide was white as buttermilk, and the sheriff wasted no time in packing Jenny off to the jail in Vidalia. When Cornelius pulled a gun on the deputy to get Jenny out of jail, he knew he was committing a crime, but the crime could be justified. What's right and what the law says are sometimes two different things.

And even though it's not decent to bother a man on the day his wife was buried, he has a feeling this won't keep, so he'd better go consult with John. He walks out into the foyer. When he starts up the stairs he sees Esther coming back down.

"Tell Miss Phony I've gone out," he says. "I've got to go see John Landerson." She nods.

He goes out to the stable where Daniel is wiping down the wet horses in the back stall. Cornelius can see the top of the boy's head, and then Daniel stands straight up and looks around, surprised to see him.

"Yes sir?"

"I need you to saddle Eagle again."

A few moments later Cornelius is galloping down Main Street toward the Elenora House. Up ahead he can just make out its round cupola above the gray winter trees, in the fading light.

When he arrives at the Elenora House, John answers the door and ushers him into the parlor. Cornelius sees at once that the Landerson home is a chaotic place of wailing children and overwhelmed slave women trying to get control of the situation. In the parlor Delphine is holding the two infants, Cyrus and Dolly, one in each arm, and both are crying. Delphine's daughter Emma, who isn't much more than a child herself, is ignoring the squabbling older boys while she tends to John's four-year-old daughter Lissy, who has a nosebleed. The little girl screams while Emma tries to hold her so she can put a cloth to her nose; blood gushes like a waterfall onto the girl's frilly white dress. Then Marcus, Delphine's husband, comes into the room and herds the boys toward the stairs.

Relics of the funeral are tossed around the room: a prayer book splayed upside down on the brocade sofa, John's black coat thrown over a chair, the broken stalk of a chrysanthemum lying on the floor. Cornelius remembers the spray of white chrysanthemums that lay atop Elenora's coffin.

"I'm sorry to trouble you today of all days, John," Cornelius says, standing in the doorway with his hat in his hand.

"I'm glad you're here," John says. "I could use some grown-up companionship. And fewer dishes of food. Ladies've been bringing 'em all day."

Cornelius waits until Marcus and the women have the children under some kind of control. When three-year-old Frankie pulls away from Marcus and heads for the door, Cornelius reaches down to take the boy's arm and holds him still until Marcus grabs his hand and leads him over to the stairs, where he shoos the boys up the steps. Delphine hands Cyrus to Emma and wraps the tiny infant Dolly to her own chest with a scarf. Then she takes Lissy's hand and leads her into the kitchen, holding a towel to the girl's face.

"Let's go into my office," John says, and the two men walk down the hall into a small room at the back of the house. John lights the lamp and sits down at the desk, resting his head in his hands. Then he looks up at Cornelius.

"Lord, what a day," he says. "Let me pour us a drink."

Cornelius takes the glass John offers. He says in a low voice, "John, I've been told that the sheriff from Vidalia is on my tail. I've heard he was at the funeral. I didn't see him."

John takes a long swallow of his drink. "I saw him. I knew it had to be him because he was wearing a badge. Can you imagine a man wearing a badge to a woman's funeral, someone he didn't even know? He had to have a reason for being there, so I figured he was looking for you." He sets his glass down hard and the amber liquid sloshes onto the desktop, tiny mirrors reflecting the lamplight.

Cornelius tries to remember the townspeople who packed the pews. He didn't know many of them. "How worried do I need to be?"

"Well—is he coming after you? Not right now, I'd say. He'd have to file an arrest warrant with Sheriff Williams here in Adams County, and that takes time. I'll go see Jim Williams tomorrow. I think I can head your trouble off, at least for a while. Nothing happens without a warrant."

Sounds of wailing children come through the ceiling.

"John, how will you manage all this?" Cornelius asks, indicating the chaos upstairs with a sweep of his hand.

John shakes his head. "I don't know. I need more help. Is there some woman at your place I could hire?"

"There might be. I could ask out at the Dependency."

John downs the last of his whiskey. "I think you'd better lay low for a while. Some other thing might come up to take this sheriff's attention. Out of sight, out of mind. I'll handle it."

"Malachi's been after me to take him to Virginia to see his people."

"Then this would probably be a good time for you to do that."

The children are quieting, and Cornelius finishes his whiskey. He sets his glass on the desk and stands up. "Someday, let's get back to that steamboat project."

John gives a wan smile. "I'd surely like to."

Cornelius goes outside and swings up on Dixie. He gallops up Main Street, glad the city's seen fit to install street lamps. When he gets to Carefree he walks the horse around to the stable. Daniel's still there, currying Chico by the light of a lantern.

"Do Eagle too," he says.

Cornelius walks to the kitchen, stepping around rain puddles. In the kitchen Mal sits alone, whittling a stick by the light of a lamp that's turned up high. When Cornelius comes in, Mal looks up, surprised.

Cornelius leans against the wall a few feet away, his arms folded. "You're going at this a little late, Mal. Can't hardly see in the dark."

"I know. But I'm almost finished now."

"What's that you're carving?"

"A horse for little Henry. I told Dancy I'd make him one. Then I gotta make one for George too, else them two chaps'll fight. You know how boys is."

Cornelius looks around the kitchen. The logs in the fireplace are still glowing, and Esther's dishcloths are draped over a line in front of the fireplace. The aroma of roast beef reminds Cornelius that he missed dinner.

"That carving might have to wait. We need to head out for Virginia tomorrow. Can you be ready that quick?"

"Tomorrow?" Mal looks up, surprised. "Oh, yes sir, I can be ready." He sets the half-carved figure down on the table and stands up. "This'll keep. Time we get back, those chaps might've lost their interest. Gettin' to Virginny's more important in my opinion, like I told you before. My people ain't gonna be around much longer, so if I'm gonna go, I got to go."

"It's kind of rushed, I know, but I've got a need to go now," Cornelius says. "We'll have to head out at dawn to get an early start. We'll catch the first steamboat to New Orleans. I'll chart us out a route. It'll be a long trip, four or five months, so pack everything you'll need. And Virginia's way up north, so take your warm coat."

"Yes sir. It gets cold there. I remember it snowin' when I was just a li'l chap."

"Go tell Daniel to be ready at sun-up. He can drive us down to Under-the-Hill. He needs the practice."

As Mal disappears into the darkness, Cornelius stands in the kitchen for a few moments, thinking about the trip ahead. The two men will face situations new to both of them, and the last time that happened was when he made that run for Texas with Mal and Thomas two years ago. This trip will be more complicated than that one, because they'll travel on river steamers and ocean ships, and they'll rent horses to cross terrain different from any they've seen. They'll have to hire guides; Cornelius isn't sure he can find the old Georgia homestead or that Mal can find the plantation in Albemarle County. There are a hundred reasons Cornelius would like to put the trip off, but go they must, and as of tomorrow the Dependency won't be as crowded as it is right now. For a while it seemed that people were moving in all the time, especially after he brought his plantation slaves here. Then not long after that, Jenny showed up with Rosabel and May. But Jenny, Walker and Rosabel took off for Vicksburg this evening, and after tomorrow morning he and Mal will be gone too; five people subtracted in just one day.

Euphonia can run the big house all right, with Dancy cooking and Esther and Bo and Traysa doing the housework. By the time he sees Carefree again, months from now, the children will be bigger: May, Thomas, George, and Henry. It's with growing children that you really see time flying by.

But he'll miss his home. After he and Mal have whatever adventures are out there, he'll be glad to head his horse toward Natchez. It could be early summer before they get back.

He wonders about Jenny and Walker and the baby. He hopes he gets word of them once they get to Vicksburg, and maybe they'll come back for a visit. Or he can go up to Vicksburg and check on them if he feels the need. He'll probably want to do that in the summertime, if he hasn't gotten word by then. Thinking of Jenny's leaving, he has the same flattened feeling he had when she left for New Orleans two years ago. She came back, but now she's gone again. He'll miss seeing her and little

Rosabel around the place. As for Walker, plenty of people in Natchez might miss him.

He turns the lamp out and closes the door behind him. Even on this moonless night the bricks leading to the big house are shiny, a light-colored path in the milky darkness. He takes the back steps two at a time and goes inside to find Euphonia sitting in the parlor, a glass of wine in her hand. She looks up when he walks in.

"Esther said you went to see John," she says. "How was it over there?"

"About like you'd expect," he says. He pours himself a glass of whiskey and sits down on the side chair near her. "I don't know how John will handle it all."

Phony shakes her head. She's taken off her black funeral dress and put on a frock of teal blue with a deep neckline, which he likes, and she's draped an oriental shawl around her shoulders, since the room is cool and damp. He admires Phony, the way she's changed her appearance since they moved to Natchez. He can't criticize her for trying to match the other city wives in her appearance. When she lived in the Cocodrie, before he married her, she wore homemade calico dresses and a sunbonnet, and her face and hands were chapped. But now the pharmacist's concocted some balms for her, for a pretty price no doubt, and Phony's a good customer. Her face is soft and white. And she visits Miss Dolores's Shoppe of Finery to order the clothes she needs for this life. It's interesting to see the metamorphosis in the country girl he married. The pretenses of city society don't mean much to him—that's what he tells himself anyway—but whenever he goes into town Phony sees to it that he wears a well-cut suit and a string tie and carries his Spanish hat.

"It's quiet in here now. Has Thomas gone to bed?" he asks.

"Coella took him up a while ago. May too."

"It seems early for May," he says as the hall clock chimes eight o'clock.

"She's got a book to read," Phony says. "Is there anything we should do for John?"

"He'll need more help. I told him I'd ask if any of our women want to work for pay, to help out with the house and the kids. Only—" he hesitates—"you'll have to be the one who asks them. I won't be here."

"Are you going somewhere?"

He gets up and walks over to sit next to her. "Phony, there's a new sheriff in Vidalia, and he was at the funeral today," he says in a low voice.

"At the funeral? Why?"

"Because he's after me, I imagine. And if he's on my tail, John says I need to skedaddle for a while. Throw him off the scent. Beyond that, John'll take care of it. So tomorrow I'm gonna leave at sunrise, me and Mal. We'll take the first steamer headed south and catch an ocean steamer out of New Orleans that can take us to Newport, or up the Chesapeake. We'll get to Virginia one way or the other. I told Mal a while back that I'd take him to find his people, but I didn't plan on goin' just yet."

She sinks against the back of the sofa, her face creased in thought. "How long will you be gone?"

"Well, Virginia's a long way. I'd say five months, at least. But I'll write to you."

He takes her hand and kisses it. "I'll miss you."

She nods. "Let me go get your satchel. I'll help you pack."

She gets up and walks toward the door. Then she stops and looks back at him. "It seems odd, about the sheriff," she says.

"It does."

"After all this time —" She shakes her head.

Watching her walk toward the stairs, Cornelius looks up and sees May sitting on a step halfway up, her toes peeping out from under her white nightgown. The girl's been eavesdropping on them; little girls like to do that. When she sees Phony coming toward the stairs, May jumps up and runs back up the stairs, her feet making little slapping sounds on the steps and her nightgown billowing out behind her.

CHAPTER SIX

IN THE MORNING ESTHER STANDS AT THE KITCHEN DOOR drying her mixing bowl and watching Daniel drive the barouche into the yard. When he sees her he stops the carriage and gets down. He strides past her into the kitchen with a sheepish grin.

"And just where have you been this early?" she asks.

He pulls out a chair and sits down at the table. "I took Master Cornelius and Malachi down to Under-the-Hill. You made hotcakes? I'm hungry."

"Mind your manners," she says. "Your mammy know you was gone? And why'd Cornelius and Mal want t' go down there this early anyways?"

"They're catchin' a steamboat," Daniel says as Esther hands him a plate of hotcakes. "I watched Cornelius buy the tickets." He reaches for the molasses pitcher.

She frowns. "A steamboat? Where are they goin'?"

He wolfs a forkful of hotcakes and wipes his mouth on a towel. "They're goin' to Virginny," he says, "but first they gotta get to New Orleans. Master Cornelius promised Mal he'd take him to Virginny to find his mammy, and today's the day they're goin'. He said they won't be back for a long time."

Esther throws her dishrag onto the side table. What Daniel said gives her a sick feeling; here she's asked Cornelius so many times to help her find her girls who were sold off into Louisiana, and he's put Mal ahead of her, as usual. Finding Theresa and Helene is a lot more important than chasing around with Mal in some far-off place called Virginny, a place she can't even picture. It's been over three years since her girls were grabbed right out of this house, when Emile Coqterre went stark crazy and sold every slave on the place except her. Her girls might be in a cruel situation—she can't bear to think that—or they might've been sold time and again. And now Cornelius has snuck off with Malachi without a word to anybody, and not giving a thought to helping her find her girls, even though she's mentioned it to him more than once. A knot of anger seizes her, and she turns away so Daniel won't see the bitterness in her face.

After Daniel finishes eating and goes out to drive the barouche back to the carriage house, Esther goes into the big house to set the breakfast table. Her hands are shaking as she lays out the china. After she sets the last plate down she stops and walks to the window, her back to the room. She closes her eyes and laces her fingers together to steady them.

"Esther?"

She turns around, surprised to see Euphonia standing in the doorway. She hadn't heard her coming down the stairs.

Phony says, "Esther, now that Jenny's gone, clean out that back bedroom, will you? It needs a deep cleaning. I want to get all Jenny's things out of there. And open the chiffarobe so it'll air out. I want to put my sewing things in there."

"Yes, ma'am."

Coella comes downstairs with Thomas and May, and Dancy brings in the eggs and ham and hotcakes Esther's been preparing since before dawn. Esther goes to the back bedroom and stands in the doorway, gazing into the peach-colored room. It's a small room with one window that looks out toward the Dependency. It looks the same as it always has: to the right there's a bed with an iron headboard, a side table, and a dresser; and to the left, a tall black chiffarobe. The room still has Rosabel's powdery scent. But Esther remembers farther back, to the time when this room belonged to Emile's sister Sophronia, who was always a mystery. Esther wasn't sure Sophronia wanted to live here, but maybe the young widow had nowhere else to live. Wasn't it a kindness for Emile to move his sister here? But after she came here, Emile kept himself away at his plantation most of the time. Esther thought he brought Sophronia here to run the big house and look after little Stephanie, since his own wife was dead.

But Sophronia was overwhelmed by it all. She kept to this room with a bottle of Cherry Bounce on that side table. So it was Esther who took Stephanie under her wing because someone had to mother the orphan child. And what started as a duty turned into an attachment for Stephanie that wasn't too distant from what she felt for Helene and Theresa. It hurt Esther's heart so bad when Stephanie drowned.

There's always a price, she thinks. *Be careful what you love, because one day you're gonna lose it.*

When Sophronia died, nobody's heart was hurting, Esther thinks. The day she found the woman lying cold in the bed, Esther tiptoed right past the corpse's blind eyes and went straight to the dresser to open the second drawer. There under the nightgowns was Sophronia's purse, right where Esther knew it would be. Many a time Sophronia would send Esther to town to buy this or that, and she was always stern about how she wanted the buying done, telling Esther where to shop, and what to get, and what price to pay. But once Esther had that money jingling in her pocket, she shopped where and how she pleased. And Sophronia always wrote her a pass, the way the law called for, but sometimes Esther slipped into town even without a pass, and she never got into trouble for that.

Esther hid the purse in her hidey hole in the wall behind her own bed. That seventy dollars was what kept her going all those months after Emile killed himself. She still has most of it, as well as another fifty she's saved up from the wages Euphonia's been paying her every Friday since Cornelius put her free.

Sounds come from the dining room: Thomas protesting because he has to eat eggs, May humming absent-mindedly as she butters her toast. Esther turns the small brass key to the chiffarobe; it seems balky, doesn't want to catch, which is unusual. She tries it again, and this time the doors swing open. Esther stares: inside the dark chiffarobe the figure of her friend Lucy Ida is hanging in the air, translucent above the summer dresses. Little Lucy Ida was bent and thin in her ninety-third year, when she died. Now her bright little eyes are peering straight into Esther's, and she rises and sinks on the current of air that wafted in when the doors opened. She shakes a spectral finger, crooked as a discarded carrot, and says, *Helene and Theresa wore these dresses, you know. Don't you forget them.*

Esther's heart jumps. She clasps her hand to her chest and sinks backward to the bed, staring into the gaping maw of the chiffarobe. The image was made of dust and it carried the musty odor of old clothes. Now it's gone. All she sees are May's summer dresses hanging there alongside two of Jenny's old dresses that used to belong to Helene and Theresa: a green one with bows sewn over the buttons, and a plain gray one with a white collar.

Esther thinks, *I've got to find my girls.*

CHAPTER SEVEN

TWO DAYS LATER VICKSBURG FINALLY RISES in front of Jenny and Walker, a skyline of slate-gray rooftops stabbed with the pencil silhouettes of steeples and rising to a columned courthouse at the top of the hill. Jenny thinks it's a miracle that the horse didn't give out and the wheels didn't fall off the buggy, and mercifully it didn't rain on them. And no slavers threatened them.

Walker turns the buggy onto a boulevard that curves up from the bottom of the hill. Then they drive along a leafy street where handsome white houses sit behind well-kept lawns, shrubs lining the front paths, and every house looks welcoming behind a wide front porch. Walker turns the buggy onto an unpaved side road, and they rattle down an alley. He pulls the buggy to a stop behind a cabin huddled in the back-yard of a two-story house.

"This is it," he says, reaching to take Rosabel, who looks at him with wide eyes, her thumb in her mouth.

Jenny looks around. So Walker's mother lives here behind the house where she works, in a cabin between a clothesline and a privy. Walker told her how Minnie, his mammy, was a house slave for Missus Martin for as long as he can remember, and how most of the time she raised her children by herself. His pappy Vinson was always trying to run away from slavery; that's why he named his first-born son Walker, because Vinson was a walker himself. He tried to walk away from slavery more than once, and finally he made it. Nobody knows where he went.

Minnie's house is cheaply built, with unpainted boards nailed up for the walls. It has only one room, and Jenny can see the whole house isn't much bigger than a single bedroom at Carefree. They walk around the side of the cabin, ducking through sheets billowing on the clothesline.

Two men are sitting on the steps of the little house. When Walker comes around the corner carrying Rosabel, the men jump up. They grin the same toothy grins that Walker has, even though they're tall men, not small like Walker.

Walker hands Rosabel back to Jenny and grasps his brothers' hands in greeting.

Beaming, they slap his back. "Welcome, brother!"

"This here's Jenny," Walker says. "And that's Rosabel."

The men look at Jenny and together they envelop her in a bear hug, which surprises her; people at Carefree don't hug much. Barney reaches for Rosabel and hefts her high, while Cooper turns around and shouts into the open door of the cabin, "Walker's come!"

Walker's brothers and sisters spill out through the door chattering like a flock of birds, washed along on a tidal wave of happiness, and they crowd around Jenny with friendly, happy faces. And then the beaming people move aside to make an open space, and a small humpbacked woman wearing a white tignon and a faded housedress appears in the doorway. *No queen could make a more regal entrance,* Jenny thinks. The woman opens her toothless mouth in surprise and holds her arms out to Walker, who grasps her in a swaying hug. This is Minnie, Walker's mother, Jenny knows.

Minnie pulls away from him. "You've come back, Walker!" Her voice is high-pitched and sweet, like a bird chirping in its early spring nest. She hangs onto Walker's arm as if she's afraid he'll disappear if she lets him go. They all push backward into the house. Minnie reaches out to take Rosabel, her eyes bright. She has to know that bright-skinned child can't be Walker's, Jenny thinks, but still, Rosabel's such a pretty baby, with her wide face and her curly black hair, and she's not afraid of strangers; any old woman would reach for her. With the friendliness in the room, and the aroma of chicken stew simmering in a black pot in the fireplace, Jenny senses the warmth that Walker must have grown up with, in this big family with two brothers and four sisters.

They talk, bursts of laughter rising to the low ceiling. Later Minnie ladles out their meal into big cracked bowls. The chicken stew is thick with cream and vegetables. They sit on the stools or on the floor, their plates on their knees. Jenny counts: there are ten people here, counting the little girls Violet and Callie who belong to Walker's sister Marie.

Jenny feeds Rosabel some of the broth, and then she nurses her. When Rosabel's eyes close she lays the girl down on Minnie's bed. Walker and his sisters and brothers talk together in a happy excited way, as if Walker had never left. Jenny looks around; the walls of the house are rough, pieces of cardboard and newspaper stuffed here and there to cover the cracks. Even though the quilts Minnie's hung on the walls are tattered and faded, they give the room a homey look. A geranium clings to life in a coffee can on a shelf near the fireplace. Even the mismatched dishes and bent old spoons have a charm. Jenny pictures how a big family of seven kids would grow up here in this cabin and turn into these friendly people: Barney and Cooper, and Walker's sisters Marie and Susie. His other sisters, Joan and Annie, aren't here.

The men sit outside on the step, talking. After a while, Cooper calls, "Come out here and talk to us, Miss Jenny." He stands up so she can sit on the step. It's dark out, but the men have set up a lantern near the steps. So Jenny goes out and sits down.

"Tell us about you," Cooper says. "We can see you ain't from around here. So tell us where you come from, girl."

"Africa," Jenny says, and she sees their eyes grow wide and white with this thought.

After a minute Barney says, "I thought I could see it."

"You a lot darker than us," Cooper says, holding out his hands to compare with hers, and they all laugh good-naturedly.

"So how'd you meet up with Walker here?" Barney asks.

"I knew him a long time ago in Natchez," she says. Walker, standing near the steps, looks at her and winks. She wonders if she should tell the whole story, but then she decides that might be more than Walker wants told, especially the part about him being captured back into slavery and dragged onto the *John Jay*.

When it gets dark Cooper and Barney drift away, saying they have to get back to their master's house. Jenny has gleaned that they both belong to the same man, a Mister Fitler, who lives on Montgomery Street. Jenny goes inside as Rosabel frets awake, but Minnie picks her up and goes to the table and sits down in the chair, feeding the child spoonfuls of a white custard she'd cooked, all the while talking to her in baby talk. Marie and Susie inch closer to Jenny and then the three young women sit on the floor in front of the fireplace, their legs straight out under their skirts.

"We're younger than our brothers," Susie says. She has Walker's wide grin.

"Yes'm, Miss Jenny, first I had the boys and then I had the girls," Minnie says from the table. Rosabel has grabbed a spoon and bangs it on the table. "My other two girls, Joan and Annie, they live too far away to come by too often. Up by Yazoo city, they is, on a big plantation. I'm just glad they together." *Enslaved together,* Jenny thinks. She remembers Esther's big fear, that her girls wouldn't be together.

Jenny likes Minnie. When the old woman smiles, her smile takes up her whole face, and her bright little eyes crinkle until they're almost closed. She likes Marie and Susie, too. Their gossip and story-telling don't leave her out. She looks from one to the other, smiling.

Jenny and Walker sleep that night on the floor of the cabin. The fireplace pops and crackles, and Jenny lies awake for a long time, listening to Walker snore. Minnie snores too, her back turned, on the small bed pushed against the wall. Rosabel is curled up beside her. Listening to the unfamiliar sounds and breathing the aroma of the wood fire and the stew Minnie cooked, Jenny feels—not happy exactly, because the trip was exhausting and she feared for her freedom the whole way—but content to be here. They've made their escape, and now they're safe in Walker's world, where friendliness and good food and safety make the air practically shimmer along the walls and around the fireplace, where the last log is winking into darkness.

Late in the afternoon the next day, Jenny, who thinks she's begun to understand the order of things in Minnie's household, stands at the kitchen table chopping onions for the gumbo she promised to make for tonight's supper. The door to the cabin is open, because it's a mild day. Rosabel is napping on Minnie's bed with a light quilt pulled over her, when Jenny hears the back door of the big house slam, a sound that startles Rosabel out of her nap.

As she goes over to pat the girl back to sleep, she looks around, and Walker is standing in the doorway.

"Jenny." He's out of breath and he wears an expression she's never seen before. His eyes are big as anything in his old face.

"What?" she asks as Rosabel's cry catches in the air.

"Jenny, I got to go."

She's never seen Walker look afraid like that, not even on the steamboat when he'd been snatched back into slavery. She picks Rosabel up and puts the baby to her shoulder. "What happened?"

"I gotta hurry," he says. He leans out the door, looking in both directions. He eases the door closed.

"Go where?" she asks.

"Anywhere. I gotta get outta here. Bernadine's gonna go for the authorities, and they'll grab me quick. I'll end up at the slave auction, and that's if I'm lucky. If I ain't, I'll swing."

"Why? What happened? We just got here."

He whispers, "Vicksburg ain't safe for me, Jenny. I done caused some trouble for my mammy."

"What kinda trouble?"

He crouches down to drag his satchel from under Minnie's bed. "Jenny, listen, it happened so quick I didn't hardly know what I was doin,' and now I'm in trouble big."

"Will you please tell me what?" Jenny asks, as Rosabel, unhappy because her nap was interrupted, whimpers into her neck.

Walker throws his clothes into his satchel. "Mammy went to hand Bernadine a platter, that big silver one that's so heavy, I remember it from when I was a kid here. I could hardly lift it myself. But Bernadine told Mammy to get it down from the high shelf, but when Mammy tried to hand it over to her, the heavy old thing, she dropped it. It put a big dent on the side."

"Well, that ain't so bad—"

"But, listen. Then Bernadine started whackin' my mammy with her ridin' crop, just grabbed it up off the table where it was layin', and beat her 'bout the shoulders. That was the exact minute I walked into the kitchen. Oh, Jenny, my poor mammy was whimperin' and cryin', and Bernadine was madder than I ever seen a white woman be. I couldn't let her beat my mammy, I just couldn't, Jenny. So I grabbed that whip out o' the old lady's hand. She pulled against me, all shocked to see me doin' that, but I tell you, she weren't goin' to hurt my mammy."

"Did you strike her?" Jenny asks in a low voice.

"No, I didn't, but I held it up over her like I was threatenin' to." His voice is a hoarse whisper.

It's so easy to get into trouble if you're around slavery, Jenny thinks. And she and Walker haven't been around slaves much since they lived at Carefree, because Cornelius freed everybody there and didn't really pay much attention to what they did.

"I gotta go, Jenny. I'm goin.' You stay here. Remember that paper you got ain't nothin' but paper. It might keep you safe, or it might not." He reaches out and takes Rosabel from Jenny and kisses her forehead. He hands her back to Jenny.

"Take some cornbread," Jenny says. She sets Rosabel back down on the bed and grabs a pan from the table. She stuffs the cornbread into a sack. "If you runnin', you gotta eat." Then she says, "Walker, wait! I'm comin' with you."

"You crazy, gal," he said.

"You said we'd go to the free soil. So let's go."

"Jenny, I ain't even sure I can make it out of slave-land. I didn't count on bein' arrested. I ain't never broke any rules in my whole life, and now I done this one thing. Just 'cause I couldn't stand for my mammy to get beat." He heads out the door.

"Wait! I'm comin' too." Jenny grabs her own satchel from under the bed and stuffs her few things into it, along with the baby's clean diapers. She takes the sack that holds the dirty diapers too. She runs out the door to where Walker is already hitching up Dun. He climbs up to the seat, the reins in his hands, and reaches down to take Rosabel. Jenny climbs up next to him and takes the baby. Then he shakes the reins hard, and Dun pulls away. They're off to free soil for sure this time, Jenny thinks, although it's a shame they have to run, and not even tell Minnie goodbye.

CHAPTER EIGHT

BUT THE ROAD NORTH OUT OF VICKSBURG is hard to find, and Walker doesn't know the way. After they take two wrong turns, they finally seem to be headed out into open country. But by nightfall Jenny knows that two slavers are tailing them. She looks over her shoulder and watches the white men move their horses together so they can talk, and then ride apart; then together again, talking, and all the time getting closer and closer to the buggy. The woods seem to swallow the road on each side. There's no town up ahead, no cabin with a lamp in the window, no country church with a revival meeting—nothing. No place to pull off the road and take refuge, to double-check their freeing papers. The men know this road better than Walker does.

At a place where the road forks, Walker has to make a judgment which way to go, and he chooses wrong; Jenny senses it immediately. Because a minute later the two men beat their horses into a lather and overtake the buggy, cutting them off. Walker shouts at them to leave, and Rosabel wails; Jenny holds the baby tight to her chest. The men yank Walker down.

"We're free people!" he shouts, but Jenny knows at that moment they aren't free at all. They're arrested, and these two hard-bitten men with fierce eyes probably couldn't read a freeing paper if their lives depended on it. Walker, his hands shaking, pulls his freeing paper out of his pocket and holds it out. One of the men yanks the paper out of his hand and throws it down, grinding it in the dirt so it's ripped and shredded, and then the other man stalks over to Jenny.

"You got one o' them papers too?"

She won't look at him, just keeps her eyes down and fixed on Rosabel. "I ain't got one," she says.

"I bet you do." He yanks at her dress and then pushes her back. Her bodice buttons pop loose. She falls over onto her back while Rosabel wails.

She grabs her bodice and holds her dress closed. "It's in my satchel," she mumbles as she reaches over to open the satchel and fumble for the paper. She hands it to him.

He spits on it and rips it in two, and then drops it on the dirt.

"Guess you ain't free after all," he says, chuckling.

The other man has ropes, and he gets up onto the buggy next to her. He points her to the back of the buggy, and then he takes rope and ties her ankles together as she crouches there, but not before he pushes her skirt up over her knees. Rosabel wails. The other man shoves Walker into the back and ties his wrists behind his back. Then he climbs up onto the seat and shakes the reins to turn the buggy around.

"This is one miserable nag," he says.

"Hey, Tom, it's three for one," the driver says, chuckling.

"Oh, ain't this terrible, Jenny," Walker mumbles. "The worst thing of all. Worst of anything."

Jenny closes her eyes and in her mind she kneads a dough for bread, pushing and pounding the pliant dough and breathing in the yeasty fragrance as it rises around her.

But fear rises more.

Jenny had pictured a slave auction often enough. In Natchez she once walked past the auction house of Franklin and Armfields; it sat on an unpaved street over on the east side of town near the place known as Forks of the Road. And even though she didn't see any slaves being taken inside the building, she remembers the foulness of the air that enveloped the place. She'd never been traded in an auction, but she'd been taken for a price twice, once in New Orleans and once in Natchez, sold man to man. But she'd never been inside an auction building until today.

The driver pulls the buggy to a stop at a wooden building built halfway down a hillside. When he gets down from the buggy, Jenny sees he's a stubble-faced old buzzard wearing a ragged shirt. The man who squeezed her thigh must be his son. The old man motions them to get down, which is hard for Jenny to do with her ankles tied. But she hops down clumsily, clinging to Rosabel. They stand tied beside the buggy, as the two men walk a little distance away from them.

"I think they might let us go, Jenny," Walker whispers.

"They ain't gonna let us go, Walker! We're money in their pockets." She's flabbergasted that he would say such a thing. Walker's looking every which way, but she stares straight at the two men who're watching them from ten feet away.

"They're figuring a price for us," Jenny says.

The older man goes inside the building and then returns a few minutes later to talk to his partner. Jenny can't make out what they're saying.

Then both men walk over to them. The younger man says, "Auction's tomorrow. Ya-hoo! Y'all are goin' in there."

He pushes them toward the door and they stumble into a large empty room with a raised platform at one end. *This is the place I've been warned about,* Jenny thinks. Even though no one is in the room, Jenny thinks she hears the sounds of ghosts chattering like monkeys in all the corners and up by the ceiling.

The jailer jerks Walker toward a door off to the left; a stench rises as they get closer. Rosabel buries her face in Jenny's shoulder as they go into another room at the back. This room is already crowded with a dozen men and women huddling in groups.

The slaves shift around to make room for them. She sees why the place stinks; a bucket in the corner serves as a toilet. The expressions on the faces of the waiting men and women aren't the masks slaves usually wear, Jenny thinks. They're trying to hide what they're thinking, but they can't. Those stony faces are bleak. Walker guides her to one corner of the room, where they have a little more space and can stand together. The other slaves glance at them and then look away.

Jenny tries to calm her racing mind. The imprisonment they're in hardly seems real to her. Only a few hours ago they were on the road, in the sweet smelling air, and now they're here in the stench, and the air is drenched with fear.

Her chest feels so tight it's as if some iron band has encircled her, and she can barely breathe. Jenny thinks, *What did we do to be in this prison?* And Rosabel—what will happen to her? If I'm sold off to be a slave, what if Rosabel's left behind? It's the most horrible thought she can imagine. But it's reality; Rosabel is in this prison too. Why?

Everything can change so suddenly. In an instant you can be done for. There's no escape from this room; the only door is guarded. She looks around; the walls are dim in the lamp light. There's one grimy window, hardly bigger than her hand, high on the wall behind Walker. They made that window so small so no one could get out, she thinks. But Rosabel could. For a second she considers hefting the child up to it and letting her drop through it to whatever is on the other side. Some kindly stranger might find the child.

She can't think that! Dogs are barking out there, and Rosabel is afraid of dogs. No, whatever fate Jenny has as a slave woman, she'll have to face it for Rosabel too. As long as she has breath in her body, she'll stay with her child.

That night she sits cross-legged on the filthy floor with Rosabel curled up in her lap like a cat. Jenny wants to stay awake, to watch, but she can't keep her eyes open. As she drifts off to sleep, a dream begins to play across her brain; a sudden bright image, but with no backwards or forwards, the way dreams are. Like all dreams, it says: *You know everything. There are no questions in dreamland.*

She startles awake. She can't dream that whole dream, not here in this slave-auction room. But the whole story is in a space as small as the head of a pin. It's her memories, turned into a dream.

She remembers Dahomey, West Africa. The curve of the thatch huts that form a semicircle that is the village—she can see that clearly. Is the village still there, an African place that was its own den of misery?

When slavers came it was the start of a war. Her name was Abena then. The village warriors were always watching, their eyes flashing in the night. Her brother Kofi wouldn't remember. He was only seven. But she was a girl of ten; she remembers how afraid the whole village was.

Her mother Esi cared for an old man she called uncle, but whether he was her uncle or not, Abena couldn't be sure. Perhaps he was her mother's uncle, he was so old. His white hair was like a cloud around his head. His back was so weak he could barely stand, but sometimes he had to get up to hunt. He was hunting in the forest the day she and Kofi were taken. The slavers would have taken the old man too, if he'd been caught out in the forest alone. She pictures him coming back to the village, and the children not there. Was he the only one who helped Esi look for her children? All the other men were cowards. If Jenny could say something to Esi in her dream, she'd say Mother, listen—the slavers are about.

Did Esi and the old man go looking, traipsing through the forest till they came to the river? A sandy bank curved along the river there, and Esi would have seen where Abena and Kofi made a play village, scraping the sand into little heaps. Abena and Kofi used sticks to scrape out roads and piled up little mounds of sand for the houses. Surely she would have seen the marks where heavy boots had ground up the smooth surface. Wouldn't she have knelt down and touched the sand? She might even have seen a palm print Abena pressed into the sand. Esi would've wanted to save this little hill of sand, the last thing she'd ever see of her children, just as Jenny wants to save every brown curl she clips from Rosabel's hair before the girl slips away from her and is grown. But when Esi touched the sand, wouldn't it crumble, just as Rosabel's wispy hair flies off into a breeze as she clips it?

Esi was never liked in the village, a woman with children but no husband. Now the women treated her as an untouchable, because she was a woman whose children were snatched. The witch woman in the next village would tell the other women their own children might be snatched too, if they talked to her.

Esi never trusted that witch-woman, never paid her for her foolish sooth-sayings. But some villagers paid the old crone in secret, whenever they needed a hex to blind a husband's wandering eye, a potion to scald a troublesome mother-in-law, or an amulet to hang on the hut of a widow whose children vanished. Abena knew the talk in the village, more than her mother knew. The villagers dropped their eyes *when Esi passed them and their voices fell silent when she came to the well where the women were. It would have been lonely. After a while she moved into the old man's hut. Everyone knew the slavers could come again. And then one day they did.*

Jenny opens her eyes to stop the story playing in her head. A candle, burning low, sputters on the floor a few feet away. Rosabel doesn't like to sleep in the dark. Jenny sits awake for the rest of the night, thinking Dahomey is right outside her window, in the cool night.

At the first light of morning the iron lock on the door clangs open, and a guard comes in. He hands a tray of biscuits to a woman near the door. It's a silent meal, as the slaves eat the hard biscuits and then one by one go to the water bucket to drink from the dipper.

When the guard returns, he bustles through the door holding some towels and a bucket.

"Y'all fix yourself up," he says, handing a towel to a woman standing near him. "Wipe your faces." He sets the bucket on the floor. "You men oil your hair with this grease," he says, pointing to the bucket. "You need to look shiny."

The men glance around uncertainly and then they line up and pass by the bucket one by one, dipping their fingers into the bucket and smearing the grease on their hair. The guard goes back out and returns a moment later with a pile of dresses across his arm.

"You gals get changed. Put on these here dresses." He hands them out to the women.

No one in the room speaks. The women turn their backs to the men and pull off their clothes and slip the dresses over their heads. Jenny wrinkles her nose at the greasy dress he hands her. She takes off her own dress, which isn't ragged at all, and drops the flimsy dress over her head. She buttons the cheap buttons down the front.

They wait. A few of the men begin to talk in low voices, glancing around the room and then looking down at the floor. *Those men must have come from the same place,* Jenny thinks. *Maybe they'll get sold together.* An older man says to a young man standing next to him, "Robert, if we don't go to the same place, I just want t' say, I enjoyed gettin' to know you. If ole Master Ben was still livin', we wouldn't be here. It was that boy of his, that Frank. Master Ben wouldn't 've called the slavers in."

Robert nods. "I enjoyed gettin' to know you too, Harry. I hope you get to someplace they don't work you too hard. And I hope you get a kind master."

"I hope you don't have to go to the cane fields," Harry says.

"You neither. I pray to the Lord we don't, neither one of us."

Jenny glances at Walker, but it seems bold to speak to him. He's crushed because he's been made into a slave again, after all he's gone through to get free. *It's because he never made it to the free soil,* she thinks; and neither did she. If you're in slave-land, you can't think slavery won't reach up and get you. But she didn't go to the free soil when she had a chance; when she was on the steamer *John Jay,* she had a ticket, a chance, and she didn't take it. And when she was in New Orleans, there wasn't anything to keep her from going. The steamers pulled out of there every morning, and she could have taken Rosabel and May and just gone. But she didn't.

Slave-land is where she is; it's all she knows, and that's why she didn't go north. Her brother Kofi's here somewhere. Now she's only as far up the river as Vicksburg, and it's still a long way to Cincinnati.

The morning drags on; the jailer comes in after an hour to look them over. The slaves look at the floor with no expression on their faces. Everyone's just waiting to see what happens, Jenny thinks. There's no point in wailing or making a scene. All that would get you is a smack from the jailer in some place where it wouldn't show through your clothes.

Finally there are noises from the other room, doors opening and closing, and the low rumble of voices. The auction is starting. The slaves in the waiting room tense. Then the door opens and the jailer motions for three slaves to pass through the door.

A few minutes later the jailer points at Walker and motions him through the door. Walker grabs Jenny's hand. "Cornelius bound t' come rescue us, Jenny," he whispers.

"You are dreamin', Walker! How's he gonna do that?" she whispers. "He ain't even gonna know where we're at."

"You hang close to me," he says as he moves toward the door. He turns to the guard. "Sir, this here's my fambly."

The guard wordlessly motions Jenny through the door too. Rosabel clings to Jenny's shoulder, her face buried in her neck. Through the thin slave dress, Jenny can feel the child's heart beating fast as a bird's.

As they go into the next room, Walker whispers, "Hold tight. We might get lucky here."

But she sees how he looks around nervously, studying the crowd of buyers. She wonders if he really slept at all last night.

Jenny looks around. It's a relief to be in a larger room where the air doesn't reek, but when she sees the buyers she feels faint. She tries to stand next to Walker, but it's hard to stand close to him, because he's pulled to one side and the other, as buyers inspect him. Most of the men are standing around watching the auction as one after another slaves are summoned to stand on the dais. The men look well-to-do in their suits and string ties.

"Y'all go stand up thar," the guard says, pointing to the dais. The white men in the room are shuffling around, talking and pointing. The only people not moving are the slaves who wait, their faces unreadable. A man in a top hat comes over and without a word pulls Walker's lower lip down to look at his teeth; then he squeezes his upper arms. Walker glances at Jenny and turns around when the man orders him to.

"You're strong enough," the man says. "What's your name?"

"I'm Walker Jackson, sir. A free man."

"No, you ain't free," the man says.

"This here's my fambly," Walker says, motioning to Jenny and Rosabel. "I'd be most appreciative, sir, if we could stay together—"

"Walker, don't say anything," Jenny whispers. The man glances at Jenny and Rosabel, and then turns his back and flicks his finger up at the auctioneer, pointing at Walker. He motions Walker toward a line of slaves who stand along the wall.

"You're goin' to Texas," the auctioneer says to Walker.

A sound comes from Walker's throat as he's yanked away and pushed toward the group of men near the door. Then a man opens the door and orders the men out. As he disappears out the door, Jenny calls out, "I'm sorry, Walker!" He looks around at her and says nothing, and the door swings shut behind him.

Jenny is alone, and the weight of that is so heavy she thinks it could stop her heart. These men looking over the slaves like cattle—what did they know about Walker, the things he's done, how he worked hard for five years to buy himself out; or of herself either, the places she's been, the people she's known. Nothing protected her and Walker; not the freeing papers, not a law written down anywhere. Her skin is black, and a long time ago Mal told her, "If your skin's black, you a slave, and that's it." There's no escaping it unless the abolitionists could hold sway, and there's only a few of those.

She moves forward when she's ordered to, clinging to Rosabel who's digging her fingers into her neck. She's determined not to look at anyone; she keeps her eyes fixed on the floor. A moment later, a pair of expensive riding boots come into her sight. The boots stand there for a moment and then shuffle away. The jailer tells her to turn around. The boots scuff back, and then stand close to her again. When she turns back around she glances up at the man in the boots. He looks her up and down and his hand flashes up toward the auctioneer, signalling a buy. He walks over to the podium and signs a paper the auctioneer holds out to him. *I'm bought and paid for*, Jenny thinks. As he walks back to her she looks at him. He's a young man with a round soft face and a swelling belly under his expensive suit. He's a slave buyer, that's all she needs to know; and except for Cornelius Carson, every one of those men, in her experience, is evil.

At least she has her child. She presses her face to the girl's damp hair. It's the one thing she couldn't bear, if she lost Rosabel.

The buyer motions her to follow him, and when they get outside she breathes deeply of the clean winter air, wanting to get the stench of the holding pen out of her lungs. The sun is just rising over the trees to the east. He motions her toward a buggy parked nearby, and she climbs up and settles Rosabel on her lap. He shakes the reins and drives along the dirt road and turns up into Vicksburg proper.

Jenny hates the slave dress she had to put on back at the auction.

He glances over at her. "My name's Milton Crum."

Her voice has failed her, but after a minute she croaks, "Yes sir. I'm Jenny, and this is Rosabel."

"My wife needs help with the house. You know how to cook?"

"Yes sir."

"We live over here on Cherry Street."

She nods. The houses and shops of Vicksburg pass in a blur. When they reach Main Street, Jenny says, "Sir, I need to stop up here at Missus Bernadine Martin's house. It's where I was before. I left some things there in the slave house out back for my baby, her diapers and such all."

He glances at her and says, "Awright. But don't dawdle."

"No sir." She sets Rosabel on the seat between them and points out Mrs. Martin's house. "It's that white house over there, with the fence. The slave house is in back. There's an alley you can drive down."

Crum drives into the alley and pulls the buggy to a stop. Jenny gets down. When she reaches back for Rosabel, he says, "She stays here."

Jenny sprints around to the door of Minnie's house. When she looks back she sees Rosabel sitting on the seat whimpering, and Crum scowling as he holds the hem of the child's dress. Jenny pushes the cabin door open and slips inside.

Minnie looks up, the whites of her eyes flashing in surprise, as Jenny comes in. The old lady's halfway dressed, putting on her house-dress for the day's work.

"Jenny? What you doin' here, girl?"

Jenny takes a deep breath. "I got to grab the rest of Rosabel's things, Minnie. And then I got to go." She swallows hard. "Minnie, we got caught back into slavery, and I was sold at the slave auction to be a house slave for Milton Crum over on Cherry Street."

Minnie puts her wrinkled hands up on her face, and her eyes are big. "How'd you get caught back into slavery? You had your freein' papers!"

"Didn't make no difference."

"And where's Walker?" Minnie's voice rises.

Jenny puts her finger up to her lip, to quiet her. Milton Crum can't hear this. "He was sold off and took to Texas," she whispers.

"Took to Texas?" Minnie says, sinking to the floor with her face in her hands. "Lord, don't tell me that. I ain't never gonna see my boy again."

Jenny reaches down to help her up. "We couldn't do anything about it, Minnie. We got caught. But I'm gonna be right here in Vicksburg. I'll come see you. I gotta go now. He's waitin' out there in the buggy with Rosabel." After Jenny stuffs the baby's clothes into a sack, she runs out the door. Minnie, her dress still unbuttoned, runs out behind her and stands at the fence, watching as the buggy rumbles away. When Jenny looks over her shoulder, she sees Minnie standing there, hunched over with her hand over her mouth. Jenny gathers Rosabel close to herself and they sit as far away as they can from Milton Crum, two humps of misery.

CHAPTER NINE

Natchez
March 1844

BY LATE MARCH A WARMTH HAS ENVELOPED NATCHEZ, and the dog-wood trees are bright as bride's bouquets in the lime-green woods. Squirrels hop from branch to branch, and birds call endlessly.

In the mornings Esther likes to walk out to the bench behind the kitchen, where the pond reflects the sky like a round mirror. Normally the pond reminds her of Lucy Ida, her old friend who died on the same day Miss Stephanie eloped with Cornelius; Lucy Ida used to enjoy sitting and staring at the pond too. But that was more than ten years ago now, and her memories of Lucy Ida are fading, a comfort gone. Now Esther sits, twisting her hands together slowly. She feels alone, even though there's plenty of company to be had at Carefree if she wants it. She knows that Jane, Margaret, and Virginia are sitting in the spot they've claimed on the other side of the kitchen, where there's a log bench that's long enough for the three old women. If Esther were more sociable, she'd go sit with them; but she holds herself a little apart from those women. She's never found common ground with them; it's the distance between Natchez and Rapides Parish. Those women even cook their own food over fires they build behind the Dependency; it's food Esther doesn't recognize, but all the slaves brought from Louisiana—except for Dancy—prefer it to what she cooks. Dancy's learned how to cook the Natchez way, and she's in and out of the big house almost as much as Esther is. The old women almost speak a different language from a person who's spent her whole life in Natchez. So Esther's satisfied where she sits, where she has room and space to think her own thoughts.

She can't get her girls out of her mind. *Where are they?* Helene, short, round-faced and rambunctious, was Raynard Fanning's daughter as sure as that sun rising. And her older girl Theresa, tall and lanky, a hundred times more reliable than her sister. When Theresa was born, the baby gave Esther hope that she could have a living child after August and Littleton died. It wasn't right the girls should've been yanked away from their mammy just when they were coming into their own as grown women. They were in the blossom time of their lives. If they were here, Esther would've found them husbands—she used to be known as the matchmaker for this whole house—and there could've been babies and laughter and they could've been free just like she is now, because Cornelius won't keep slaves. But Emile Coqterre took all that away from her when his brain went crazy and he sold everybody off.

And it wasn't like Master Emile was a cruel man; he treated her decently before he started thinking all wrong about everything. It was after Miss Stephanie got married, and then Miss Sophronia died, that his mind went wrong. Esther could see it happening, day by day, him losing his way. She served his meals and made his bed, and when you live that close to somebody you notice the little things going wrong. By the end he was living like a wild man in the woods, him the owner of the finest house in Natchez; his hair grew so long it hung down his back and over his face too. She almost didn't recognize him on those few times when he'd come up to the house. Then he opened the house to the goats and let them destroy it as much as they could.

So she's decided she just needs to go. Mister Cornelius is a kind man, but he's gone to Virginny so Mal can see his people, and he didn't say a thing about taking Esther to find Helene and Theresa. Euphonia has never once asked Esther anything about herself, her life. And Cornelius has other things on his mind.

I've never been anything more than a shadow to them, she thinks; *every day I'm in the house, picking up and cleaning and winding the clocks, but Mister Cornelius and Miss Euphonia don't give me a thought. I'm just a fixture, like the lamps and the draperies, and they probably figure they're doing right just by paying me that puny salary every Friday.*

She smooths her skirt down and stands up. She's made up her mind. She walks over to the big house and goes inside. The house is quiet. After Cornelius and Mal left four months ago, the house settled into a different rhythm. Every day Euphonia meets with Elliot Badeau to discuss the things that need to be repaired or repainted around the place; and she still visits with her friends and works on her embroidery projects. Only two letters have come from Cornelius, and none for a while. When the letters came it caused a lot of excitement; Euphonia called everyone into the parlor and read the letters out loud to them. But it has been some weeks, Esther knows, since any letters came.

Esther goes upstairs to May's room. The girl is sitting on her bed playing with an old French doll that used to be Stephanie's. A few days ago Esther found it tucked away on a shelf in a chiffarobe, and she got it down and dusted it off. It's a pretty doll, expensive looking, with a porcelain face and a soft brown wig. Its lips are parted in a little smile to show two pearly teeth, and when you lay the doll on its back its eyes swing shut. Esther gave it to May, and right now the girl is dawdling over it in her dreamy way, her spelling book lying closed on the counterpane.

"Where's Coella?" Esther asks.

May looks up. "She took Thomas down to the creek, but I didn't want to go. And Miss Phony's gone to the dressmaker to get a new dress."

Esther sits down on the side of the bed next to May and fiddles with the girl's hair, which hasn't been brushed.

"You want me to tie a ribbon for you?" she asks.

May nods. Esther opens the dresser drawer to find a ribbon to match the girl's brown dress. After she brushes the girl's hair and ties the ribbon, she says, "Now May, listen. I need to tell you somethin'."

The girl turns to face her. *You're growin' up*, Esther thinks; the girl's features are becoming more distinct, but she won't ever be pretty. Her chin is narrow and she has chipmunk cheeks.

"I'm gonna be leavin' for a while," Esther says. "Dancy can see to it that you get your coffee, and while I'm gone you can go sit in the kitchen with her like you do now."

"I don't like Dancy."

"Well, you better get to likin' her if you want her to fix your coffee every mornin'. You can't pick who you like and who you don't in this world. She'll look after you all right." Watching May pick at her fingernails, a habit which Esther's tried to break her of, Esther thinks, *I'm sorry, May, but I have to go. I know Coella ain't payin' you much mind, not with Thomas runnin' wild like he does. And Euphonia don't spend time with you like she should, 'cause she really never spent time with anybody but Cornelius, and he ain't here.*

"Can I go with you?" May asks.

"No, child, you can't. I'm goin' over to Vidalia. How would I explain why I'm travellin' with a child that ain't my own? When I get to Vidalia I'm gonna ask ever'body I can find if they know of two girls named

Helene and Theresa. And if I can't find 'em there, I'm gonna go further, and ask at the next town. My girls are bound in slavery over there, and it ain't right."

"How long you gonna be gone?"

"Long as it takes to find 'em."

"How you gonna get 'em out of slavery? Their owners ain't gonna just let 'em go."

You know a lot about slavery for an Irish ragamuffin, Esther thinks, but of course May listens to every conversation in the Dependency, and Dancy and Bo talk a lot about the times when they were in slavery. They want to get their husbands back, but Esther doesn't see how that can happen. But Cornelius knew Helene and Theresa when they were just kids growing up here; and if she finds her girls and can't get them back with the money she's saved, she'll come back here and tell Cornelius where they are, and he'll go buy them out for her. He's been gone all winter, and he should be coming back just any time now. He hasn't written for a long time, but Esther has a feeling Miss Phony really doesn't care much whether he writes or not.

The next morning Esther doesn't say goodbye. She just up and goes, and May finds out about it when she goes to the kitchen after breakfast to get her coffee, and Dancy says, "Esther's gone."

That afternoon May wanders down to the ferry landing at Under-the-Hill for the first time, and nobody stops her. She wants to watch for the ferry to see if Esther's coming back. Today she decided she won't wear hair ribbons any more, because that's just what little girls wear. And she didn't want to put on a pinafore, but she did because she knew if Coella saw her without a pinafore she'd pop her on her arm. She's figured out that one good thing about having everybody gone—Cornelius to Virginny and Jenny to Vicksburg with Walker, and now Esther over to Louisiana—is that nobody's really keeping tabs on her. Especially since Thomas has turned into such a runner. Give that boy a chance and he barrels away from Coella. And Coella will think May's out in the kitchen with Dancy and Bo, and Dancy and Bo will think she's with Coella. Miss Phony doesn't even think about where May is; she just leaves it up to everybody else to watch her. So May can just mind herself.

She saunters down the road into Natchez, and nobody stops her, so she just keeps going, down Main Street, past all the shoppers. When she gets to Broadway Street, she can see the river, that wide gray streak. She walks down Silver Street. People are driving buggies and wagons up and down, so she walks at the side of the road. Three flatboats are pulled up to the shore there, and right now there's a steamer too. The big old flatboats look like deep smooth-topped barges, but they have a hole in the top where the boatmen can go up and down. May wonders what's inside, down in the dark. The boatmen are just lollygagging around on the top, smoking and drinking whiskey; another boat steers in and ties up, and the boatmen hop off and go over to talk to the men on the other boat. May wonders if they know each other. Then some of the men leave to go see what there is to see in Under-The-Hill, but one man stays behind to be the watchguard.

Out in the river right now the little ferry is chugging across to Vidalia. *I bet Esther rode on that ferryboat this morning*, May thinks; she squints across the river to see what Vidalia looks like, but from here it looks like nothing but trees. Off to the side of Silver Street is a grassy slope, so she walks over there and sits down, her legs straight out in front of her. She'd like to see a steamboat coming in. Two boys about her age are sitting there watching everything too, but they ignore her.

She looks up and down the river. After a while some clouds cover the sun, and May thinks she'd better head back. When she stands up, brushing the grass off her skirt, she hears a tinkling melody. Another flatboat is pulling up to the shore. The boatman steers it up to the riverbank, and a man in bright green pants hops off and ties it to a tree. This boat looks different from all the others; it's got a flat stage built right on top and some poles sticking up from holes cut in the top. Once it's tied up at the shore, a man in a black jacket hoists a big sign upright and stands it up right on the top of the boat: "Minstrel Show. Five o'clock. Five cents."

May looks for the name of the boat, and there it is, painted on the side: "Merry Belle."

So it's a showboat. Coella's told her about them, but she's never seen one. The boys have gotten up and wandered closer to have a look, so she skips along behind them. Other people are already heading over that way. The man in the black jacket ropes off a big square on the grass. He sets up a table with a sign: "Tickets 5 cents."

As a line forms at the ticket table, the man in green pants hoists two big poles and sets them straight up into two holes in the top of the flatboat. Then he unrolls a painted canvas and hooks it to the poles. He sets two more poles at the front connected with a rope and hangs a red curtain across the rope. A woman in a pink fluttery dress comes out from behind the curtain and talks to him as he works. She's the prettiest woman May's ever seen, with her cascade of yellow hair down her back. The man looks at her and laughs when she says something funny, which May can't overhear. The woman motions for him to pull the curtain open and then close it again. Then she ducks behind it.

May doesn't have a nickel, so she crouches down to watch the show from behind a big elm tree that's just outside the roped-in area.

The man in green pants goes back behind the curtain. More and more people come to pay their money at the ticket table and find a place to sit on the ground.

After everyone's paid their money, the man in green pants comes out from behind the curtain. He stands on the stage and blows a big whistle. May knows this means the show's about to start. He says, "Y'all come sit down close." The people get up and shuffle closer and then settle themselves again just a few feet from the boat. A few more people pay their money and find a place to sit.

The man in the black jacket pulls the rope across the opening. Then he goes down to the boat and hops on board. He goes behind the curtain and then comes out again with a big drum hanging from his neck with a strap. He beats the drum in rhythm, a deep *boom-boom* that rolls up over the slope.

The blond-haired woman comes out from behind the curtain and stands at the side of the stage. She opens her arms wide and says in a loud voice, "Friends, my name is Celestina." She points to the man in green pants. "And that is Anton. The other man over there is Henry. And I would like to sing you a song."

Anton and the other man pick up cymbals. Celestina folds her hands together and starts to sing. She has the prettiest high voice May's ever heard. She sounds the way an angel would sound, May thinks. The song's about a man who writes sweet letters to his lady, and he starts each letter with "My bonny my lass." At the chorus, the two men shake the cymbals to keep time. By the last stanza, Celestina drops her voice, as she sings of how the man receives a letter from the sweetheart's mother. Without even opening it, he knows what it says; the sweetheart is dead. Then Celestina finishes her song and curtsies to the audience, dipping low so that her skirt spreads around her like an angel's wings. Then she stands up and the audience claps, even though some of the women are dabbing tears from their eyes.

It's wonderful. May loves every bit of it. The woman goes behind the curtain and then Anton picks up a rope while Henry pulls out a carved wooden calf on a rolling platform. He drags it to the side of the stage. Anton swings his rope and it sails up across the stage with a whoosh, making shapes like soap bubbles that hang in the air for a second until the rope lands with a thunk around the calf's wooden head. Everyone applauds, and May does too, thinking how hard that must be, to rope a calf's neck that far away. Then the man in green pants comes out juggling some red balls. May's never seen anyone do that before. The audience applauds but not as loudly this time; May thinks they want to hear Celestina sing another song, and then here she is again, stepping out from behind the curtain. The men are going down into the belly of the boat, hoisting the wooden calf down the steps.

Celestina stands in the center of the stage.

"My friends, we have a special treat for you tonight." She looks around. "We have travelled many many miles on our little boat, and while we were passing by the great city of Saint Louis, a man came to us and asked us if we wanted a pet. And naturally, we said yes, because"— she pauses—"naturally, we thought a little kitten or puppy would make a nice companion on our travels down the river. And so he gave us a pet. And since she reminds us of the Garden of Eden, we named her Evie. Would you like to see her?"

The audience nods and applauds, and the kids squeal "Yes!" Celestina goes to the curtain and pushes it aside as Anton comes up slowly from the bottom of the boat. First his head appears, and then the rest of him emerges. Henry is below him, and they're twisting and struggling as they come up onto the stage.

Between them they're holding the biggest snake May's ever seen. The wicked animal is as thick as a man's leg, and it writhes between the two men, coiling about their shoulders. Its head, which is big as a shovel, undulates back and forth, and its tongue flicks out, testing the air.

The audience is silent; every man and woman is transfixed at the sight.

Celestina says, "Now, we've been talking about whether we should keep Evie, or if we should just let her go. She lives in a pen we've built for her belowdecks, but wouldn't she be happier if we just turned her loose, right here on the riverbank? She'd like living free."

"No!" a woman in the audience squeals.

"Don't do it!" a man shouts.

May claps her hands over her mouth. Evie's getting restless, May can see it. Her twisting and coiling's gotten more determined, and Anton is struggling to keep the big snake's head away from his own face.

"Oh, all right, I guess we'll just take her back down to her cage," Celestina says, and the audience claps as the men wrestle the unruly snake back down into the darkness of the boat.

The people in the audience whisper together, excited about the snake. After a few minutes the two men come back up without the snake. Each goes to a corner of the stage and they pull out another curtain, this one painted with a picture of a castle on a hill, and below the castle are some trees.

Anton stands in the middle of the stage and tells a story about a stagecoach driver who gets trapped in deep snow in the mountains—he gestures behind him at the snow-capped mountain where the painted castle sits—and a strange creature appears out of the snowstorm. The creature looks like a man but he really isn't one, being all hairy; and the creature shows him the way back home, to his wife's warm arms. But when he gets home and tells his wife about the creature who led him home, she scolds him. He mimics her high squeaky voice: 'You are just imagining things. There's no such things as snow monsters—unless you been hittin' the bottle too hard, Theodore.'

'Oh, no, I ain't been hittin' it, Louise. Ain't had a drop,' the man says, and the audience titters. Anton goes on, relating how the man lies down in his bed to go to sleep, but in the middle of the night he wakes up and looks outside his window. He sees the hairy beast looking in at him and his wife as they sleep. But he thinks, *That can't be real; my wife says there's no such thing as snow monsters.* So he rolls over and goes back to sleep. Then his wife gets up and says, 'I think I'll close that window since it's so cold outside'; and the next time the man looks, his wife and the monster are gone.

There's more applause.

Now it's time for the next act. Celestina walks out from behind the curtain holding a large red apple. She stands in front of the painted tree.

Anton says, "Celestina, why are you in my orchard, pretty lady?"

"I'm just out for a stroll, sir," Celestina says in a high pitched voice, swinging her hips from side to side.

"You're stealing my apples!" he says in a gruff voice.

"Oh, no, sir, I wouldn't!" she squeals.

The audience gets quiet. Celestina sets her apple up on top of her head, where it rests in her nest of yellow hair. She opens her arms wide open, as if she'd like to give the man a hug if he walked across the stage to her.

But he doesn't. She stands very still so the apple won't tumble off. Then all at once he pulls out a gun and slowly lowers it, aiming straight at Celestina.

May holds her breath. "No," she breathes. He's mad at Celestina for stealing an apple, and now he's about to kill her dead.

May looks around at the people sitting on the ground. *Don't they care?* But they're all watching the stage, their eyes fixed on Celestina in her white dress standing right in front of the painted tree. Some of the men point and lean over to whisper something to their wives. Even the rowdy kids get still, waiting to see what happens.

He fires the pistol. There's a big cloud of smoke, and Celestina twirls around, her back to the audience, and everyone thinks she's dead for sure in that cloud of smoke. Then she whirls around to face the audience, not dead at all. She curtsies. The apple lies in shreds on the stage floor, and Celestine picks up what's left of it and holds it up by the stem for the audience to see. The people in the audience start to giggle and chatter, and they clap and clap. Anton blows the smoke away from the barrel and drops the pistol back in its holster. May lets out a long breath, relieved that Celestina is still alive.

The men pull the curtain closed, and that's the end of the show. Celestina and Anton come out from behind the curtain and bow to the audience. The people in the audience clap again, and then they get up, the women brushing down their wide skirts and rounding up their kids. They walk back across the grass to the top of the hill, talking and laughing together as if seeing the show brightened up what's left of the day.

May waits until everyone's gone. Then she gets up and walks down to the boat where Celestina is crouching on the stage, brushing some shreds of apple off the boat. She picks up the core of the apple and tosses it over the side. Standing on the shore, May sees marks around the lady's eyes, like blue paint, and red paint on her lips. May's never seen anyone as pretty as Celestina.

Celestina straightens up and brushes her hands together. Then she sees May.

"Well, who're you?" she asks. Her voice is deep and throaty.

"I'm May," she says.

"Did ya like the show, May?"

May nods.

"Don't ya think ya better just run on home? It's gettin' dark."

May takes a deep breath. "Can I be in the show?"

Celestina laughs a little laugh, turning her head to look at the men rolling up the canvas curtain. "Well, I reckon you might could, if we had need of any other person right now. How old are you?"

"Ten."

"You don't look that old."

"I'm little for my age." May swings her skirt out to the sides and holds it out wide, like Celestina did when she was singing. "I'm just the runt o' the litter, everybody says."

"What a mess," Celestina says, wiping her hands on a towel. Anton unhooks the curtain and smooths it out on the floor and then rolls it up.

Celestina looks at May again. "Well, I tell you. What's your last name?"

"Carson."

"What would your mammy say if you went away to sing on the showboat?"

"Ain't got a mammy."

"Or your pappy?"

She shook her head. "He's dead."

"You a orphan?"

May nods. The woman pulls the net shawl from around her shoulders, leaving her neck and arms bare. May's never seen a woman show so much of herself that way; even Coella, when she puts on her nightgown, turns her back and hunches over away from May's eyes, like she's hiding something shameful.

Up and down Celestina's white arms are an array of blue and black bruises, some fading to yellow.

"What happened to your arms?" May asks.

"Oh, nothing," Celestina says, adjusting her shawl. "Well, May Carson, can you sing?"

May nods again.

"You gotta sing real loud," Celestina says. "Let's hear it." Celestina wipes her hand across her shiny forehead and then hoists herself up to sit on a barrel at the side of the stage, her ankles crossed.

May starts to sing, and she makes her voice as loud as she can. It's a song Coella taught her; but when Coella heard May singing it for Thomas, she changed her mind and told her it wasn't a nice song, and a girl like May shouldn't be singing it.

"Sla-a-a-ck your rope, hangman!
Sla-a-a-ck it fer awhile
I think I see my father comin'
Comin' many a mile
Father! Have you brought me h-o-o-ope
Or have you paid my fee
Or have you come to see me
Hangin'—hangin' from a galla's tree?

Celestina claps. "Yoo-hoo! Ain't that somethin', Anton! Look at this! This young'un is tiny as all get-out, but she can sing like thunder!"

Anton walks over and stares at May. "That's somethin' awright."

May thinks he has a mean face, the way his eyes squinch down.

Celestina says, "Well, I tell you what, May. We're hovin' out of here tomorrow first thing, but we ain't got too many stops and then we'll be in New Orleans. You ever get down to New Orleans, you come see me. We'll let you sing in the show."

May thinks that's the best thing she's ever heard.

Just before sunset Dancy looks out from the kitchen and sees two horses she doesn't recognize walking up the road. They turn through the gate. All at once she sees who it is: Malachi on the lead horse with the reins of the second horse tied to his saddle, and on the horse that's following sits a form slumped over like an old man. Mister Cornelius Carson.

"Oh my Lord," she whispers to no one. And a second later she's running up the path to the big house, where she knows Euphonia will be sitting in the parlor, a glass of wine in her hand.

She hurries into the parlor without knocking. "Missus, come quick!" Dancy points toward the front of the house. "Mister Cornelius is back!"

"Oh —." Euphonia sets her wine glass down on the table and jumps up.

"But, missus —" Dancy starts to say, but Euphonia is already running toward the front door, and a second later it slams shut behind her.

"It was the most God-awful trip you ever seen," Mal says that evening as he sits with Dancy in the kitchen. Some of the others have come in to hear about the trip, and they stand along the wall watching him with keen eyes: Bo, Daniel, Traysa, Jane, Margaret, Felisa.

"It weren't nothing but trouble, especially after we got to Virginny," Mal says. "That's where things started to fall apart."

"What happened, exactly?" Dancy asks, leaning forward.

"Well, we got to Albemarle County all right," Mal goes on, "but then just as we was ridin' up that big hill to the place where I was born, Master's horse went lame. It was a sunny mornin', and everything was all right 'til then. So anyway, we left the horse and double-rode on up to the old place, and it was all deserted. The fences was all fallin' down and everything. And I did find my mammy's cabin, and that was a awful sight, with the roof half off and cavin' in. It was the sorriest-lookin' place you ever saw. I was ashamed for Mister Cornelius to even see it. And then we went on up to the big house, where my ole master used to live. Nobody was there, but the house just didn't look the same. 'Course the old master's long gone, but there was a caretaker there, and he said the old place got pretty run-down, but somebody's bought it, and they're fixin' it back up. Upstairs, there's a fine hall, and mirrors hangin' on the walls just like I remember. But I could hardly stand to see it. It's just been too long."

"Did you find your people?" Dancy asks.

"Well, I didn't really know how to find my brother James, so we went into the town that was nearby, and Mister Cornelius asked around. We found out James was workin' on a farm outside of town, so we rode on out there. I recognized him right off, since he was only two years older than me. But you know, he's still in slavery, and it's made him different. He's got a hard face now, and a rough way about him. I dunno if he was glad to see me or not, me bein' a free man. He told me our mammy done passed on." He looks out at the window, where the sky is darkening. "But I reckon he was glad to see me. He just didn't say much about it. We rode down to the cemetery below the hill and James showed me where our mammy's grave was. It weren't marked at all, so Cornelius and me hammered a cross made out of wood and he asked me what her name was. I said Lucy. So he wrote it out for me, what the letters looked like, and he told me to carve it on that cross, and I did. We pushed the cross down into the ground as far as we could, so it set solid."

He looks down at the floor, remembering.

"I appreciated him helpin' me honor my mammy that way. Then James pointed out our old Master's grave in the other cemetery right next to it. It's got a tall monument standing' straight up, but it's all chipped out ugly. James said people been comin' up there all the time to chip out a piece of Masta's monument, 'cause at one time he was the executive of this whole country. So then we were gettin' ready to head out to Georgia, and that's when Mister Cornelius fell sick."

"The doctor went upstairs to see him a while ago," Dancy said. "I wonder what he's got."

"I dunno, but I was afraid we wouldn't even make it back here, and I'd end up havin' to bury 'im somewhere out on the road." He shakes his head. "Then I'd have a hard time gettin' back here by myself. I wouldn't even know the way."

"Good thing he had you with him," Bo says.

"I reckon so," Mal says. "He's a sick man. I sure hope that doctor can do somethin' for 'im." He looks around at the people standing along the wall. "Law, I sure am glad to be back here. I don't never want to be out on the road again."

CHAPTER TEN

THE SOUND A CHILD'S FOOT MAKES when it hits a rug in the middle of the night—no mother will miss that sound. In her bedroom at the end of the hall, her eyes will fly open and fix on the dark ceiling as she lies motionless, listening. If there's some shift in the air in the house, the mother will sit up, stare at the black rectangle of the door, and wait for the next sound.

Carefree's a large house, and it has its share of creaks. Ghosts hover in the corners of the rooms; Euphonia's known that ever since she first came here. She can't see the ghosts, though; they're no more than shadows. But she knows they creep along the walls and slip over the gold-striped wallpaper; they put their feet on top of the walnut chest and brush their phantom fingers through her jewelry. They're the shades of earlier men and women who were tied to this house, and to Cornelius: Josephine, Stephanie, Hattie, and old Emile himself. And even an old slave or two. Euphonia can't let them know she knows they're here. They'd torment her if they could.

But if the mother's not really the mother—

And if there's a father, but he's not really the father, just a kindly man who took responsibility for the child when no one else would—would he hear a child's footfall?

And what if he lies sick, sweat pouring from his feverish face and bile rising in his throat? And the wife is exhausted from wiping his face with a cool cloth, cleaning up his messes and changing his clothes and trying to get him to sip the physic the doctor prescribed?

Is there really anyone who could hear?

Perhaps then the child can get out of bed, stand in her nightgown for a few minutes, and slip through the house as quietly as a mouse running.

Because a house with grave illness is a house in storm.

In the darkness before dawn on a June day, May stands in her bedroom humming the scraps of a tune. No candle is lit, but that doesn't bother her; she's seen darker dark than this. No rooster is crowing yet, so dawn is at least an hour away. And she knows how many steps it takes to reach the top of the staircase that curves down to the foyer below. She doesn't even have to think about it. She tiptoes out into the hall, her light nightgown billowing out behind her.

At the top of the stairs she stops and listens. All she hears are low snores coming from the back bedroom where Mister Cornelius and Miss Phony are sleeping. Their door is closed, and so is the door to the room next to theirs, where Coella and Thomas sleep. If the grownups wake up, they'll stop her, and Coella will send her back to her bed. And tomorrow Coella will hand her the spelling-book with an assignment, just as if it's an ordinary day, and Thomas will want her to run horsies along the play-road they've built in the dirt behind the house. And today will be just like every other day.

Humming the not-nice song Coella taught her, she creeps down the steps, not cringing at the sounds the old stairs make, because every night Carefree is a house of squeaks and groans and murmurs anyway. She's used to the sounds.

Halfway down the stairs she stops and swings first her right foot and then her left up and over the bannister, so her feet dangle above the black and white marble floor below. This is her favorite trick; she's been scolded about it a dozen times by Coella and Miss Phony when they catch her at it, but when no one's around she always does it anyway, loosening her grip just enough to let her hands slide on the polished bannister. She slides down and a second later she lands with a smack of her bare feet on the floor, without the bother of the last few steps.

Exhilarated as she always is by her successful landing, she stands up and skips down the hall toward the back door. Off to the right is the back bedroom where her clothes are hanging in the chiffarobe. It's easy for her to find her way in the dark because she's hardly ever gone anywhere else for the past two years. She goes into the bedroom and feels her way to the bed, patting her hands along the counterpane to reach the matchbox on the table. She fumbles a match out and strikes it to light the candle.

She looks around. Phony's sewing basket sits on the dresser, almost buried under a pile of embroidery scraps and white crocheted squares which Phony plans to make into a bedspread, once she gets about a hundred more made, if she ever does.

May looks at her reflection in the mirror above the dresser. She's a girl with tangled hair that reaches down to her flat chest, but she can tell she's looking more grown up lately. She's older than everybody thinks she is. She might even be ten years old, like she told Celestina she was. One night she overheard Phony say to Cornelius, "I think May might be older than we think. She's at least nine, I think. She's just small for her age."

"Why would that be?" Cornelius asked.

"Probably because when she was younger she was underfed," Phony said.

Even her real mammy in Ireland once told her she was small for her age, and now, looking at herself, she can see she's still kind of little. Little but hard. And growing.

She goes over to the black chiffarobe and turns the key that's hanging loose in the keyhole.

Here are her dresses, neatly lined up on hangers, dresses Miss Phony ordered for her from the dressmaker. Most of them are too frilly for her liking. She pulls her nightgown over her head and throws it across the bed. She reaches for a simple plaid dress and puts it on, buttoning the bodice buttons quickly. She goes over to the dresser and opens the top drawer, taking out an old hairbrush. She tries to brush the tangles out of her hair, but she can't tie a ribbon in it like Coella does. So she brushes her hair straight down. It's light colored hair, not perfectly straight like Miss Phony's or curly like Thomas's; it waves all the way down, and it's wispy when it reaches her shoulders.

The candlelight jumps, and there's a creak somewhere in the house, but she ignores it. She rummages through the jumble of clothes lying at the bottom of the chiffarobe and sees her old blue dress, the one she wore when Jenny brought her here from New Orleans. It was a summer day, she remembers, and she wore a white pinafore too. Jenny told her to keep her dress clean, but that was a long, hot boat ride. She remembers how Jenny brushed her hair with her fingers and tied her hair ribbon, wanting her to look good when they got off the boat. Then they came up to this big house called Carefree that looked like a mansion to May, with its red brick sides and four white columns on the front. It was as grand as the houses she saw in Ireland, houses she never entered.

That day she learned that Carefree was to be her new home. And she met Esther, who hugged her when she wandered out to the kitchen the next morning and poured her coffee and fixed her something to eat.

Esther talked to her all day long in the big smoky kitchen, even though back then May couldn't understand but a few words in English. But it wasn't long before she knew more English than Irish.

Esther told her all about the people here at Carefree, Dancy and Felisa and Bo and that scrap Daniel, who thinks he runs the place even though he's only fourteen, and scrawny.

"You talkin' just like a Natchez child now," Esther said to her not long ago. Esther's old, and her arms are wrinkled like her face, but still, May loves her. Last spring, when May got sick, Esther took right over, sitting by her bed and holding her hand while she had the fever, and talking to her while Miss Phony was out in the hall with the doctor. May wanted to hear what the doctor said, whether she was about to die or not, but Esther kept talking, and she couldn't overhear. But she got better, drank the lemony tasting liquid they gave her to drink, and it did the trick; a week later she was well again. She wasn't nearly as sick as Mister Cornelius is now. He's got the malaria, and you don't get over that so quick.

Jenny didn't stay at Carefree, which didn't surprise May too much; she always knew Jenny was unreliable. And sure enough, one day last winter Jenny took her baby and left with Walker Jackson, and she's never come back.

Now Esther's been gone a whole week; she just packed up her satchel and left one day, saying Mister Cornelius wasn't ever gonna help her find her girls, and she guessed she better go find them herself. Esther talked about them a lot, Helene and Theresa, those grown-up girls. Esther saw a sign; she said the sun just went dim one day even though there wasn't a cloud in the sky, and it wasn't even a foggy day. Nobody noticed it but her, but she said it was a sign telling her she had to get her girls before something worse happened to them and they got scattered even farther away than they are now. She wanted Cornelius to go with her to Louisiana to look for them, and he said he would some day, but first he had to take Malachi to Virginia. And he already helped Jenny find her brother; but as for Esther, he put her last. And now he's lying sick, and Lord knows he can't go with her now.

So Esther left.

"Don't worry, child, I ain't leavin' you forever," Esther told her the day before she left, but May's not sure she really meant it. Dancy said she'd be back, and Coella said so, too. But it hurt May's heart when Esther left. Esther was always putting her arm around her shoulder, cooking something good, and making sure May ate something. And letting her drink coffee piled high with cream and sweet with sugar. If May didn't like what Esther cooked, Esther would find something else for her to eat. And Esther talked to her all the time. Dancy and Bo and Malachi would come into the kitchen, and they'd all sit around the table and talk, laughing about this or that. Sometimes May played tricks on them, sneaking into the kitchen and crouching down behind the spice cabinet and eavesdropping on what they were saying, until Malachi or Esther or Dancy would say in a high voice, "Oh, I think I hear a little mouse over there behind that cabinet!"

"I better get the broom to chase that mouse away," Dancy would say, and then May would pop out and they'd all laugh. Sometimes when they sat at the table, Dancy or Bo would give her their boys to hold, but George and Henry were getting so big, and half the time their bottoms were wet, so she didn't much like doing that.

Esther let her stay in the kitchen most every day after her lessons were over with Miss Coella. Coella taught her how to read and spell, but Esther showed her how to thread a needle and sew a seam, although she wasn't good at it yet. She remembers Esther's long knobby fingers laying over the fabric like crooked sticks as she showed her how to take small stitches, one after the other in a straight line.

For the first two days after Esther left, May stationed herself at the kitchen door, watching to see if Esther came up the road, thinking any minute that she would. But anyway, what if Esther never found her girls? Would she just keep looking for them forever? Then she might never come back.

When Esther left, she didn't even say goodbye, and that hurt more than when Jenny left. May remembers another mother she once had, and a girl who lost her mother once before isn't going to just wave goodbye and say, "So long," as if it's just anybody that's leaving. No; a girl who's lost her mother before will go stand in the kitchen door and watch, every day, to see if she's coming up the drive, her skirt rustling about her legs the way it always does. She'll be wearing one of her shiny dresses that came down from Miss Sophronia, the lady who used to live in this room. May doesn't know this Miss Sophronia, but she's not here anymore, so May thinks the lady must be dead. It was nice of her to give her pretty dresses to Esther, even if she's dead.

May brings out her old satchel from the bottom of the chiffarobe. Now, her voice just above a whisper, she sings absent-mindedly, with half a melody, as the things she'll take with her, her green dress and her stockings and her handkerchief, come out of the chiffarobe and disappear into the satchel.

The house is quiet again, and still dark. May grabs a hair brush and a plaid brocade ribbon from the dresser, and she drops those in the satchel too. She pulls on her stockings and her high-top shoes and ties the laces. She looks around the room. She sees her old dolly—a ragdoll with one button eye hanging by a thread—where it's fallen half under the bed, and decides to leave it. It's not as nice as her new doll with the eyes that close, but that one's back upstairs, and she won't go up there to get it. Her spelling book is on the side table. Last winter she wrote her own name inside the cover, right underneath Stephanie's name, making the same extra loop on the "C" just like Stephanie did. She drops the book into the satchel and buckles the bag closed.

She goes to the back door. The sky is just beginning to show flickers of light. That rooster will be crowing any minute now, and as soon as he does Dancy will be getting up to go out to the privy.

May slips across the back gallery and stands on the top step for a moment. The night air smells clean and dewy, and she can just make out the brick path. She goes down to the kitchen and opens the kitchen door as quietly as she can and goes inside. It's strange to see the kitchen so dark and still; it's usually got people coming and going, talking and eating. But now it's just a dark room with a big black fireplace where a thin line of white smoke is rising straight up from the ashes. May lights the candle on the table. Looking around, she sees a biscuit tin sitting on the sideboard. She pries the lid off and peers inside; sure enough, there's one leftover Whiskey Lizzie inside. She takes a dish towel and wraps the sweet in it and sets it in the satchel on top of her dress. She carries the candle outside and tiptoes down the short path to the Dependency. All the doors are closed, so everybody must still be sleeping. So many people live in these rooms—Dancy and Bo and Henry and George and Malachi and the others—and they'll all be waking up soon. Esther's room is the closest one to the kitchen, and May walks over to it and pushes the door open. She holds her candle up, to make sure Esther didn't suddenly come back in the night. But the room looks just as empty as it's been the past week, with the quilt pulled up neatly over the bed. Esther's not here.

When she gets back to the kitchen, her candle's flickering and almost out. She sets it down on the table. When Dancy comes in, which won't be long now, she'll see the flickering candle and she'll know May was here.

She eases the door shut and swings her satchel as she half-skips around the big house and out to the road that leads into Natchez. At the turn in the road she stops and looks back at the house, but all the windows are still dark. The rooster crows, and May spins on her heels and runs, skips, down the street and into Natchez, where before her eyes the streets are turning blue.

She hears the whistle of a steamer. When she comes to the top of Silver Street, she can barely make out the boat. It's all lit up, and it looks like a toy out on the big river. It turns and then whistles—two short toots and one long one—so she knows it's pulling into the dock. By the time it reaches the dock she can see it clearly, because it's almost dawn.

Silver Street's a long way down, and wagons rumble past her; but no one stops to give her a ride, which she thinks is rude but she really doesn't mind. *When I get to New Orleans, I can sing in the show*, she thinks, and the thought makes her giddy. She hums her song about the hangman as she goes down the hill.

CHAPTER ELEVEN

WALKING AHEAD OF HER IS A TALL WOMAN holding the hand of a little girl. At one point the woman loses her footing on the uneven ground, and the girl looks up at her, startled. But the mother catches herself before she falls, and she doesn't break her stride.

Seeing the woman stumble reminds May of her own Mam. All these people passing her, whether they're riding in buggies and on horses or just walking faster than she is, can't imagine who she is, a girl from so far away they can't even picture it. She has all kinds of secrets they'll never know. Because before she was May Carson, she was Maeve O'Malley, and there was a time she went to a boat dock with her mammy.

She remembers that time, but the memory is faded now, because she was little back then. Her Mam was walking down the road holding her hand to her stomach. She was sick. Maeve walked close behind her.

She remembers they lived in a ditch beside some green woods. Every day they waited by the side of the road hoping a carriage would go by, and sooner or later it always did, rumbling down the road between the big trees. It made a hopeful sound, and Maeve would suck in her breath; every part of herself would start to quiver. She'd point down the road and Mam would get to her feet. Then a minute later the shiny black carriage pulled by two big horses would come around the curve, and inside would be the English lord and his lady. When they saw Mam and Maeve, the driver would beat the horses so they'd go even faster. Maeve remembers how the English lord looked, with a face so blank you could write a story on it; and how his lady looked angry, as if she was mad to see the ditch people. But Maeve and Mam would run to keep up with the carriage until their legs gave out and they were out of breath, and the whole time they had their hands out. Most of the time the carriage wouldn't stop, and they could never catch it. Then she and Mam would crouch by the side of the road till it got dark, and if it started to rain they'd pull their holey capes up over their heads.

But once in a while, the English lord or his lady would call out something to the driver and the carriage would slow down, and Maeve and Mam would be right there reaching their hands out. A gloved hand would come out from the carriage window and drop a coin or two, which would land on the ground more often than not, and she and Mam would scrabble for it. It would buy them a loaf of bread in the village. They had such handsome full faces, did the English; Maeve thought all the English lords must look like that. Mam looked like a ghost with her big eyes and her narrow face. Once Maeve saw her own face reflected in a pool of water, and her eyes were big too.

But one day the carriage stopped in front of them, and the English lord stepped right out onto the ground. Maeve had never seen such shiny high boots, such a coat with tails. And such a neat beard on the man's pale white face. He handed Mam two pieces of blue paper, and Mam nodded as he talked. He pointed down the road, and she looked that way. Then he got back into his buggy and it rolled away. Mam showed Maeve the two papers; there was a picture of a boat and some words on both papers, and Mam must have understood what he said, because then they started walking down the road the way he pointed. They slept in a field that night, and the next day they came to a city where some boats were.

She remembers how the road wound over a hill and down to a river. It was a rocky path, and by then Mam could hardly walk. She just skittered and stumbled all the time. Mam tried to straighten her shawl around her bony shoulders, and she tied her kerchief over her hair. She smoothed down her skirt and splashed Maeve's face with water from a well by the side of the road. Maeve remembers how cool Mam's fingers felt, brushing her face clean, her forehead, her cheeks and chin, and how the water smelled like old moss. Mam held herself straight and tall as they went down to the ship, because she said the captain wouldn't let them on the ship if they thought she was sick.

After they got on the ship, they went down some steps into the bottom of the boat, where it was dark and wet and stinky. There was only one lantern down there, and once Maeve's eyes got used to the dark she could see that the place was just a framework of boards with bunks built into every open space. Men and women with big eyes were already lying in most of the bunks. The women had scarves tied around their heads, and they tried to keep their squalling kids quiet. Mam climbed up onto a bunk no wider than she was, and Maeve squeezed in beside her, listening to her raspy breath.

After a while Maeve whispered, "Mam, where are we going?"

"America."

"Why?" Maeve asked. But Mam didn't answer.

For a long time she lay beside Mam on the bunk, staring at her face. The boat started to creak and groan, and it shifted this way and that. Maeve heard shouts from the sailors over their heads, and she could feel the ship begin to move. Then they were out on the open sea, which rocked the boat all night. The passengers jolted back and forth with the pulling waves, which didn't feel good. Some people got sick, and then the air stank even more. They had a bucket, but the sick ones couldn't always reach it in time. Late in the night the sea got still. Most of the passengers were asleep, except for some of the men. Maeve watched the shadowy forms move as the men reached for the women in spite of the too-small beds, and then the wives weren't sleeping either.

Mammy's breathing got rattly. Maeve brought her a dipper of water from the barrel and tried to get her to drink, but most of it just ran off her chin. She dipped the corner of Mam's shawl in the barrel and wiped her hot face.

"What's wrong down there?" the woman in the bunk above them asked, poking her head down over the side.

"My mam's sick," Maeve said.

"Well, keep her down there," the woman said. "We don't want no sickness up here."

But later in the night, her mammy's breath was no more.

In the morning, when the lantern was flickering low where it hung by the stairs, Maeve sat up in the bed and pulled herself up straight so she could touch the snoring woman who'd spoken to her in the night. She tugged at the woman's blanket.

"What is it?"

"My mammy died."

The woman raised up. "*Jayzus*, child. Don't tell me that. We don't need no sickness and dyin'. Are you sick?"

May shook her head.

"Well, lemme get up and get the captain. We only been at sea one day, and there was one died yesterday, and here today we ain't even awake yet, and there's one more." She lunged up out of the bunk, and Maeve stepped back, not wanting to be knocked over, and stood against the wall by the water barrel.

A few minutes later the captain came down the steps cursing. He clumped over to where Mam lay. The bed's still warm, Maeve thought. He bent over Mam and then straightened up, shaking his head. He went back up the steps without a word, leaving Maeve standing by the bed. She looked at her Mam, whose eyes were closed. She wondered if she should lie down again so Mam wouldn't get cold.

Two sailors came down the steps. "Who goes with her?" one of the sailors asked. He looked at Maeve. "She yours?"

She didn't know how to answer, so she stuck her fingers in her mouth and stared at him, or what she could see of him by the lantern.

"You better come up too," he said. They wrapped Mam in a sheet and took her up the stairs, one sailor hauling her head and one her feet.

Maeve scrambled up after them so she wouldn't lose sight of Mam, who was wrapped head to toe in the white sheet. When she got to the deck one of the sailors turned to her. "What's your name?"

She didn't answer.

"What's your mama's name?"

She said nothing.

The other sailor swore and got out a book and opened it to a certain page. He glanced down at it. "Bridget O'Malley," he said. He turned to Maeve. "Your last name O'Malley?"

No answer.

"Bound to be," said the other sailor. "That's the only name that was a woman with one child."

"Captain's got his prayer-book," the other sailor said. They laid Mam on the deck right by the rail and pulled up the gate. Then the captain, his face bleary, read some words out of his English prayer book, but Maeve didn't understand the words. She stood back, afraid to be too close to the open gate when right below was the churning sea, the chopping waves.

They had put Mam there with her head so close to the gate.

When the captain said "Amen," he motioned to the sailors who were standing there. They pushed the long slender wrapped body right through the gate and it went down to the water. When Maeve heard the splash, she put her hands up on her face.

"Mam?" she called. But she knew Mam wasn't coming back out of the water. The boat just kept going.

"You better go on back below," the captain said to her, pointing to the steps that led down into the dark hold. So she went back down the steps to the bunk, which should still be warm. But Mam wasn't there to keep it so.

And so two months later she came to New Orleans.

CHAPTER TWELVE

SHE'S FIGURED OUT HER PLAN. She won't buy a ticket. She only has two dollars in her pocket anyway, money Esther gave her for picking blackberries. Every scratch and bug bite on her arms and legs told her blackberry picking wasn't a good job. She'll hold on to her two dollars because she'll need some money when she gets to New Orleans.

She just has to get on a steamer, and she's already figured out how she'll do it. There'll be some lady with a passel of kids, maybe six or eight of them, and she'll just slip in alongside them. The ticket taker won't have time to count so many kids, and she'll find some that look just like her, so nobody will know she doesn't belong. She'll stand close to them, and when it comes time to get on the boat, the kids'll be milling around, and she'll just walk up the gangplank with them. Nobody will notice one more kid in a bunch of kids, and once she's on the boat she's on her way.

When she reaches Under-the-Hill, it happens just as she figures. There's a woman with a bunch of children, and they're ragged enough, so they're bound to be deck-passengers. The woman squints at her ticket and May can tell she can't read, so May reads the ticket for her and points to the black letters painted on the side of the cabin house: *Colonel Charlie*. And when the woman starts to go up the gangplank with the kids, May goes with them.

"My name's May, and I seen a snake that's the biggest one you ever saw," May says to the girl who's about her own age. "It lives in this river."

"My name's Dorsy," the girl says.

"This snake is so big, two men can't even hold him," May says as they go up the gangplank. "You better watch out for him, you might see him swimmin' right along with this boat."

Dorsy's eyes get big. "Where'd you see a snake like that?"

But May doesn't answer, because they've reached the deck, and now she needs Dorsy to go help her Ma with the other kids. May knows the woman will find herself a place behind the cabin house, and her kids will squabble and run wild around the deck. May doesn't mind, because once she's on the deck she doesn't have to stand close to them. Just getting up the plank onto the boat—that's all she needs to do.

Once she's there she ignores the woman and the kids. She moves away and won't talk to the girl she was talking to when she came up onto the deck. Dorsy can find herself some other friend, she thinks. She turns her back when the girl comes over.

She goes to the front railing and watches white plantation houses come out of the jungle like ghosts. The boat stops at Bayou Sara—for a minute May thinks about getting off there, since it looks like a bustling town—but then she thinks *No, there are flatboats here, but none are the* Merry Belle. Then later they're at Baton Rouge, but something tells her this isn't the place either. *Colonel Charlie* ploughs south.

It's late in the day when the boat comes to New Orleans. May remembers the city, the white cathedral with its three spires, the big square, and the boats crowding in at the riverbank. When the *Charlie* nudges up to the dock, May remembers what the dock was like, and it hasn't changed: the dockhands rolling barrels and hoisting baggage, and cats and dogs everywhere, and rats scurrying along a fence. There's nothing happier than a cat that lives by a dock, May thinks. There's always fish heads or something a cat can eat. Which reminds her that she's hungry. She remembers how New Orleans smells, too, sweet and fishy at the same time; like lemons and wet bricks. The *Merry Belle* must be here somewhere.

She goes down the plank and then stops at the bottom. An egg of uncertainty grows in her chest. Now where would a showboat be, in this long line of boats? She's forgotten how big New Orleans is, but then, she was just a little girl when she was here. She's big now, practically grown, and what she wants more than anything is to sing on that showboat stage. And she wants to be away from Coella, who's always telling her what to do and whacking her arm if she doesn't do it fast enough. And Miss Phony, who pays her no mind. And Mister Cornelius, who's a nice man, but then he got sick; and now she's just in the way of everybody. She knows she doesn't really belong at Carefree; she just washed up there, right out of the river.

She walks toward the cathedral. Ship passengers lie around on the green grass in the square. They look tired, she thinks. Looking back toward the dock, she can see the long line of boats—high-masted ocean-going ships, river steamers, and flatboats.

She's tired and hungry. She wanders down the streets, reading the names of the streets at the corners: Chartres, Bourbon, Toulouse. This last street looks familiar; wasn't this a street she walked down with Jenny, so long ago? She walks along the brick sidewalk under the filigree balconies overhead, looking around. Yes, it's familiar, this steaming place.

She crosses a street called Burgundy. This looks familiar too.

She walks more slowly now, carrying her satchel. Yes, this is the same street where she lived with Jenny. Across the way is the yellow house with its blue door and its too-tall roof. An old lady used to sit in a chair at the corner, watching everything. But the old lady's not there now. And straight in front of her is the house where Rosie lived. May, because that was her name in New Orleans, played with Rosie's little boy Charlie right here on this sidewalk. Here are the uneven bricks she remembers, some sinking down into the ground, some poking up high, with grass growing up between them.

She thinks Rosie might be home, so she walks over to the green door and knocks. No one answers. A spider has hung his web across the top of the door and when she sees it she ducks back, out of that varmint's way. Then she gets her courage up and reaches under the web, to knock again. No answer. She sits down on the step to wait, setting her satchel down on the bricks and pulling her knees up. Rosie will come home before long, she thinks. This street's a lot quieter than she remembers. When she was here before there were rag pickers and vegetable carts going up and down the street, and people out walking. But today the street looks deserted. She opens her satchel and takes out her Whiskey Lizzie.

An hour later no one's come to the house, and May thinks Rosie must not live here anymore, because the street is awfully quiet and that spider looks like he's been living on Rosie's door for a long time. So she gets up and walks across the street to the house where she lived with Jenny. She jiggles the door handle but the door won't open. She goes to the window and stands on tiptoe to peer in. It's dark inside, but she can make out the sagging settee in the front room.

She thinks her trip's gone wrong. She wanted to find the *Merry Belle*, but she couldn't see it; and now she's back to the one place in New Orleans she knows, but she can't find anyone here either.

She walks to the corner where St. Louis Street crosses Burgundy. She doesn't know this street, but she can see it's another street of houses set close to the sidewalk. She walks down the street and stops at a gate made of iron pickets formed into shapes like flowers. She peers into the courtyard, but when she pushes on the gate it won't move.

The courtyard looks like it belongs in some fairy castle, with palm trees waving their arms up and down so slowly you'd think they were going to be still, but then they move again. At the back of the courtyard there's a tall black cistern with a pointy top that's shaped like an onion. May hears a hollow sound as water drips into the pan under the cistern. Milky blue air fills the courtyard because it's getting dark.

She's thirsty, so she pushes her satchel through the bars of the gate and then hoists herself over it. Inside, she stands up and looks around. She goes over to the cistern, where the pan's overfilled and a wet stain of water snakes across the patio and makes a puddle on the other side of the courtyard. She crouches down and cups her hands to slurp up some water.

She stands up and brushes her hair back from her face. She sees a privy in one corner of the courtyard, so she goes in, even though it's almost too dark to see inside. When she comes back out, she goes over to the cistern and sits down beside it. She likes the look of the cistern; it could almost be a tall tin soldier wearing a pointy helmet. She puts her legs straight out and smooths her skirt down around her legs. A cat sticks its head under the fence to look around and then minces across the courtyard, its belly swinging.

"Hey, mama cat, you wanna be petted? Where'd you hide your kittens?" May asks. But the cat starts to run, arching her back as she disappears behind a bush.

The city gets quiet except for some dogs barking somewhere. The sky turns deep gray, and May lies down on her side, watching to see if the cat comes out again. But it doesn't, and she sleeps.

May wakes to the sun streaking across the patio and the sound of slippers scuffling across the bricks. She sits up and rubs her eyes as the tail end of a flowing kimono disappears into the privy and then the privy door latches shut. In a moment a woman comes out, humming and tying the sash of her kimono. May recognizes her. It's Margot, and she's walking straight toward the cistern.

When she sees May she jumps back. "What you doin'?" she says, and May remembers that voice.

Yes, it's Margot all right, a sharp-featured woman who lived with Jenny in the yellow house. And now here she is, the same Margot, even though she looks skinnier and more tired than May remembers. But May remembers her pointy nose and that honey-brown face.

Margot bends down and peers into her face. "Are you May?" Her mouth hangs open in surprise.

"Yep," May says, scrambling to her feet.

Margot straightens up and glances around the courtyard. "What you doin' here, girl? Was that gate left open?"

"No, I clumb it."

Margot stares hard at her and her eyes become slits. "You here by yourself? Is Jenny here with you somewhere?"

"No. She went away."

"Well, I *know* she went away," Margot says, her face bitter and her hand on her hip. "The last time I seen that Jenny, I could swear you was with her. I saw you walkin' down the street that day, carryin' your bags, so I knew y'all was leavin'. And that's exactly when I stopped gettin' recommendations for my business. That Jenny hexed me some way, I know she did. And then right about that time Rosie took it in *her* head to do midwifin', and she took away most of my business. Everybody who lived down that way, Miss Hedro, too, they all ganged up against me."

"So what did ya do?" May asks.

"You sure are nosy, ain't ya? Well, if you must know, I cleaned houses for a while, and my hands ain't never been so chapped and scratchy as they was back then, from that hot water and soap. And my back never hurt so bad as it did then, wringin' those mops. But then Rosie left and I wasn't one bit sorry to see her go. After that I built my midwifin' business back up from nothin'."

"Rosie's who I was lookin' for."

"Well, you ain't gonna find her here."

"Where'd she go?"

"Sold back into slavery. Serves her right. So what you doin' here? You can't sleep on the patio. Madame Devrot won't allow it. This ain't my place; Madame Devrot only lets me stay here."

"Do you know a lady named Celestina?"

"No. Who's that?" Margot looks around. "You listen, I ain't keepin' no white child here, that's for sure. I can't afford to have any more trouble. When the white ladies hire me to deliver 'em, they don't want nothin' but Margot, and they don't want Margot with some mascot taggin' along. You can't stay here."

"I ain't got nowhere to go."

"You learnt English, didn't you? That's good. Better than that Irish foolishness you used to talk." Her lips pressed together. She looks around as if she expects someone to come into the patio. "Let's go talk to Madame Devrot, 'cause you can't stay here." She holds out her hand, and May takes it, noticing how Margot's fingers are long and straight.

They walk under the gallery to a door in the corner. Margot knocks and a high thin voice calls, "Come in."

They go inside, interrupting the breakfast of a small woman sitting alone at a long dining room table. In a shaft of weak sunlight that comes through the tall window, the woman's hair shines with the same silver color as her coffee pot, May notices. She's holding a half-eaten biscuit smeared with strawberry jam, and May is hungry, so the aroma distracts her. The woman sets the biscuit down and brushes her fingers together.

"Excuse me for bargin' in so early, but I found this ragamuffin young'un sleepin' on the patio," Margot says. "She used to live 'round here, years back, and I guess now she's run off from wherever she was. She used t' stay with a gal I midwifed."

"Hmph," May says. "That ain't so. Jenny told me you was gone off somewhere when she needed a midwife." She tries to pull her hand free but Margot holds it tight.

"That was a long time ago," Margot says. "Two—three years anyway. So now she's showed up here again and what am I gonna do with her?"

Madame Devrot frowns and looks from Margot to May and back. "Well, I don't know—"

"You can't just let her hang around here," Margot says. "She'll be wanting' scraps and everything out of the house."

"Oh, no, we can't have that." Madame Devrot's eyes get big. "Can't she just go back to where she come from?"

"If you can get her to say where that is."

Madame Devrot turns to May. "Where you come from, child?"

May looks at her. She smells something sweet and spicy in the air here, and she's hungry as anything. All she had to eat yesterday was one Whiskey Lizzie.

"Tell you what, May," Margot says, her eyes darting over the girl's skinny frame, her dress hanging loose around her waist. "You a big girl now. How old are you?"

"I'm ten."

Margot leans right into May's face, her eyebrows pulled high. "You don't look ten. I 'member you from before, and I know you wasn't more than six. I guess you just a little short." She turns to Madame Devrot. "I bet she could be a housemaid, if you know anybody who could use her."

Use me? May thinks, but she's distracted by the aromas in the air.

Madame Devrot's high voice squeaks, "I might be able to find somebody who's lookin'." She looks at May and then gazes through the window, where the weak sunlight is filtering through the curtains. "Maybe my friend Lacey Parlenge —"

"I'm hungry," May says. Margot glares at her.

Madame Devrot flutters her hands toward the hallway. "Delie's in the kitchen out there. Go ask her if she'll give you somethin'."

May pulls her hand loose and walks toward the hall. Margot and Madame Devrot are watching her, so she tries to walk softly on the shiny wood floor.

The kitchen is at the end of the hall, a room with a sloping ceiling built onto the side of the house. May sees a woman sitting at the kitchen table sipping a cup of coffee.

"Can I have a cookie?" May asks.

"I ain't got no cookies, chile. Have one of these," Delie says, sliding a plate of beignets across the table as if a strange girl showing up in the kitchen is something that happens every day. May takes two beignets, stuffing one into her pocket for later. The one she eats is soft and mushy, golden on the top and floured with sugar.

After she finishes eating, she brushes the sugar from her mouth with the back of her hand and goes back out through the side door to the patio. She leans against the wall, thinking it would be good if she could live inside this house with Madame Devrot. This house is smaller than Carefree, and it doesn't look like anything on the outside, but with its back gallery draped with wisteria and that flashing big cistern and the palm trees dipping their arms as if saying *hello*, it seems like a good place; a place she could stay while she waits for a chance to look for that showboat.

A moment later Margot comes out and motions for May to follow her. They go across the patio to the small wooden building that looks like a shack on the outside, but it's Margot's home. When they go in, May thinks it looks like a different world. There's a thick rug on the brick floor and a silky white bedspread. A little white dog is curled up in the middle of the bed, almost disappearing into the creamy counterpane.

May brushes the rest of the crumbs from her mouth and sits down on the side of the bed, petting the dog. "What's his name?" she asks Margot.

Margot ignores the question. She turns her back to May and tosses her kimono onto a chair; then she pulls her nightgown over her head. She steps into a petticoat and pulls a corset around her waist. After she laces the corset as tight as she can, she drops a red dress over her head. Then she sits down at her dressing table and looks at her face in the mirror, pulling the sides of her face back to make her skin tight and smooth. But when she turns her fingers loose, her face goes back to the way it was. She tosses her head back, making her hair fly out down her back; then she parts it down the middle, rolling it into a big bun on the back of her neck.

She stands up. "Listen, May, I'm going out for a while. You stay here. I'll be back."

"Are you gonna help a lady have a baby?"

Margot doesn't answer. She goes out, closing the door. May hears the click of the lock as Margot turns the key. May bends over the dog and pets it; then she stretches out on the counterpane, her head on Margot's silk pillow, and sleeps.

The next thing she knows, Margot is shaking her by the shoulder.

"Come on, it's time to go. I found you a place with Miss Parlenge, and Madame Devrot's gonna drive you over there. She's waitin', and she ain't gonna wait for no dawdlin' girl."

May gets up and stumbles outside, rubbing her eyes. Madame Devrot's buggy is waiting on the patio with a young slave boy holding the reins. When he sees Margot and May come out, he gets down and opens the gate. Madame Devrot comes out of her house dressed like she's going to a funeral in a black crepe dress. She gets up on the buggy and motions for May to sit beside her. Margot goes back into her shack and shuts the door.

May grabs her satchel, which is still sitting next to the cistern, and climbs up onto the buggy.

"Immanuel, take us to Myrtle Grove," Madame Devrot says.

As the buggy rumbles into the street and they turn the corner, May looks around at the familiar houses on Burgundy Street. She turns to Madame Devrot. "Was Antoine took into slavery too?"

"Antoine? Who's that?"

"Rosie's husband. Her and Antoine lived in that house over there, the one with the green door."

The old woman shrugs. "I don't know 'im. But all of 'em went, so I guess he was sold off, too." May stares at her, trying to imagine how Rosie and Antoine would feel, being sold off into slavery.

"Are you really ten?" Madame Devrot asks.

May nods.

"You don't look it."

"I'm small for my age. How old are you?"

"I'm 'bout a hundred," Madame Devrot says.

"No, you ain't."

"How old you think I am?"

May shrugs. "Seventy?"

"Not quite, girl."

"Oh." May glances up at the woman's wrinkled face, wondering what it feels like to be that old.

"You gonna have to learn to watch your smart mouth," Madame Devrot says. "My friend Lacey ain't gonna want some smart-mouth girl around. You say 'yes, ma'am' and 'no, ma'am.' Ain't nobody ever taught you your manners?"

May ignores the question; she can see they're driving into a new part of the city, because the houses look new and all the trees are planted in rows. She hopes they drive close to the river so she can see the *Merry Belle*. The buggy rumbles out of the old quarter and across a wide boulevard. May turns around once, to watch the cathedral's spires grow smaller and then drop behind the rooftops. Then they come to a street lined with saplings, where new houses are going up.

"Now, over there is the asylum for orphan girls," Madame Devrot says, pointing to a large frame building. "But you ain't goin' there. My friend Lacey lives right over here on this other street. Oh, and she's a spinster."

"What's that?"

"A maiden lady."

May nods, trying to look knowing.

"And she smokes a pipe. Don't stare."

May nods again.

The buggy comes to a stop at a tall narrow mansion with a deep porch across the front. An iron arch over the walkway spells out "Murtle Haven" in ornate letters. Madame Devrot gets down and straightens the folds of her heavy skirt.

May climbs down and looks at the house. She still hears the whistles of the steamers, so she knows she's not too far from the river.

Lacey Parlenge opens the door to greet them with a half-smile on her yellowy wrinkled face. She motions Madame Devrot inside and points May to the wicker settee on the porch. As the screen door swings shut, a tobaccoish aroma wafts out.

May sits down on the settee and swings her legs as she looks up and down the street. She hears the clink of china from inside the house and knows the women are having coffee. She wonders if Lacey is smoking her pipe. She pulls the smashed beignet out of her pocket and nibbles at it, ignoring the sugar that cascades down over her dress. She scoots down to the other end of the settee so she can hear the women talking.

"Now Marie," Lacey says, "You've brought me another Irish housemaid?"

"I heard your other girl died last week and left you here with nobody but Lulie. You think you could take this orphan girl on? She just showed up at my place. Margot knowed her. She's little for her age, but she says she's ten. She probably can't cook but she could do laundry and cleanin' and such."

After a moment's silence and then more clinking sounds, May hears Lacey say, "Well, bring her on in and let's see 'er."

Madame Devrot comes to the door and motions for May to come in, but when she sees the sugar that's cascaded across May's skirt, she hisses, "Brush yourself off, girl." May brushes her skirt and follows her into the parlor and looks around.

"And what's your name, girl?" Miss Parlenge asks, holding her fancy pipe out to the side. May stares at the cloud of white smoke filling the cavern of the woman's mouth. Miss Parlenge is missing some of her teeth. May knows it'll just be a moment before the pipe goes back in her mouth.

119

"May Carson."

"And where you from, May?"

"Natchez."

Lacey waves the pipe in the air. "Oh, that's good. My last girl was from Mississippi too, and she was the best cleaner I ever had. I don't mind that. I can't pay much, though, you bein' just ten. You got any family?"

May shakes her head.

"Well, Lulie—she's my other girl—she'll show you what to do. There's a room upstairs you can sleep in. It's where Martha slept. It's got a little bed but it's big enough for you. That all right with you?"

May glances at Madame Devrot, who nods. "Yes ma'am."

"You better learn to speak up. My hearing ain't good."

"Speak up, you rude child," Madame Devrot says, scowling. "There ain't nothin' worse than a sneakery servant who won't speak up."

May looks at the two women, a lump growing in her throat. This wasn't what she wanted, but it seems like she's on a train, and it's pulling her forward, and she can't stop. She's come all the way to New Orleans, thinking she might find the showboat, just to land here at this old lady's house. Lacey's older than any lady she knows, and her house smells too, some bitter smell mixing with the sweet smell of her pipe. This house isn't near as nice as Carefree. *I shoulda stayed there*, she thinks, *but it's too late. I left 'cause I didn't want t' get whacked by Dancy, and I wanted to sing on the showboat. I'm here now, at this house that must be named Murtle Haven because that's what's written on the arch over the gate out front, and Lacey must not even know how to spell.*

"I just live here by myself, but I have company a lot of the time," Lacey says. "My niece and her kids come from Mobile every Christmas. And Lulie could use more help. So you make yourself useful, and we'll get along just fine."

"Do you know somebody named Celestina?" May asks.

Miss Parlenge shakes her head. "Who would that be?" she asks.

"Somebody I know. I was looking for her."

"Well, I doubt you're gonna just run into her. But you might, you never know." She reaches out and grabs May's hand. "So you Irish, huh? You all good workers, I say, if you don't take to drink. Just leave it be."

"Yes ma'am. I'll leave it be."

A big girl comes into the parlor and stares at May, who stares back.

"This here's Lulie," Missus Parlenge says.

Lulie's tall, so she must be nearly grown, May thinks. She has a square face and her hair is a brown mop. Her limp calico dress looks like it hasn't been starched in forever. She wears a stained apron.

"Lulie, you show May where to go," Lacey says.

Lulie motions her to follow and they go down the hall to a staircase at the back of the house. Halfway up the stairs May stops and listens to the women talking in the parlor. *This is a good listening spot*, she thinks. But she can't stop to hear what they're saying because Lulie is motioning her to come up the steps.

"This here's your place," Lulie says when they get to the top.

May looks into the room; it has a bed so small it looks like it was made for a baby. The room itself is so narrow the bed runs from wall to wall. May lies down on the faded quilt to try it; her feet are up against one wall and her head rests against the other wall.

"Too short," she says, getting up.

"You don't need to stretch way out," Lulie says. "Just curl up. Put your satchel on that chair and then come on back downstairs. We gotta mop the kitchen."

The stairs creak as Lulie goes back downstairs. The house is quiet, so Madame Devrot must have gone back to her house.

May thinks, *Now I gotta work for this old lady, and she'll pay me something, but it won't be as good as singing on the Merry Belle. So maybe I'll just walk on outta here and go look for that showboat.*

She goes back to the stairs and stops when she's halfway down. From there she can see the front door, where the morning sun is shining through the leaded glass and throwing diamond-shaped designs on the foyer floor. She knows that front door's gonna be beckoning her every day she's here. But she won't leave, not today. The showboat'll still be there another day when she has time to go looking for it. And at least here she has a bed, and that's better than sleeping by the cistern.

She creeps almost to the bottom of the stairs and sits down, listening. Madame Devrot is still here after all, and the women are talking.

"Now, this May Carson, Marie. I'll give her a try. If she's an orphan, what other life is she ever gonna have?" Lacey says.

"Housekeeper till the day she dies," Madame Devrot says. "It's good of you to take her on."

"Well, it's my Christian duty," Lacey says. "Her bein' an orphan. She reminds me of Trella, who cleaned the upstairs. She was an orphan too when she started with me. Did I tell you she died last week?"

"Yes, I heard it."

"She was only thirty-one. You know, when she died I went over to her house and asked her husband Bennie what kilt her, and he just looked at me so unkindly and said, 'She died of not wantin' to clean out your chamber pot anymore.' If you can imagine him sayin' that rude thing to me. And all those years I was *good* to Trella."

"You could get some slave women," Madame Devrot says. "It might be simpler."

"Oooh, Lord, no," Lacey says. "I couldn't stand to have an African village walkin' through my house day and night." May pictures Lacey scrunching up her long face, but from where she sits on the top step, she can't see into the parlor. "But this girl May, startin' young, I can train her right. I trained Lulie, and I tell you, if I could train Lulie, I could train anybody. That girl's not bright at all."

May looks around to where the steps disappear above her at a dark room that'll be her room now. She starts to hum, too low for the old ladies to hear, the only Irish song she remembers, but she's not sure what the words mean any more.

"Ach go drail lamb..."

CHAPTER THIRTEEN

Vicksburg
April 1845

JENNY STANDS FOR A MOMENT AT THE DOOR of her cabin, watching as the shadows thrown by the chinkapin oak dance across the white clapboard wall of the Crum house. She doesn't remember the tree shading the house last year, but it's grown a lot, after a rainy spring. Last year it was hardly more than a sapling that sprang up in the yard. But nobody in this house would think to take a saw to those low-growing limbs. But it could just be a trick of her memory; her mind hasn't been clear enough or free enough to consider what foliage is swallowing the house of Milton and Verna Crum.

Although it's a new house for Vicksburg, the Crum house already has a shabby look. Seeing the house washed by what should be hopeful morning sunlight gives Jenny a sick feeling like a fist in her stomach, knowing her whole day will be spent inside.

On the day she came here a year and a half ago, James Crum drove the buggy up to the big new house and pointed her to the slave house in the back, behind the well. Jenny's heart sank when she saw the little cabin, but it's been her home ever since. It's inside the Crum house that she spends her days, with one eye on her daughter and one eye on Verna Crum, who's quick to scold. And the Crums' twin boys, who are a year younger than Rosabel, already act like they know they're better than Rosabel. Those boys can't talk clearly yet, but just seeing them reminds Jenny every day that if she's caught back into slavery, her daughter is too.

Jenny's life is used up hour by hour, and she has little time to spare for Rosabel. Right now the second-story shutters are already open, so Verna is up. And Milton will be lumbering around the upstairs bedroom as he pulls on his clothes—his expensive suit, his shined shoes—but he always manages to look rumpled in spite of his nice clothes.

She knows what the work in the house is before she sees it, the scuffed kitchen floor, the windows halfway open so the flies buzz in, the orange cat mincing across the floor in the slant of sunlight, yowling for his milk. Verna will be waiting for her coffee in the dining room, her fingers drumming the table hard and looking at the doorway, expecting Jenny to walk through it any minute with the coffee pot. It ought to be a pleasant morning, she thinks, but there's no comfort in it, not for her and not for the Crums, either. The Crum house is a place of terse conversations, of doors closed hard, of awkward silences. You could bottle up the unhappiness in that house if you slammed the windows shut.

She has to hurry; she's a slave woman and her time to think her own thoughts is short.

She ties her apron and puts her hands up to push her hair back into place. She looks around for Rosabel, who's sitting on the side of the bed pulling up her socks. The little girl puts on her shoes and then holds them out so Jenny can lace them. The child's shoes are tattered and scuffed, but someone gave them to Verna, and she handed them to Jenny, saying a child coming into her house had to wear shoes, that she couldn't stand a barefoot child in the house, it wouldn't look right. Jenny was glad to take the shoes, since Rosabel's outgrown the baby shoes she brought from Natchez. But she wishes she had better shoes for Rosabel. If these brown leather high-tops were ever polished to a sheen, that was long ago; the toes are scuffed white. They're big for Rosabel, and some of the eyelets for the ties are missing; and there's a small hole in the right sole, which Jenny repaired with some cardboard. She hopes they'll hold the child through the rest of the summer and then through the winter. Vicksburg doesn't get that much snow.

After she laces Rosabel's shoes, Jenny stands up and catches a glimpse of herself in the cracked mirror standing on the chest. She sees what slavery's done to her. Instead of the well-fitted dresses she wore when she lived at Carefree, she's wearing a shapeless gray shift—a slave's dress—and a tignon that once was white is tied around her head. The corners of her mouth turn down, and her dark eyes look droopy, defeated.

I am completely a slave, she thinks. *I went to a slave auction, and now here I am, twenty-two years old, and I have no future.* She shakes her head and doesn't even smile at Rosabel, who's looking at her curiously. In a moment she'll shuffle over to the Crum house, not hurrying in her own worn-out shoes, to do Verna's bidding. The dishpans, the dusting cloth, the hot water sloshing into the washtub, the chamber pot: this will be her slavery life forever. She goes to the door and breathes in the cool morning air. Rosabel comes up behind her and puts her arms around her mother's waist.

"Ready, Sugar?" Jenny asks.

Rosabel steps around her mother. At three years old, Rosabel's too young to be put to work, but her day will be spent as it is every day, with Billy and Albie, the Crums's twins. And Jenny's so glad it's spring; last winter she worried every day about Rosabel left alone downstairs with the toddling boys in front of that blazing fireplace with Verna ignoring them most of the time. Verna has no sense, but Jenny couldn't watch the kids because she had to spend most of her day upstairs, mopping and scrubbing, and then in the afternoon she was off in the kitchen, chopping onions and pounding meat for the Crums' dinner, because Verna wants it ready at six o'clock sharp, every day.

Milton Crum watches Jenny whenever he's in the same room she's working in. Feeling his eyes on her back makes her stomach feel emptied out and sour. But this is her life now, every day except Sunday, when she has her half-day off.

Rosabel doesn't have that sick feeling, Jenny knows, and she's glad about that. Since the child knows nothing else in her young life, she goes into the big house without complaining and tries to make the boys her play-mates.

"Let's go, mamma," Rosabel says, squeezing past Jenny and marching ahead of her down the path. Jenny smiles; yes, this is Adrien Jean-Pierre's child for sure. He's in Rosabel's features and her light complexion and in the way she swings her arms when she walks.

Jenny cautions Rosabel to stay on the bricks and not walk on the dewy grass. Verna would scold her for letting Rosabel come into the house with wet shoes, and likely as not she'd follow up the scolding with a smart pop on the arm.

Jenny opens the back door and they go inside. Milton is sitting at the table with the newspaper open on the table beside him. She knows he's been watching for her to come in. The knot in her stomach ties itself a little tighter.

"Mornin,' Jenny." He stares at her for a moment.

"Mornin'." She glances at him and then looks down at the floor.

He points Rosabel toward the parlor, where Jenny hears the sounds of a squabble between the two boys. Rosabel goes in and gets between them, snatching whatever toy caused the fight. Verna walks through the kitchen and glances at Jenny. Then she goes into the dining room to drink her coffee alone at the long table there.

The sun casts a yellow streak across the dining room wallpaper, a peach-colored tableau of French fountains. Jenny knows not to move quickly; a fast-moving slave woman is expected to keep moving fast, and there's no advantage in that. She reaches for the apron that hangs on the kitchen wall, listening as Rosabel jabbers with the two little boys, and then she saunters over to Milton to pour his coffee.

All at once he reaches out and grabs her arm and pulls her down toward him. Thrown off balance, she drops the coffee pot on the table, and the coffee splatters. Then Verna appears in the doorway, and Milton releases her and picks up the newspaper, scowling.

"I'm sorry, sir," Jenny says. She sops up the splatters with a towel and walks back to the kitchen trailing the aroma of chicory coffee.

She looks down at her arm where he grabbed it. She'll have a bruise there. Steadying herself, she washes the boys' oatmeal bowls and sets them upside down on a dish towel. This is a chore she doesn't mind, and she'll putter in the kitchen until Milton leaves for his office on Main Street. She thinks of the day in sections: when Milton is gone to his office or to his men's club, and when he's back; when Verna's here or when she's gone out to shop or socialize; or most importantly, when Rosabel is downstairs watching the boys while Jenny has to be upstairs cleaning. But it's all miserable. And she can't shake the memory of the slave auction that put her here.

I'm a bird caught in a net, she thinks. If only Cornelius could come and rescue her and Rosabel. She's dreamed of it many times. Here she's helpless, a slave, with her precious freeing paper thrown away in the dirt, and her husband sold off to Texas. Walker wasn't really her husband, but now she's lonely and she thinks of him that way though they never had even the kind of halfway ceremony she had with Adrien. But she accepted him the first night on the trip when he reached for her, and the night after that, too.

But Cornelius won't rescue her. He doesn't know where she is, and besides, he and Euphonia live in a world unto themselves at Carefree, satisfied they've freed their own people and giving no thought to all the slaves around them in slave-land. Walker told Esther to say Jenny left a long time ago; and people who once were slaves are good at keeping secrets, so she's sure no one at Carefree will ever say her name. But here she is, only a few hours away by steamer, but caught, hopeless.

Yesterday Verna told her to stew a chicken for dinner, plucked from the coop in the yard. And the very act of wringing the chicken's neck brought her down, even though she's done that a hundred times before. But for some reason when she woke in the night she remembered the headless fowl running about the yard looking for its head. The chicken's despair and doom had caught in her chest, and an emptiness settled over her. Not even the sweet face of Rosabel, who took her hand as the sun set and they walked across the yard to their own cabin, could brighten her. She's lost so much, and she doesn't know how to get it back. That sense of despair was with her all night, waking her and causing her to stare empty-eyed at the black sky outside the window.

CHAPTER FOURTEEN

EVERY SUNDAY JENNY USES HER HALF-DAY OFF to walk to Minnie's house to spend the afternoon. It's the one time of the week when she doesn't have to account for her minutes and hours. Walker's family is friendly and she's just as valuable to them as they are to her, because they're all a connection to Walker.

But today as she and Rosabel walk down the back streets toward Minnie's place, she's having trouble shaking the feeling of gloom that settled over her this week. If she stays at the Crum house for twenty years, things will never be better for her, because she knows Milton Crum is a dangerous man. And he'll be dangerous for Rosabel, too, as she grows.

When she gets to Minnie's house, expecting to be greeted by the friendly faces of Minnie's children and grandchildren, she's the first one there. She walks in holding Rosabel's hand, startling Minnie, who's sitting at the table with her back to the door. A potato sack lies on the table in front of her. Before she sees Jenny, Minnie leans forward and puts the open sack up to her face like a mask.

"Minnie?" Jenny says.

Minnie drops the sack back onto the table. When she looks around at Jenny, her bright eyes are brimming.

"Oh, what is it?" Jenny asks, going over to her and putting her arm around Minnie's thin shoulders.

The old woman shakes her head and grabs the hem of her apron to mop her eyes.

"What is it?" Jenny asks again as Rosabel troops past her and climbs up onto Minnie's bed to take the ragdoll from where it rests against the pillow.

"I'm sorry, Jenny, but you know sometimes it's just more than I can bear." Minnie shakes her head. "Bein' a slave, and not worth nothin' to nobody in this world. And my whole life taken up in slavery, and my chilrun's too—"

Jenny sits down on the other chair. "Well —" She knows this feeling. "Did somethin' happen?"

Minnie turns to face her. "Bernadine's gonna tear down my house! She wants me to start livin' in her bedroom with her. She told me so this mornin'. She wants to tear down this ole shack—that's what she called it—'cause she's too scared to sleep by herself. So I won't even have my own house."

"Oh, Minnie," Jenny says as the old woman lays her head on Jenny's shoulder and cries, holding the hem of her apron to her mouth. After a minute Minnie composes herself and lays her hand gently on top of the potato sack, fingering the rough burlap.

"This here's a sack my mammy gave me on the day I was sold away, when I weren't no more than eight years old. And I never seen my mammy again after that. I was sold off to be a baby minder, and when the Martins bought me they expected me to know how to do that. But I was jus' a child myself, and never been away from the plantation in my life."

She shakes her head and then goes on, "But while they was waitin' in the buggy to take me away, my mammy said, 'Wait, Minnie!' She took me into our cabin and got this ole potato sack out of the bin and shook it out; I can still remember how the dust flew off it. And she folded up my other dress and put it in there, and she dropped in some pecans. And then right in front of me she took her scissors and cut off a piece of her hair and put it in there, too. She said, 'You keep this sack with you, so you have a extra dress to wear. And times when you feelin' sad 'cause you ain't got me with you, you remember to look in this sack, 'cause there's a piece of me in there.' And I was cryin', and I tried to say, 'Mammy, I don't want to go'. But Master Martin was shoutin' for me to come out, and I had to go."

Minnie reaches into the sack and pulls out the lock of black hair that was her mother's. She cradles it in her palm and strokes it.

"What was her name?" Jenny asks.

"Bitsy," she says. "And sometimes now, even though I'm old, when it gets too much for me, I just gotta put my face down in this ole sack, and I breathe it in, 'cause that's my mammy's air in that sack. And I know I'm breathin' the same air she did, and I'm touchin' the hair she cut off her own head for me that day."

Minnie strokes the lock of hair for a minute longer, and then carefully lays it back in the sack. Sighing, she folds the sack closed.

"And the thing is, Jenny," she says, "I'm tellin' you, you better make a sack for Rosabel. Maybe a better one than this one. Put in things she can remember you by. And breathe your air into it. 'Cause if you a slave, she is too, and she might be took away from you any day, and you won't even see it comin'."

Jenny stands up, shocked, tipping the chair backward. She looks around at Rosabel, who's talking baby talk to the ragdoll. Jenny covers her mouth with her hands, afraid the child could disappear right out of this cabin.

It gets darker and darker, she thinks. *There's no bottom to it. How is a person supposed to breathe, with all this slavery darkness everywhere?*

Minnie's face is sad all that day, even after Cooper and Barney arrive a few minutes later, and then shortly after that, Marie and Susie appear. It's not the happy kind of afternoon they usually have, although the others don't know why Minnie's face is so sad. Minnie doesn't spoil the day by telling them about Bernadine's plans, but Jenny can't get Minnie's sack out of her mind.

The next week Minnie is sweeping the parlor floor in Mrs. Martin's house when she hears a dog barking in the normally quiet street. She goes to the window and pushes the lace curtain aside. She can't see the dog but she sees Carlton, Mrs. Martin's slave boy, striding along the sidewalk in his loose-limbed way, whistling. He's carrying a package wrapped in brown paper. Carlton's tall as all get-out, and he's a good-natured helper around the old woman's house. He ducks along the side of the house, and Minnie props the broom against the wall and waits for the sound of his shoes on the polished floor. A moment later he stands in the hallway.

"What's that you carryin?" Minnie asks.

"Somethin' come for Miz Martin," Carlton says. "The man at the post office said it just come in yesterday."

"You best let me give it to her." Minnie takes the package and goes into the parlor, where Bernadine is sitting at the piano, plinking her way through "Home Sweet Home." When Bernadine sees Minnie standing in the doorway with the package, she pauses halfway through the last line. The notes of the unfinished bar hang empty in the humid air.

"What?"

"Package come." Minnie walks into the room with Carlton right behind her.

"It come from Natchez," Carlton says.

"Well, let me see it," Bernadine says, spinning around on the piano stool. She takes the package and holds it up, squinting at the address. "All it says is *Mrs. Martin, Main Street, Vicksburg.* I don't know who'd be sending me somethin', especially if they don't even know my address."

"The man at the post office said it must be you," Carlton says. "'Cause there ain't no other Mrs. Martin on Main Street, and everybody knows you."

"Well, get me my scissors," she says, fluttering her crooked fingers at Minnie.

When Minnie brings the scissors, Bernadine says "Well, I don't reckon I know anybody in Natchez." She snips the twine and the package falls open in her lap. The paper snakes to the floor.

"Well, I never—" She holds up a garment and shakes it out. It's a child's blue dress, not new, and frayed at the hem. "This is plainly a mistake. It must be meant for somebody else."

Minnie looks at the dress. She wonders if this has something to do with Walker, who lived in Natchez all those years.

"It's come to the wrong house, since there's nobody in this house that's under seventy, and we certainly don't have any little girls living here. Well, that's it. Wrong address. I guess whoever was waitin' for this dress is just gonna have to keep waitin'." She fingers the fabric. "It feels kinda dusty anyway, like it ain't been washed good. It's kinda nice made, you know, but it's worn out."

"I might could find some young'un that could use it," Minnie says.

"Take it." Bernadine folds the dress roughly and thrusts it at her. "And pick up this paper. Now I'd like to finish my music, if y'all don't mind.

If my old fingers will find the right keys. I do love to play these songs. Ain't they just beautiful, Minnie?" She spins around to the keyboard.

"Yes'm, they are pretty," Minnie says, noisily crumpling the paper into a ball.

Bernadine pushes the music to one side and opens a different sheet, shaking it so it stays open. She squints at the music and lays her little monkey fingers on the keys and plinks into the heavy summer air, singing with an old lady's warble, *"One mornin', one mornin', one mornin' in May, I met a fair couple, they were makin' their wa-a-a-y..."*

Minnie takes the dress back into the kitchen and refolds it and lays it on the table. Carlton follows her into the kitchen.

"You want a piece of cake?" she asks him.

He nods and she carves him a piece of the spice cake she'd made for dinner. He sits at the table and eats it with his hands. When he's finished, he brushes his fingers on his pants and heads out toward the stable behind the house.

Minnie sorts through the pile of sweet potatoes in a bowl; she wants to make a pone, even though it's too hot to start baking this late in the day. She picks out half a dozen yams and peels them. As she starts to grate them, her arm sawing back and forth, she eyes the dress lying folded on the table. Why would somebody in Natchez send a child's dress here, with no explanation? But the parcel was addressed to Mrs. Martin, and it found its way here. That means something. Mysterious as this is, if Walker were here, he'd know. He lived in Natchez all those years, and he knew most everything that went on down there.

She wonders where he is now. Jenny said he went to Texas. Minnie hopes he's got a kind master and an easy position, that he's not sweating out his days in some cane field or cotton field. She hopes someday before she dies he'll come back. She swallows back the lump that rises in her throat whenever she thinks of Walker, her one child that's lost to her. All the others are in slavery, but at least they're here in Vicksburg or nearby.

But Jenny and Rosabel are a connection to him. It makes her feel she hasn't really lost him forever, because Jenny and Rosabel are his family. As long as she can see them, she feels close to Walker too.

By the late afternoon she's finished peeling the sweet potatoes and scraped the peelings out to the chicken yard, and the pone is sitting steaming in a pan on the table. She carries a dinner plate upstairs for Bernadine, who likes to eat light in the evenings, sitting with a tray by the window. As Bernadine eats, Minnie folds back her coverlet and plumps the feather pillows. It's sunset by the time the old woman's been bathed and helped into bed. Sixty years of working together has made the two women work in the same rhythm, even though Bernadine can screech and threaten when she feels like it, and her smacks are sharp and hurtful. But as Bernadine's gotten older she can't hit that hard, and Minnie knows to duck her head and say "Yes'm" without reacting.

Bernadine'll be going to sleep soon—she drops off early—and so far she doesn't expect to have Minnie at her beck and call in the middle of the night. She hasn't mentioned tearing Minnie's house down again; she only mentioned it that one time. She might have forgotten all about it, but Minnie knows that day's coming, as feeble as Bernadine's getting. It's coming. She dreads it.

Minnie takes the dress and goes out to her house and lights a candle. Tomorrow's Sunday, and she'll be glad to see her children.

The next day when Jenny walks into Minnie's house, she sees the blue dress on the table, folded neatly. She glances at it and hugs Minnie, whose outlook seems to have brightened since last Sunday.

"What's that?" she asks, pointing at the dress.

"It come from Natchez. Somebody sent it to Bernadine," Minnie says without getting up. She holds out her arms to Rosabel, who climbs onto her lap. "I told her I might know some young'un that could wear it. I was thinkin' of Rosabel. It musta been a mistake, though. Nobody here knows anybody in Natchez." She puts her cheek down on Rosabel's hair.

Jenny takes the dress and shakes it out. She holds it up and studies it. "Oh, it ain't a mistake. I know this dress."

"You know it?"

"I've seen it before." The blue dress looks a little more faded than she remembers, but it's the same dress with the lace-edged collar and the three lines of pin-tucking above the hem. "This was the dress May wore when I brought her to Natchez from New Orleans. Rosie gave me this dress so May would have something nice to wear on the boat."

"Who's May and who's Rosie? I ain't heard you talk about them before."

"May was a white child I saved off the dock in New Orleans, and Rosie lived across the street from me. She's the one I named Rosabel for. She midwifed me."

"You sure this is the same dress?"

"Well, look at this worn-out place, right here along the hem. The dress May wore had that same frayed place. The exact same."

Rosabel fiddles with the rag doll. "I'm gonna sew that eye on for you sometime," Minnie says, touching Rosabel's hair lightly.

"But I can't figure out what it means," Jenny says. "Do you think it was Esther who sent it? But why would she?"

"Jenny, I don't know them Natchez people, Esther, Rosie, May," Minnie says. "You rattle 'em off as if I oughter know, but all that does is make me sad. Makes me remember Walker."

"I think Esther must've mailed this so I'd get it, and she didn't know the address. I bet she just took it to the post office and told the man there to send it to Missus Martin on Main Street. She must 'a figured I'd get it, and I'd know what it means, but I don't."

"Maybe she thought Rosabel could wear it."

Jenny frowns. "I wouldn't put a ragged dress on Rosabel. She'd have nicer dresses than this. Esther knows I can sew."

Barney comes in a moment later, and then all the others, so Jenny folds the dress and slips it under the quilt on Minnie's bed. Seeing the old dress has given her a shiver. She almost wants to put it up to her face, the way Minnie did with her sack, because it came from Carefree.

Later, she sits outside on the step with Cooper, watching the moon rise in a golden wash of clouds.

"What you thinkin' about, sweet Jenny?" he asks. He leans over and kisses her, but then she leans away from him. Cooper's sweet on her; she's known that for a while.

"I'm thinkin' about a little girl's dress that somebody sent here from Natchez. I bet it was Esther that sent it."

"Now how would you know that?"

"Because it was May's dress. Esther was tryin' to tell me somethin', I bet. I hope nothin's happened to May. I felt bad leaving' her the way I did. Now I feel bad seein' that old dress."

"I dunno know who this May is, but you wouldn't 'a left her if you didn't know she was all right where she was at."

"No, I wouldn't. Not after I rescued her in the first place. Esther took to her and was treatin' her just like her own child. And she was learnin' to read and everything. I had no way to keep her." She looks up at Bernadine's house, a gray square shape in the moonlight. "But it hurt my heart to leave her, anyways, even though I knew Walker and me couldn't take her, a white child."

"You right about that. So she had to stay. It sounds like it woulda been harder on her to leave Esther than it was for you to leave her, you bein' busy with the baby and all. Whoever this Esther is."

"But I know Esther's tryin' to tell me somethin.'"

"So what you gonna do?"

"I can't figure out why she sent it, that's all. I guess the only way I can find out is to go back there. To Carefree."

"How you gonna do that? Last I saw, they wasn't lettin' slave women roam up and down the roads of Mississippi."

"You're right, but I might have to take that chance. I been here over a year. I imagine things at Carefree's settled down some. It's odd that I ain't heard a word from that place from the day we left 'til now. Not a word. But I been thinkin', Esther could've asked Cornelius to find out Minnie's address, and he would've written it down. But that wasn't his writin' on the package, so she must 'a wanted to keep him out of it. I got a bad feelin' about it." She looks at him. "Cooper, could you help me? Come with me if we made a run for Natchez?"

He leans back and shakes his head. "I can't do that, Jenny. You know I'm bound to Charles Fitley, and there ain't no gettin' away from that man."

"Don't you want t' get free?"

"There ain't no gettin' free. You know that."

"I'll tell you there is. All it takes is to find a white man that's got the right spirit in his soul. Not that there's many of 'em around, I get that, but if you come live at Carefree, Cornelius Carson ain't gonna keep you in slavery."

"He ain't got a legal right to do nothin' about it. I'd be a runaway."

"He'd do it. He's got connections with the law. He freed me and Mal. And Walker got free down there by payin' off his old mistress. Cornelius would figure it out." When Cooper doesn't say anything else, she goes on, "We'd need a buggy. I think I remember the road."

"You be careful, gal. That's how you got caught before, bein' out on the road. That's why you in slavery now."

"It's where I'm gonna stay if I don't make a run. The reason I got caught is 'cause we were runnin' to the north, and Walker didn't know the way and neither did I. But I do remember the road to Natchez."

"Ain't you worried about the sheriff that's after you? The one you told me about?"

"Right now that don't seem like as big a worry as stayin' in slavery with Milton Crum. Let's us just go on back to Natchez. It's been so long since I was there. And all I got here's a moony-faced white man who's lookin' at me hard, and 'fore you know it, and it could happen any day, Milton Crum's gonna have me up against a wall, and I'm gonna end up with that man's young'un. And then I couldn't ever leave 'cause I wouldn't leave my child. That's what's gonna happen if I stay with the Crums. I can see it. He's a no-good man. He'll get me under 'im one way or the other, and he won't mind forcin' me. He's already grabbed me rough." She pulls up her sleeve to show Cooper the bruise on her arm. "And he's mean to Rosabel. He brought a sweet to his boys last week and even though Rosabel was standin' right there, wantin' one, he told her she couldn't have one. And if he gets a child on me, I won't never be able to go. So I got to go pretty quick."

"I don't know, Jenny. You gotta think about Rosabel."

"I am thinkin' about her. I'm thinkin' about her all the time. As long as I'm in slavery, she's gonna end up in it too. Can't you come with me?" When he doesn't answer, she scowls, "Cooper, are you *sure* you Walker's full brother?"

He looks at her in surprise. " 'Course I am. Can't you see we look just alike? Except Walker was little, and I'm normal size."

"'Cause Walker wasn't somebody who'd wait and worry about things. Somethin' come along, Walker'd just up and do it. That's why me and him got along so well, 'cause we was just alike that way."

Cooper looks around. A long minute passes. Then he leans toward her and kisses her, harder than before. "You got a mighty sweet kiss, Miss Jenny. Well, if you promise to kiss me while we're on this crazy run, I guess I could try it, since I ain't the one with the sheriff on my tail. That's you."

She puts her arms around his neck and kisses him again. "Ain't Fitley got a buggy he ain't usin? Out behind the barn or somewhere?"

Cooper thinks. "Matter of fact, he do. Got a old nag of a horse too. Name of War Face. But War Face so old, he done fit his last war. But he might last til we get to Natchez. He might drop down dead once we get there, though."

"When can you sneak off?"

"Well, it ain't gonna be tonight. But I guess there ain't gonna be a better night than tomorrow night. Fitley told me he's goin' to Nashville on business this week. And his wife goes to bed at six. She's about to spring with the third kid anyway. It wouldn't be hard to go tomorrow night."

"I'll pack up my things and Rosabel's too." Jenny jumps up. She reaches down and takes his face in her hands and kisses him. "Cooper, now you actin' like you and Walker's related."

"We get catched on the road, I'm warnin' you, Jenny, I'm gonna say I ain't never heard of you."

"Minnie told me you know how to write."

"You ain't s'posed to know about that."

"Is it true?"

"Well, I ain't good at it. I can do it a little. I don't know how to spell a t'all. I'm just guessin' at words."

"You could write me a freein' paper."

"Naw, I couldn't do that."

"Well, nobody else's gonna help me. Won't you try?"

"Nope. But you want t' go to Natchez, I guess I could sneak off. I'll get Barney to tell Missus Fitley I'm sick out in the slave house. She ain't gonna check up on me."

In the night, a dream comes to Jenny, sick and rancid: the slave holding room is before her eyes, its sickly yellow candle-light flickering on the walls. Its stench is in her nose, and Rosabel is a soft burden in her arms. Hopelessness is in the air.

She opens her eyes to the dark cabin. The slave auction is a hard kernel of shame inside her chest. *I will never speak of it again in my life,* she thinks.

CHAPTER FIFTEEN

COOPER SHOWS UP BEFORE DAWN with a beaten-down horse and a two-seater buggy that looks like any of the four wheels might fall off any minute. Jenny, who's been standing in the alley with Rosabel for an hour watching for him, holds up a lantern as he pulls the buggy to a stop.

"I was afraid you changed your mind," she whispers as she helps Rosabel up onto the seat.

"I had to wait 'til Fitley set off for Tennessee," he says, grinning. "The place was real quiet when I left, so I know nobody seen me leave. So hey, let's go, Miss Jenny, Miss Rosabel. We gonna see some new sights."

"I brought us somethin' to eat. Verna won't miss it."

As they drive away, Jenny turns around and looks at the Crum house, but the windows are still dark. Milton and Verna won't be up for another hour.

"I'm just gonna walk old War Face 'til we get outta town. Don't want to make noise," Cooper says. The Vicksburg streets are still empty, the sun just coming up.

Jenny says, "Now listen, Cooper, if anybody looks at us like they're wonderin' who we are and what we're doin', you just look straight ahead down the road. Don't look back at 'em. But if they look like they're gonna stop us, I'll climb in the back seat, and you tell 'em I'm sick with the yella jack, and you got to get me to your master's other plantation, where the doctor is."

She tells him where to turn to get to the Natchez road. By the time the sun comes up, they're on the road, the sun throwing shafts of light across the clay tracks. Jenny remembers how the road goes down into gullies and then curves back up again into thick forests. At this early hour no one passes them.

Rosabel wakes up and leans against Jenny, rubbing her eyes. Jenny hands her a peach she brought from the Crums' kitchen, and then holds a towel under the girl's chin to catch the dribble. She thinks, won't the Crums be surprised when they wake up, expecting her to come into the kitchen like she always does, and when she doesn't, they'll go out to the little house and Jenny won't be there. It's a thrilling thought.

Still, it's frightening to be running away, and all day Jenny watches the riders who pass them on horseback, remembering the slavers who took her and Rosabel and Walker to the slave auction. But Cooper is a confident driver.

That night they pull far off the road into a field, and Jenny spreads the quilt on the ground for them to sleep on. Rosabel whimpers, so Cooper tells her a story about a fish that swims out of its pond and walks away to the next pond.

"I heard there is fish such as that," Cooper says seriously.

"No, there ain't," Jenny says.

"Well, I heard there is," he says.

Rosabel sleeps, and Jenny lies on the quilt, looking up into the sky. She can just make out heavy gray clouds scudding overhead, but she hopes the clouds will stay high up, so it won't rain on them. Cooper sleeps stretched out across the buggy seat, snoring.

She thinks about Cooper. He'd probably like to come over to the quilt with her, but he can't. She's kissed him more than once on this trip, like she promised him she would, but she's told him she thinks Walker's coming back, and she's saving herself for that day. Which made Cooper look disappointed, and she's sorry about that, but that's just the way it is. And she can't imagine where Walker is tonight, except that he's off in Texas somewhere, a place she can't even picture.

It's late in the afternoon two days later when they come up the hill to Carefree. Cooper pulls the buggy to a stop as the big house comes into view.

"It looks different," Jenny says. "And littler."

"It looks mighty big to me," Cooper says. " 'Course, I always heard that a place you come from, when you go back to it, it looks littler than you remember."

It looks defeated, Jenny thinks. Yet it's the same place: the four white columns, the drive that curves around to the front, the black shutter hanging off kilter at one window. And the late afternoon sunlight is glinting on the tiny leaves of the shrubbery.

"What's wrong with it?" Jenny asks.

"I dunno. Where do we go from here?"

"Go on through that gate. Let's see if Esther's here. She'll know what's going on."

"Maybe you ain't gonna like bein' back here," Cooper says.

"I'm gonna like bein' out of slavery," she says. "And Cornelius'll let us stay."

Rosabel starts to whimper and Jenny sits her up on her lap and fans her with her hand. Cooper shakes the reins and they drive onto the drive and around the back toward the Dependency.

"I wonder where everybody is," Jenny says.

He pulls the buggy to a stop near the kitchen. They get down and Jenny opens the kitchen door. Cooper, holding Rosabel's hand, follows her inside. Dancy is stirring a pot at the fire, and when the door opens she turns around, mopping her glistening face with a towel. Jenny smells gumbo.

Dancy puts her hand on her hip. "Well, Jenny, I do declare," she says. "Is that you?"

Jenny walks over and hugs her. "It's me all right."

Dancy steps back. "And look how big li'l Rosabel's grown!"

"She has," Jenny says. She brushes Rosabel's black curls back from her forehead. "And this here's Cooper, Walker's brother." Cooper smiles his crooked smile. "Is Esther here somewhere?" Jenny asks.

Dancy shakes her head and walks over to the table and sinks into the chair. Jenny sees sagging lines on her face that weren't there before. Dancy's voice drops. "Jenny, we had all kinds of bad things happen since you left. It's been mighty hard."

Jenny sits down opposite her. "What?"

"Esther ain't here no more," Dancy says. "She went off to find her girls 'bout six months ago. She went out once before and couldn't find 'em, so she come back. But then she was just so sad, she said she had to go look some more. This time I ain't sure she's ever comin' back."

"Where'd she go?"

"Across the river, out by Vidalia."

Jenny lifts Rosabel to her lap. "Wouldn't Cornelius help her?"

"He did help her, much as he could. He sent Mister Badeau to Franklin and Armfields to see if they had any records, but he couldn't find any. It's been a long time since those girls was sold. It was back before I came here."

"Is everyone else here? Bo, Daniel, and all the others? It seems so quiet."

Dancy looks at Rosabel. "That's a pretty child, ain't she?" She sighs. "Well, we got more trouble than that, and that's why everybody's tryin' to keep quiet. It's what Phony wants. Coella's still watchin' Thomas, though with all the trouble we had lately, I wouldn't be surprised if she don't up and leave one day. That'd serve Phony right, if she had to see to Thomas all by herself. Everybody else is here, 'cept for Cassie. She went to find her husband in Texas. I don't know how she's gonna find 'im though, because all she knows is the men went to Texas, and it's a big country. And Jane and Margaret both died. So we ain't crowded like we used t' be."

"I'm gonna wait outside," Cooper says. He goes out to sit on the bench beside the door.

Jenny asks, "Is Cornelius in the house?"

"He is, and so's Phony." Dancy's voice gets low. "Jenny, Cornelius's been real sick. He's had the malaria."

Jenny stares at her. She can hardly picture Cornelius ailing, because as long as she's known him, he's never been sick. "Is Malachi here?"

"He's somewhere hereabouts. Right when you left, Cornelius took Mal to go find his people; but when they got to Virginny, Cornelius took sick, so they come back. Mal says he might go back there someday, just not right now; but I don't think he's ever goin' back. That's just him talkin' about somethin' that ain't gonna happen."

"Ain't his people in slavery?"

"His brother is, but his mammy's passed on." She shrugs. "He says his brother's a hard-faced man, but you know, kin's kin." She gets up and walks back to the fire, scraping the last of the logs around so only a thin thread of smoke rises. Then she comes back and sits down again at the table. "We had somethin' else happen here that's bad, and we don't know what to do. I sent you a dress for Rosabel. Did you get it?"

"Oh, it was you who sent it. I thought it was Esther. I got it. It came to Walker's mammy. When I saw it, I knew right off it was May's dress. I had to think awhile, though, before I could figure out what it meant. I decided y'all wasn't just sendin' me a present. Y'all was signallin' me to come back."

Dancy looks at her a long while, studying Jenny's face. "Gal, you lookin' older since you left here. I don't mean you're ugly. You're still pretty, but you do look older."

"It's 'cause I was caught back into slavery, Dancy. The worse thing in the world."

"You was in slavery? Where's Walker?"

"He's in slavery, too. Took to Texas is all I know. I was kept in Vicksburg. Cooper's in slavery too. We snuck off."

Dancy glances out through the door, where Cooper sits on the bench, fanning himself with his straw hat.

"There's one other thing," Dancy says. "You won't hardly believe it, cause none of us could. But May's gone."

"Gone where?"

"She run off. We got up one morning, not long after Esther left, and she'd disappeared." Rosabel wriggles off Jenny's lap and goes outside to sit on the bench with Cooper.

"Did y'all look for her?" Jenny asks.

"Of *course* we looked. Cornelius was just beside himself, sick man that he was. He got a lot sicker after that. We looked high and low all around Natchez, and we got up a search party. I can't tell you how much it troubled us. It was all we talked about, for the longest. Ever since then, it seems like there ain't nothin' goin' right 'round here."

"You think she was snatched?"

Dancy shakes her head. "We think she ran off. She took her satchel, and some of her clothes. We even went for the sheriff, which we knew was dangerous, but Cornelius said we had to do it. Sheriff got up a posse. I think we covered every square inch of ground in Natchez, lookin' for that child. And we put up posters all over, even on the lamp posts on Main Street. 'Missing Child,' they said. Miss Phony read 'em to me. And they told what May looked like. We're pretty sure she snuck out by herself in the middle of the night before anybody got up. Just snuck past Coella and Thomas, and out the door she went."

"Where could a child that age go?"

"She couldn't vanish into thin air, but it seems like that's what she did. Just disappeared like a ghost. That was almost a year ago. It's like she weren't never here."

But she was here, Jenny thinks. *May a real, breathing child, studying her spelling-book, fastening herself onto Esther as if Esther were her real mother.*

But Esther was gone. *Maybe May went to find Esther.*

"Why'd you send me that dress?" Jenny asks.

Dancy shakes her head. "I dunno. One day I was cleaning out the chiffarobe, and I seen that blue dress. And it just come to me, I'd send it to the house where Walker's mammy works, and it might get to you. Then maybe somehow you could help get May back. Everything here was hurtin', and hopeless, and Cornelius was so sick—I was just tryin' to make somethin' *happen.*" She smiles, wanly. "And I guess I did, 'cause you come back. And that's good. But don't think you come to a happy place, 'cause you ain't."

Dancy puts her hands up over her face, makes a sound like a strangle in her throat, and when she looks at Jenny, blinking her eyes dry, Jenny sees nothing but bewilderment in her face.

Holding Rosabel's hand, Jenny walks to the big house. When she opens the back door, she senses how quiet the house is. It was a noisy place when she lived here before, but now the air inside feels hollow, the place empty of life.

She walks down the short hall to look in at her old room. The peach-colored bedroom where she stayed with Rosabel is still a pleasant room with a dresser and a large chiffarobe; but lying on the counterpane are pieces of fabric cut into squares and triangles and circles, laid out in an orderly design. A sewing basket sits on the dresser, a pair of scissors next to it. Someone—Euphonia, probably—is making a quilt. It doesn't look like she'll be moving back into this room.

She walks across the hall to Cornelius's office, where the door is slightly ajar. She pushes it open.

Cornellius is sitting at his desk. He looks up at her, and Jenny is shocked at his watery eyes and his pale face. He stands up unsteadily.

"Jenny, you've come back," he says, and his voice is the scratching low voice of illness.

"Yes sir, I have." The words catch in her throat. She swallows hard and sits down in the leather chair opposite the desk.

Cornelius sits back down and stares at her. "It's good to see you. And Rosabel—look how she's grown. How old is she now?"

"She's almost four," Jenny says. She looks at Rosabel, not wanting to stare too hard at the changed, sick man. After a moment she says, "Dancy told me about May."

Cornelius nods. "She's been gone a long time," he says; his rheumy eyes are sad. "I guess you heard how we searched."

"Yes sir, Dancy told me."

152

Euphonia, a tall pencil of a figure, appears in the doorway. She stares at Jenny. "Jenny? You've come back?"

Jenny stands up. "Yes'm."

Euphonia brushes her hands together. "Well, we'll hear your story some other time. We can't disturb Cornelius. I only let him sit here in the office for an hour every day. Then he needs to go back upstairs to rest."

"Yes ma'am." Jenny nods at Cornelius and takes Rosabel's hand and follows Euphonia out into the hall.

"I'm using Sophronia's old room for my sewing. You can probably find something in the Dependency. There's some empty rooms out there now," Euphonia says.

Jenny takes Rosabel's hand and leads her back outside to the kitchen. The evening air is stirring, a welcome breeze. She goes into the kitchen and gets Rosabel a cookie from the biscuit tin; then they go back outside. Cooper is still sitting on the bench, the buggy parked where it was. He has a bowl of gumbo on his knees. He raises his hand when he sees her.

"Jenny, I'm gonna head on back to Vicksburg," he says.

"Wait, Cooper. Ain't you gonna stay and be free?"

He shakes his head. "No, I been thinkin' about it, and I can't leave my mammy and everybody up in Vicksburg. And if I head back tonight, I can get there before Fitley gets back from Nashville, and I won't be in trouble. He won't even know I left. So soon as I finish this gumbo, I'm headin' out."

She sits down beside him on the bench. "Listen, Cooper. Now think. This is your one chance to get out of slave-land. You see where you sittin' right here, this is the only place in Adams County that's free soil. Maybe in all of Mississippi. Cornelius has got freein' papers for everybody on this place. Him and Miss Phony, they don't stand for slavery."

"You might be right, but if this is free soil, it ain't big enough. It ain't like you can live your whole life right here at Carefree, and never set foot outside. And I don't want to leave everybody I know."

I was right about you after all, Jenny thinks. *You ain't Walker's true brother.*

He wipes his mouth with his fingers and hands her his empty bowl.

"You tell Dancy that was mighty good," he says.

He goes over to the buggy. "Dancy give me some apples and pears and some fried chicken for the trip. And a loaf of bread. So I'm mighty appreciative."

The basket covered with Dancy's checked dishcloth is sitting on the seat. Cooper hands Jenny her satchel. Jenny and Rosabel watch as he climbs up and shakes the reins, and the buggy wobbles down the drive. At the gate he looks back at them and waves his straw hat. Then he drives down the road. A dark cloud promising rain is rising in the western sky.

"Bye, Cooper," Jenny calls. As he disappears down the road into Natchez, Jenny says to Rosabel, "I hope we get to see him again sometime."

She sits down on the bench and looks up at the big house. She's come back to a changed house. Still, it's a little patch of free soil, and for the moment, she and Rosabel are safe.

She needs to choose a room in the Dependency, so she leads Rosabel over to the room on the end that used to be hers. Pushing the door open, she can tell that Jane and Margaret once lived in this room; it still has their close smell, and their old lady dresses are hanging limply from a nail. She hopes they didn't die right here on the bed, but they probably did. She smooths out the quilt and Rosabel climbs up on the bed and curls herself into a ball.

We've been through too much, Jenny thinks. *But when Rosabel's grown she won't even remember the hard trip, how we slept in the field and made it to Carefree without getting caught by slavers.* But the child's exhausted, and Jenny lies down beside her. They both sleep restlessly, unaccustomed to the bed. She wakes in the night as a dog barks, and there's a closer snuffling sound outside the door; a raccoon, probably. She sleeps again. Suddenly, in the wee hours, before the sun rises, Jenny startles awake and sits up in bed.

Maybe May went to New Orleans.

She can picture it: the yellow house she lived in on Burgundy Street, second door down from the corner, right across the street from where Rosie and Antoine and Charlie live. Would May remember that house, that street? She was only there for a few weeks, and that was nearly three years ago.

Rosabel whimpers, afraid of the dark, so Jenny lights a candle. The walls of the room brighten with the dim yellow light. She lies down again and weariness blacks out the room. Her dream plays again in her mind.

When the slavers come there's an alien sound in the forest, a crack of boots on the forest floor, and the animals in the forest go silent all at once. Esi pulls the rug down over the door and kneels beside the old man. There's no escape. The slavers have weapons, and there are so many of them. The old man stares at her without really seeing.

Villagers are wailing. When Esi hears the intruders stomp close to the house, she jumps up to save herself. She flings herself across the old man's body and rolls down into the narrow space between the bed and the wall, where she lies pinned, breathing in the aroma of the white-washed wall.

A slaver pushes the curtain aside and comes into the house. Esi, her face pressed to the wall, hears the cooking pot clatter to the floor.

There are more noises and the old man whimpers, just once, and a
moment later the intruder is gone.

Esi lies still for a long time, afraid her mind has tricked her; the
raider might still be in the house, standing silently, waiting. But when
she smells smoke, she knows she has to move, and she pulls herself up
from her hiding place. The slaver's gone.

She creeps to the door and peers out. The whole village is burning,
the half-circle of thatched houses falling into ashes.

She turns back to the old man. His blood has soaked his bed and
dripped down to the floor. His eyes are fixed on a different world, so
she pulls the cloth from under his body and snaps it above him in the
smoky air. It floats down to settle across his face.

She must go. She picks up a couple of boiled yams from the floor
where the slaver scattered them and she tucks them inside her dress.

Jenny can see her clearly. Esi's face is seamed with lines now, and her
cheekbones are sharp. She's old and her cheeks are sunken. She's past
the age of attracting men, but somewhere in this world she knows she
has two children alive. There's a road they travelled, and even if it leads
to the slave ships, she'll walk that same road.

Esi goes outside and pulls the rug back into its place over the door,
and then she walks past the collapsed houses, where fires flicker and
sputter in the ruins, past the well where women used to gossip. She
had no friends among them, those witch-following women.

Now they're all gone. Above her head the sky is blue with white
strings of clouds sailing past where the smoke is thinning.

'Damn you, King of Dahomey,' she mutters as she strides toward
the path that leads into the forest. 'Damn you for not saving us from

the slavers. I curse you, you and your women warriors.' She should be shouting her fury, but by this time her voice is soft, no more than a whisper above the popping and sputtering fires of the village.

Jenny sees the dream through to its ending, because it's the only way she can quiet her mind. She wakes again, and looks through the one high window, where the round moon is floating, a cold white stone; but the Natchez heat is stifling. She turns her back to Rosabel and sleeps again.

The sun is above the trees but the air smells like smoke when Jenny and Rosabel go to the kitchen the next morning. Dancy is drying the breakfast dishes. She motions them to the table and puts plates of hotcakes in front of them.

"This is all I had time to make this mornin'. I saved 'em for you," she says. "We was busy all last night, carryin' water buckets. That old corn crib behind the stable caught fire and burnt to the ground in the middle of the night. Guess we'll be buying our corn fresh for a while."

CHAPTER SIXTEEN

THE NEXT AFTERNOON JENNY GOES INTO THE BIG HOUSE to see if Cornelius needs anything, but the door to his bedroom is closed. So she walks downstairs again and finds Euphonia sitting alone in the parlor, her wine on the table beside her and a stack of papers on her lap. Euphonia looks up when Jenny taps at the door.

"Cornelius is having a bad day," she says. "Mal's up there with him."

"I could go up and stay with him," Jenny says.

Euphonia shakes her head. "Mal's just gone up."

Jenny sits down on the sofa. Phony looks out the window but when she turns around again her cheeks are wet. "Jenny, it's hard when I remember how strong he was before he got sick. Before he went away."

"Yes, ma'am."

Euphonia presses her lips together. "He never should've gone to Virginia," she says.

Jenny thinks, *But Phony knows he had to go, to get away from the sheriff. And she knows the trouble with the sheriff was my fault. But it wasn't my fault I was took into slavery. What on earth does the sheriff think now, with Cornelius's name on posters all over Natchez?*

"The sheriff ain't comin' after him any more, is he?" Jenny asks.

Phony shakes her head. "No. John—John Landerson—has it all

under control. He's spoken with Sheriff Williams and he'll see to it the other sheriff doesn't get a warrant. I think we're safe."

We ain't never safe, Jenny thinks. *That's just white people's foolishness.*

Phony takes a deep breath. "You come back after all this time? Why?"

" 'Cause I was workin' for a dangerous man, and I knew I'd be safe here with you and Mister Cornelius. And I had Rosabel to think about."

"What happened to Walker?"

"He went to Texas. A long time ago."

"How old are you now?"

"I figure I'm twenty-two."

Phony studies her face. "You don't hardly look that old. You people don't ever show your age." She touches her forehead. "Wrinkles don't come on your face like they do ours."

"I never thought about that."

"Anyway, I need to put up these new posters." She straightens the stack of papers on her lap. "The old ones are gettin' all ripped and rain-wrinkled."

"What do they say?"

Euphonia picks one up and reads it out loud: *Missing Child, white girl about nine years old*—she looks up at Jenny—"but we don't really know how old May was, do we?"

"No ma'am. I never knew."

"Well, we had to put something for her age. And it says, *Disappeared on June 30 last year from the house of Cornelius Carson, Natchez. Light brown hair to her shoulders, hazel eyes. Slight built. If whereabouts known please contact Sheriff Jim Williams, Natchez.*

The hopeless words float in the air of the parlor, around the door, and out into the hallway. The two women are silent until they fade, out of respect. Phony sets the posters on the side table.

"Miss Phony, do you think May could've gone to New Orleans?" Jenny asks. "That's where we lived before I brought her here."

Euphonia shakes her head. "I hardly think so. She was just six or seven when y'all came here. I doubt she'd remember anything about it."

Jenny stares at the floor. "I can help you put the posters up."

Phony looks surprised. "Okay, you come over to the house at six. We'll get this done before the heat builds up. I don't want anybody to see me doin' it. Maybe we can think of some new places to put 'em, although they don't hardly seem to help. We can drive down to Front Street and start there."

In the morning Jenny takes Rosabel to the kitchen to stay with Dancy, who's making breakfast for Cornelius. Walking up the path to the big house, she thinks of the house in Vicksburg where the Crums live. In a way she's glad Cooper went back to Vicksburg as he did, so he wouldn't get in trouble and he wouldn't get Minnie in trouble either. Cooper didn't look like a person who'd stand up when things go wrong; he'd just fall over, and Minnie at her age didn't need more worries. She had to deal with Missus Martin, too. No, if anybody was gonna get in trouble, it'd better be her, but she's safe here now at Carefree. Or at least as safe as she can be.

Daniel waits in the barouche in front of the house. He greets Jenny with a tentative wave. When Euphonia comes out he helps her up into the barouche.

"I've got the hammer and nails in the bag," she says. "First stop is the post office."

Jenny climbs up and sits beside her. Daniel shakes the reins and the buggy rumbles through the quiet dawn streets.

"Daniel, here's a place," Euphonia calls when they reach the post office.

He pulls the buggy to a stop and the women get down. Jenny takes the hammer. Euphonia sets the posters on the seat and takes one. They walk up the steps to the red brick building where a wooden billboard next to the door is plastered with notices. Phony pulls down a poster that's faded and water-spotted.

"You want me to hammer it for you?" Daniel says, starting to get down.

"You stay there," she says. She holds the poster up and expertly hammers all the corners and smooths the paper down.

"May, where are you?" she says, looking at the poster.

They put up posters on the front of a dry goods store and then on a fence behind an open market where a farmer setting out baskets of eggs and tomatoes watches as Euphonia hammers furiously.

She steps back and looks at the notice board. Then she walks over to peer at another poster, which obviously has just gone up. It looks crisp and white.

"What's this?" she asks. She reads, "'Runaway slave. Known as Jenny. Has a small child with her. Very black skin, child is lighter. Comely shape, impertinent manner. Escaped from the household of James Crum, Vicksburg. If you will bring her to Vicksburg to the Crum residence on Cherry Street, reward is $25.'"

As the farmer brings out a crate of cheeping biddies from his wagon and sets them on a table, Euphonia wheels around and glares at Jenny. "You're a runaway?"

Jenny glances at the farmer who's staring at Phony. "I guess I am. There weren't no other way to get out of slavery. And I wasn't supposed to be in slavery anyhow, 'cause I had my freein' paper."

"I cannot have any more trouble brought to my house," Euphonia hisses. She yanks the poster down and stalks back to the buggy with Jenny following.

"Let's go," she snaps at Daniel. "Back home. And be quick." Jenny barely has time to sit down before he shakes the reins and the horses trot up Main Street. Jenny glances at Phony's pinched face from time to time.

I ain't goin' back into slavery, she thinks. But Euphonia's anger has made her whole body quiver.

When they get back to Carefree, Phony stalks into the house and Jenny walks around to the kitchen, where Rosabel is sitting at the table swinging her legs and dribbling oatmeal from her spoon back into the bowl. George, Dancy's four-year-old son, is sitting at the end of the table scribbling a picture with a pencil gripped in his chubby hands.

"I don't think Rosabel's all that hungry this mornin'," Dancy says.

"C'mon, Sugar, let's finish up," Jenny says. Rosabel eats another bite and then stands up on the chair.

"Maybe these chilrun could run play outside," Dancy says. "George, y'all go on out." George holds his picture up.

"I drawed a moo cow," he says. Rosabel hops down from her chair and goes over to look at his picture.

"I want it," she says. He clutches the picture to his chest and twists away from her.

"George, let her look at it," Dancy says.

He hands it to her. She takes the picture and lays it down on the table and hunches over it, studying it.

Mal comes in holding something behind his back. He goes over to George. "Ooh, I carved somethin' for you, Georgie." He swoops it out and hands it to George. "It's a horse! I made one for Henry too," he says. "You can tell him, when you see him."

George takes the horse and gallops it across the table, making little clicking sounds.

"What you say to Uncle Mal?" Dancy prompts.

"Tanks," George says.

"You better make one for Rosabel too," Dancy says. "I bet she'd like one."

"I could carve you a doll. A real pretty one," Mal says to Rosabel.

"She might rather have a horse," Dancy says.

"I want a horse," Rosabel says.

"There ain't no figurin' kids," Mal says. "Okay, I'll carve you a horse, Rosybelle."

Cornelius is propped up in bed when Euphonia comes in. She yanks at the knot that ties her shawl and when it won't loosen she pulls the shawl over her head and throws it across the chair.

"I didn't want to wake you," she says. "I took Jenny and we put up new posters for May, since the old ones are gettin' worn out. But look." She slaps the missing slave poster across the bed to him.

He picks it up and studies it. "Well —"

"Did you know she was a runaway?"

"No, I didn't. But I didn't think too much about it. I'm not really surprised."

"Well, what are we going to do? First May's gone, and now some owner wants Jenny back. How'd she get herself into slavery in the first place? She was free when she left here."

He shakes his head. "Anything can happen, Phony. It's pretty obvious she was captured. Slave catchers ain't too careful who they get their hands on."

"And where's Walker?" Phony asks.

"She said he went to Texas."

"By his own will, or against his will?"

"I don't know," Cornelius says. "I didn't ask her."

"I think you should send her away from here," Phony says.

A minute ticks by. "Away to where, exactly?" he asks.

"I don't know. Back to New Orleans, maybe. Or up to the free soil. Didn't you try to send her there once?"

"I did, but she didn't go."

"Well, I think she should go now."

"I don't."

"Cornelius —" she slaps her skirt in exasperation—"I can't stand the way you favor that girl."

"Phony, listen, she's been with me since she was ten years old. When she had no family at all, and not even a name. I won't turn her out."

Phony looks at the window, where the branches are scratching at the glass. "I wish it was May we were talking about."

He reaches out to cover her hand with his own. "So do I."

"Let's have John come over," Euphonia says. "We'll discuss it with him and he'll tell us where we stand. I'm not paying for Jenny's ransom, though, if I can help it."

CHAPTER SEVENTEEN

WHENEVER JOHN COMES TO CAREFREE, he goes upstairs to see Cornelius, feeling increasingly that the man may never regain his strength. Cornelius is still the frail, ailing man he's been ever since his return from Virginia. Today when he comes downstairs Euphonia meets him in the hall and motions him into Cornelius's office. She slaps the "Runaway Slave" poster down on the desk in front of him. He picks it up and reads it over.

"What do we do?" she asks.

He shrugs. "Well, I could give you the same advice I gave you before. Lay low. Or else send her off to the free soil. But really, since she's free, this Milton Crum was holding her in violation of the law. I can get you another copy of her freeing paper."

"She won't go to the free soil, or anywhere else," Euphonia says. "I'm sure of that."

John says, "Then just hold tight. I'll take care of it. And meanwhile I'll check around town to see if there are more posters put up, and I'll get rid of them. We can make short work of this Milton Crum if he shows up, but he probably won't. Blacks don't have many rights, but not being enslaved if they've been set free is one of them."

Euphonia takes the poster from the desk and rips it up and drops it into the wastebasket. John stares at her for a moment and says, "Don't worry, Phony. Posters don't usually find a lost slave."

She nods. "They don't usually find a lost child either, do they?" she says bitterly.

A few days later Malachi notices the closed door to Cornelius's office, and he opens it, just to keep it aired out. When Cornelius is well, he'll want to use that room again, and Dancy needs to keep it ready for him, not just close the door and pretend it's not there, one less room to dust. Mal thinks the women hover too much, and Phony has the doctor here about every other day, so the poor man hardly has room to get better. Because even though Cornelius has this terrible malaria, he's still a man of importance here in Natchez, a businessman and a steamboat builder. Before his illness, society people came to the house, and men tipped their hats to him when they passed him on the street.

On a quiet afternoon a week later, Mal climbs the stairs to the room on the second floor where Cornelius is resting. For a month Cornelius hasn't left his room. He's getting weaker; the whole household whispers about it. And every day Mal pulls up the chair beside the bed and sits with him. Mal knows that even in his illness Cornelius needs more in his days than just being sick and getting his mouth wiped off, and trying to sip the soup and brandy Miss Phony brings him. He needs companionship. Mal always taps at the door before he goes in, to see if it's decent for him to enter. Miss Phony always looks like she's relieved when he shows up, and she goes right out. Well, the poor woman needs a chance to see to her own needs, Mal thinks.

But by the end of October, the pall of sickness that's fallen over the house seems to be lifting with the bracing autumn air that sweeps in through the open windows of the big house. Cornelius's eyes are clearer, and a week later he's even recovered enough to sit for a few minutes on the gallery with Phony.

They watch Daniel ride up the road toward the house. Cornelius asks, "Where's he gone?"

"He's been to town," Phony replies, and Cornelius senses how he's lost track of the comings and goings of the estate. Before his illness he knew everything; now it's Phony who keeps track, and he's become a spectator.

Daniel swings down from the horse and strides over to the gallery, holding a letter out to Cornelius, who takes it and looks at the return address.

"It's from Aulie Aikins," he says. The address is written in an old person's shaky script. He opens the envelope and reads the letter.

"She's asking me to come get Coffee, and his friend Harriet, too. She says she's ill, and she plans to go to Jackson to live out her final days with her sister," he says.

"You'll have to tell Jenny," Phony says.

Cornelius stares out across the lawn, where the Spanish moss is sweeping the ground in the soft breeze. "Jenny should be the one who goes to get him. But she can't go alone. I guess Mal could go with her."

Phony shakes her head. "They can't go by themselves. Neither one can read a word, and it's so easy for people to run into trouble. I'd better go."

"I'm not up to such a trip myself, but Miz Aulie's house isn't hard to find. It's close to the river. It won't be hard for them to make the trip by steamer."

"I'll go," Euphonia says again.

Cornelius looks out toward the skyline of Natchez, where the rooftops are swallowed in trees. "All right, you three can go. When I went there with Walker Jackson, a few years back, we met Kofi. He seemed likeable, and he looks like Jenny."

"I wonder what Jenny'll think when she sees him," Phony says. "They came together all the way from Africa, didn't they? That goes a long way back."

"It does."

Cornelius starts to add, "They came by way of Cuba," because that's what the slave trader told him on the day he bought Jenny out of the coffle. But he sees that Phony is gazing off across the horizon, and probably not thinking about Jenny any further than that. So he says nothing more about it. He stares down across the lawn like Phony does, imagining Africa.

Later, when Jenny comes out to the gallery with Rosabel skipping along behind her, Cornelius says, "Jenny, I've had a letter from Mrs. Aikins, down at Windrush. She's leaving the area, and she wants us to come get Kofi and his friend Harriet. So you and Mal need to go get them."

Jenny's eyes flash up. "Oh, yes sir. I'll go."

"Miz Phony will go too. Y'all can take a steamer there and back. I'll give you a letter of introduction, and a pass, just in case. 'Course, you'll need to carry your freeing paper."

Jenny beams, her eyes flashing. "It's about time I saw Kofi again. It's been more than ten years; I probably won't even recognize him."

"He looks a lot like you."

"Yes sir, you told me that. When can we go?"

"Soon as you can. Coella can watch Rosabel while you're gone. You know how to signal a steamer to stop?"

"Would a steamer stop for us black people?"

"That's why I'm coming too," Phony says. She delicately brushes her hands across her skirt. "I've never ridden on a steamboat."

"I have," Jenny says. "It was the *John Jay*. Sorriest lookin' boat you ever saw."

"It didn't sink, did it?" Cornelius says. "So count your blessings. I'll write Missus Aikins today, to let her know you're coming." He gets up and goes back into the house, and Phony follows. When they close the door, a whirlwind is swirling about Jenny, but only Rosabel can see it.

At mid-day a week later Jenny, Mal and Euphonia are standing together at the front railing of the *Star of Ohio* as she ploughs down down the river. Phony is holding a printed map of all the plantations along the river, and as they pass each one she checks it off on her map. Finally she points up ahead.

"I think that's it. There it is. 'Windrush,' " she says, pointing to a jetty built on the riverbank some distance away. "I'll go tell the captain."

Jenny grips the railing. After all these years, she'll see Kofi again. She remembers the night they came off the boat holding hands; Kofi was seven and she was ten. A minute later a man hauled him wailing off into the night, his legs windmilling. She was astonished; she thought they'd stay together after the boat docked, because they'd been together since they were snatched, in Dahomey. But as she watched him go, calling his name, she was yanked aside by another man.

Remembering that dark night, her arms and legs begin to quiver. Will Kofi remember her? When Cornelius and Walker came to Windrush, they said Kofi remembered her name. *Abena*. She stares straight ahead down the gray-brown river, hoping her unsteadiness doesn't show. Mal stands next to her, watching the steamer pull closer to the dock.

"You know, Jenny, a brother can be an interesting thing," he says. "I found my brother, James, and, my lands, he was different from what I thought he'd be. 'Course, he was a lot older than your brother. All I'm sayin' is, your brother's had a whole life that's different from yours, so don't expect him to be just like you. He might not be like you at all."

The steamer pulls over to the jetty and they walk down the plank. Jenny looks around; so this jungly place is where Kofi's been living all this time. Up ahead is a straight path leading between two rows of young oak trees.

Phony strides ahead of them. "Y'all stay behind me," she says, smoothing her shawl and holding her purse close under her arm. "We don't want this old lady to think we're an army on attack."

Mal and Jenny walk a few feet behind her. A scream comes through the jungle. "If I didn't know better, I'd think that panther was some woman screamin'," Mal says.

"We used to hear 'em on the Cocodrie," Jenny says.

"I remember that," Mal says. "I hope we don't run into one o' them black cats out here. Walker told me when he came here with Mister Cornelius, he never saw such a place. Snakes everywhere. And he said there weren't but one house like Windrush all around here, with columns on every side. We'll get there, Jenny, don't you worry."

"I ain't worried. I think I can see it up ahead, peepin' through the woods."

"I got plumb good at findin' my way to places when Cornelius and me went to Virginny. Especially after he took sick. Sometimes I think I could find my way most anywheres by myself, if I had to."

"I couldn't," Jenny says. "Neither could Walker. We got lost just tryin' to find our way out of Vicksburg."

The white house, wrapped in columns, appears like a ghost out of the autumn woods. "Well, I never," Phony says, staring at the house.

The small woman who answers Phony's knock has the grayest complexion Jenny's ever seen, and the deepest eyes. She holds the door open and stares at them.

"Y'all come to get Coffee, ain't ya?" she asks.

"Yes, ma'am," Phony says. "I am Missus Cornelius Carson, and this here is Coffee's sister, Jenny. And Mal, who's come to help us find the way."

Mal, who thinks Phony might be making fun of him, steps back behind Jenny.

Mrs. Aikins leads Phony into the parlor. Mal and Jenny stand on the gallery, listening to the muffled conversation inside the house.

"Well, I'll have to go get him. He'll be out at the stable," Mrs. Aikins says when she comes out to the gallery a few minutes later. She motions for them to wait, and they watch as she totters around the side of the house, leaning on her walking stick. A few moments later she returns. A young man and woman walk behind her.

Kofi walks with the same determined walk Jenny remembers now, but he's so much bigger. But it's him, with the same nose and bright eyes. His inky dark skin matches her own. He's smiling wide; she remembers that big grin.

"H'lo, Abena," he says.

She walks over and takes his arm. "Kofi." she looks up into his round face. "That is you, ain't it?"

"It's me." They stare at each other for a long moment. Then he puts his arm around her shoulder. "Wouldn't our mamma be proud we got back together?"

Jenny blinks; there's a catch in her throat. She glances at Harriet and then looks back at him. "You remember our mamma?" she asks.

"A little bit. Not really what she looked like. Just that she was. Just like with you, I didn't remember what you looked like either, just that you was you. But now I seen you, I can say, 'Yep, it is you.' How you doin', Abena? It's been a long time. And yet it seems like it ain't been no time a'tall."

"No time a'tall," she says, blinking hard. "I'm glad you comin' to Carefree."

"I hope I like it there. Is it a good place?"

"It's a big ole house in Natchez, full of ghosts."

His eyes widen. "Ghosts? Land a mighty, now you tellin' me that to scare me."

"It ain't so bad. They don't hurt nothin', much as I can tell. They just there, livin' in the attic. And Mister Cornelius 'll give you your freein' paper. He don't keep slaves."

Kofi looks around and puts his finger to his lips. "Shhh. Don't talk like that. Missus Aulie shouldn't hear you sayin' that. Might hurt her feelings."

Jenny shrugs. "She shouldn't be keepin' slaves."

"She's always been good to me. And she's gonna let my wife Harriet stay with me."

Jenny looks at the tall young woman standing behind Kofi. "Well, that'll be good, Kofi. Harriet'll get her freein' papers too."

"I told you, quit talkin' about it."

Mrs. Aikins goes inside and then comes back out onto the gallery and hands Kofi a sack. "Here's some things for the trip," she says to him, her voice breaking. Harriet watches with wide eyes. "Harriet, did you pack your things up?"

"Yes, ma'am, I did. I'm all ready to go."

"This ain't hard for Harriet," Kofi says to Mrs. Aikins. "She's got no family here anyways. But me, I feel like you're my second mother. Or my grandma." He hugs the old woman in a swaying bear hug. "I hope you don't mind me huggin' you," he says. "You always treated me so kind, and I so appreciate it."

Tears flow down Aulie's wrinkled cheeks. "Kofi, you are the next thing in my heart. And there ain't no way I'd send you away except I know I ain't got long. I gotta go see my sister 'fore I pass."

"I don't really want to go to Natchez," Kofi says. "Can't we go with you to Jackson?"

No, Jenny thinks. *We came all this way to get you. You comin' with us.*

"No, it wouldn't be best," Aulie says, pulling away from him. "Yall go on, now. 'Bye, Harriet."

"'Bye, Missus," Harriet says, "you take care of yourself." And Jenny thinks, *At least there's somebody here with some sense.*

"Everything in this world gets taken away," Aulie says, pulling a handkerchief out of her bodice and holding it to her eyes.

That's true, Jenny thinks. *Unless you fight like a tiger for it.*

"Wait!" Aulie says suddenly. She goes into the parlor and takes a white scarf from a hook on the wall. She hands it to Euphonia.

"Tie this to the post out there," she says. "It'll signal the next steamer comin' upriver to stop for y'all."

Missus Aikins stands on the veranda and watches as they walk down the path toward the river. Jenny turns around once to wave at the old woman who's standing on the veranda, holding herself up with a column. Aulie waves back, her handkerchief fluttering in the still air.

All her other slaves gonna be sold off, Jenny thinks. *That big house will probably fall down into one of these black pools around here.*

When they get to the river Phony ties the scarf to the post at the jetty and a few minutes later a steamer coming upriver toots a short whistle, and the five people standing on the dock wave. After the steamer pulls over, they clamber aboard. Phony finds herself a chair on the foredeck and Jenny, Mal, Kofi and Harriet stand at the back railing watching the sternwheel churn.

The boat goes around a turn in the river. Jenny puts her hand on Kofi's back and says, "You and Harriet's gonna be free people now. Cornelius'll see to it. Y'all should be happy."

"Abena, I been with Miss Aulie since I was seven years old," Kofi says. "And now I ain't never gonna see her no more." He buries his face in his hands, and cries.

CHAPTER EIGHTEEN

November 1845

A COLD WIND IS BLOWING the day Esther comes back to Carefree, and she's not alone. Watching her walk up the drive, Mal tries to read her face. Esther's thinner than she used to be, and her face is narrower. A thick waisted girl with a round face is with her, and Mal knows that must be Helene. He's heard Esther talk about her often enough.

He walks out to meet her. But it's not the happy homecoming Mal thought it ought to be, because Dancy sees her too and she runs right out from the kitchen and blurts out the news that May's run off. And when Esther hears that, she drops to the ground.

Mal reaches down to take her arm. "Now, come on, we can't have any of that wailin'," he says. "Get on up."

Helene says, "Who's gone?"

"May."

"Who's that?"

"A child who used t' live here," Mal says. "Cornelius took her in 'cause she had no family. But now she's done run off, or disappeared anyway, and we don't know where she went."

"How old was she?"

Mal shakes his head. "I don't know. About eight." He studies the girl for a minute. "You Helene, ain't ya? Your mamma talked about you often enough, so I knew you before I ever seen you."

She nods. "Mamma come found me in Jonesville. We don't know where Theresa ended up, though. We couldn't find out."

Mal looks around at the slope of the lawn, where the big house sits like a monument to despair, at this moment, and he tries to imagine how Esther feels, to come back to a house with a missing child, and a master still so ill. *What are we turning into?* he wonders, as he's wondered so often lately. He turns back to Helene. "Your master just let you go without any pay?"

"Mamma bought me out."

"That's good. We're all real happy you're back here with your ma, Helene, but you come to a most unhappy place. Cornelius is down with the malaria, and 'course we still don't know what's happened to li'l May. So this is mostly a sad house now."

"It was sad when I left it too," she says, reaching down to take Esther's elbow and help her up. "The day Emile sold us all off. Me first. And who are you?"

"Malachi Carson," he says. "I been with Mister Cornelius for the longest."

"I was born right here at Carefree," Helene says. "It's where I grew up, too. I never thought I'd see it again, though, after I got sold."

"Mister Cornelius 'll put you free. He ain't one for keepin' slaves. Which is a recommendation. He's a fine man. He'll get you your freein' paper."

Esther struggles to her feet and grabs the front of his shirt. "Mal, I been over to Louisiana, across the river, to places I ain't never been before. But I was too late for Theresa. I don't know if I'll ever see my other girl again."

He pats her back. "You might, Esther. Try to think that way, not the other way. You gotta have hope. Look at me, I spent most of my life hopin' I'd be free one day, and now I'm old, but I'm free as a bird."

But later that evening, climbing the stairs in the big house to go sit with Cornelius, Mal thinks he might have been wrong to tell Esther she had to have hope. Hope's a funny thing; it can bring you up or bring you down. For himself, he had hope when he went with Cornelius to Virginny to find his brother, and he did find him; but James was all changed, like he'd been handled hard his whole life. James didn't have hope, Mal saw it right off. That was what slavery did to a person.

As he grips the bannister rail to half-pull himself up the stairs, he thinks something's missing in the house, and then he remembers: nobody's thought to wind the clocks, and Esther's been gone, so the house is quiet. He thinks it's odd he didn't notice the quiet until now, when Esther's come back. It's like the house is just waiting for that lost child to come back.

Then he hears Cornelius groan, sickness rising in his throat. When he goes into the sick man's room, he can tell Euphonia's been waiting for him. She stands up when he comes in, and then she wipes Cornelius's face with a damp towel and tosses the towel onto the pile that's rising in the corner.

In the late afternoon John Landerson rides up to Carefree. He dismounts in front of the gallery and stands for a moment looking up at the window where he knows Cornelius is lying in bed, suffering. He's been coming here regularly in recent weeks, to see about the sick man and about Euphonia.

His life is lonely now, and if it weren't for the steamer he's planning, he'd be completely adrift. Maybe he is anyway, he thinks. His house, which used to be full of the chatter and squabbles of children, back when Elenora was alive, is quiet now. The children are scattered and so are the slaves who cared for them; Lissy and the oldest boy Freddy farmed out to his sister Dinah in Tupelo, and the two middle boys to his brother in Hattiesburg. Baby Cyrus and the littlest child, Dolly, are gone to his uncle and aunt down in Saint Francisville, where they have two small children of their own to keep the babies company. He sent Delphine and her daughter Emma to St. Francisville, too. What is a man to do, if his wife dies so unexpectedly, and leaves him with six children? He tried to cope, but a few days after Elenora died, a kind of desperation set in; he'd tried to manage on his own, but the slaves couldn't really handle so many kids without a woman to tell them what to do, and his sister didn't want to move to Natchez to take over his household. So he persuaded his family to take the kids in, and he parcelled them out two by two. He'll take them back when they're older, he's told his relatives, once he gets on his feet again. He does miss the kids, though, especially Cyrus, his favorite. But Cyrus is undoubtedly thriving under the care of his aunt Rebekah. He'll go visit them in a few months. The children might forget him, at least the youngest ones will; but in the meantime he gets letters sporadically telling him how they're doing. That will have to hold him for now.

Because he has a boat project to plan for. It would've been done by now but for the twin calamities that struck Carefree. Illness is so common, even if a child vanishing isn't, and he almost resents Cornelius for complicating the schedule the men agreed on when they started planning the steamer, back before Elenora died.

It's to be a finer steamer than any afloat right now. It will have three decks of balconies with white filigree railings, and a large salon lined with a double row of tables covered with white tablecloths. The boat will be well staffed; waiters will pour the best French wines into crystal glasses. Ticket prices will be high, but he and Cornelius think there are enough people of means to cover the cost. The better class of passengers will be much more comfortable if they don't have to accompany yearlings and bales of cotton on an excursion down to New Orleans. There are already enough scrubby river runners to take care of the cargo trade. Passengers are cargo of a different sort, and they'll need the luxuries the new steamer will provide. A pleasant river trip, the breeze of the open river and the panorama of the passing plantation houses: wealthy people up and down the river will want to experience what the *Euphonia* has to offer. And there'll be entertainment, too. John envisions a string quartet playing Mozart as the passengers dine.

John thinks he might have to go up to Pittsburgh to see the progress in person, but the builder, McCann, is a good letter writer, and he seems to have a clear understanding of the concept John laid out to him. From McCann's letters, John knows the keel's been laid and the frames assembled, and the lumber is stacked, ready for the sides.

As months went by, and then a whole year, John's been alarmed by Cornelius's illness. But it's really Euphonia he hopes to see when he comes to Carefree, although he always goes upstairs to visit the sometimes delirious man. He doesn't think he can catch what Cornelius has; it's malaria, the doctor says, and that's not catching. It's admirable the way Euphonia watches over Cornelius, although she always lets a servant take over whenever John appears, and together they go down the stairs and walk out to the gallery and sit on the settee there, talking in low tones. John reaches over and puts his hand on the arm of Euphonia's chair, and she interlaces her fingers with his. After that, their voices drop almost to a whisper, and their eyes lock. Even November can bring pleasant evenings, and there they are, two people whose lives changed, shifted, in the winter of 1843-44, in ways they couldn't have foretold.

When he arrives at Carefree today, he's disheartened to learn that Cornelius doesn't feel well enough to come downstairs. *That must be how malaria is; false improvements and then a slide back into sickness,* he thinks. The pattern's played itself out repeatedly since Cornelius returned from his trip.

He steels himself for what he'll find upstairs. "I've been getting regular reports from Pittsburgh. The steamer's coming along," John says to Cornelius, but the ailing man doesn't do more than nod from his bed; and then Mal comes in to sit with him. So John goes back downstairs to sit with Phony on the gallery. He's glad to feel her hand on his.

"Our steamer project is finally getting underway," he says.

"Where is it?" she asks.

"Pittsburgh, Pennsylvania."

"Gracious, that's a long way from here."

"It is. I'm dealing with a boat builder there, who should be finishing it up in a few months. The furnishings will soon be on their way from New York. It'll be splendid. We've spared no expense."

"I don't even want to see it while Cornelius is so sick. When he's better, though, I'd like to have a tour."

He nods. "He'll want to see it too."

"He can't travel anywhere right now."

A chill rises in the twilight. John asks, "Phony, do you think he'll get better?"

"I don't know." She twists her handkerchief in her hands and then leans closer to him and rests her head on his shoulder. "He gets better, then worse. I hope he'll rally. But we've been disappointed so many times."

He thinks how much he admires her. One tendril of her brown hair is draped over her shoulder, and she's wearing her green dress, the one with stripes and swirls woven so subtly into the fabric that the design is almost imperceptible; it's the discreet, expensive look of a Paris silk. But her pretty face is tired, her complexion paler than usual.

He turns her face to him, his hand grazing under her chin, ever so lightly. Then he kisses her.

She sighs, a long quiet breath, before she stands up and turns to go back into the house. He can't read her expression, just that it's sad. She looks at him for a moment before she steps through the threshold, back to her duties, to the husband sweating and helpless in his bed. And this house, once splendid, with the child that's gone missing and the threat of death holding its breath in the still air in that upstairs bedroom—how much longer can a household abide such loss, such sickness? It's like a swollen carbuncle. Sooner or later the festering will break open, and all this misery will spill out onto the ground.

John goes home to the Elenora House, remembering Euphonia and her kiss. He swings the big door open and goes into his parlor. No sickness is in this house, although there's been plenty enough misery in past years here. The house is silent now.

John remembers how the kids used to chatter and squabble in these rooms, and Delphine and Emma would shepherd them around. Delphine had a little one of her own, and she nursed Cyrus until he was big enough for weaning, and then he sent her to St. Francisville so she could feed Dolly, too; immeasurable, the value of a wet nurse.

The house echoes with the sound of his boots as he walks across the polished wooden floor. He misses the racket of the kids, and that surprises him. The five of them were such a trial to Elenora; and then Dolly unexpectedly came along. Elenora didn't live long enough to get to know little Dolly. He wonders if the kids remember this big house. Now he lives here alone with just Ruthy, an old slave woman, to keep the place up.

He sits down on the bottom step and stares at the empty parlor. It's really a splendid room, with Persian rugs in glowing tones of burgundy and emerald, velvet sofas in sapphire blue, and crystal candelabra on the mantelpiece. He wonders if he could bring the kids back here. He pictures Lissy and Dolly playing in the parlor. Little girls are quiet; at least Lissy is, and he hasn't been around Dolly enough to know what she's like, but little girls are likely to be quieter than rowdy boys. The only one of the kids he really misses is Cyrus, but it would be interesting to see how Dolly's growing, who she looks like. But Cyrus with his smile, his curly blond hair, is so different from the others that he looks like he belongs in some other family. Yes, he does miss Cyrus.

He gets up and goes into the kitchen to speak to Ruthy, who says she's going out to her cabin if he doesn't need anything. He nods and a minute later he hears her heavy footsteps in the back hall. Then the door closes.

He goes back into the parlor and pours himself a glass of whiskey. He sits down in the chair nearest the fireplace and closes his eyes.

He has to get a marker for his wife's grave, he thinks. That's a bit of unfinished business he needs to see to. It's been a long time since Elenora died, and her grave marker is way overdue. The children might want to visit their mother's grave someday.

CHAPTER NINETEEN

ESTON FERRIS, ON A CLOUDY DAY A MONTH LATER, decides to give his mission in Natchez one more try. He has a new horse, Ruby, a tan beast with a black mane and tail, the handsomest animal he's ever owned. He bought the mare from a horse-trader passing through, a man named Wicklow, and as near as Eston can tell, an Irishman fresh off the boat. The man's breath smelled of whiskey and he had a gambler's sneaky eyes. But Eston saw the horse's straight back, the strong rippling muscles, and he needed a horse. He couldn't really be a proper sheriff without one. And Dixie was gone, last seen galloping away down the river bank toward Saint Catherine Creek after that odd accident at the dock.

So he tried Ruby out, swinging up on her and cantering her down the one main street in Vidalia, and she rode smooth as silk. He paid the Irishman $20 for her, and the last he saw of Wicklow the man was galloping his own black mare westward out of Vidalia. Horse traders are always a slippery bunch, he knows. He's just as glad to see the man leave town.

He goes out to the stable and looks at Ruby. Yes, a fine piece of horse-flesh this is. The handsome horse nods as if she's agreeing with his assessment. He congratulates himself on his good fortune.

His work in Vidalia is so routine. He thought, when he took the job, that a town the size of Vidalia would provide him with some challenging crimes to solve, some excitement that would make his reputation, but instead he gets the usual drunks and pilferings that upset any quiet town. The drunks go right into the drunk tank at the sheriff's office. And as for the young noisemakers who drink a bit and upset the pious church ladies who never were young themselves, well, since he's been sheriff, he looks at things a little differently. He tends to let them go.

Cotton Ferguson, his deputy, is little help. Cotton worked for old sheriff Willie Haynes, and he's got Willy's slow ways. If Cotton's stomach gets any bigger, Eston wonders how the man will be able to mount a horse. He'll keep him off Ruby; Cotton might break her back.

Eston feels he has Vidalia under control, but the Carson case in Natchez still nags at him. When he pulled the daguerreotypes down from the wall, it was because he didn't want those eyes staring at him, rebuking him for failing to solve that crime. It wasn't the worst case that Haynes left hanging, but the most immediate, with those two taunting images. That man, Cornelius Carson, is still rich and free in Natchez. And he has a feeling the slave girl Jenny is somewhere over there, too.

So today he tells Cotton to cover the office. He's headed over to Natchez to clear up this Carson case once and for all. The last time he tried, six months ago, it cost him a good horse, Dixie, when the ferry rammed the dock at Natchez, spilling passengers and Dixie right through the broken railing into the waist-deep water. The flummoxed horse, flailing on her side in the river, stumbled to her feet. The last he saw of her she was galloping away along the riverbank, the reins flying out behind her. Even though he searched for a week, she was never seen again.

But now he's got an even better horse. He goes out to the stable and saddles Ruby. He's got a fine new saddle, too, which took most of his paycheck; Dixie ran off with his other one.

He mounts Ruby and rides out to the street. Main Street drowses in the late morning somnolence; a blue haze is eating away at the vista of trees across the river. Up ahead is the hotel, where a crowd has gathered, as usual, to wait for the ferry's return. The horse's withers are taut, and she lifts her hooves smartly as she prances down the street toward the hotel.

But at the street corner the horse bucks all at once and arches her back. Eston, caught unawares, flies up and then lands again in the saddle.

"Whoa," he says, pulling the reins to the right. He looks around to see what might have spooked the horse, but all he sees are townspeople standing with their mouths open, watching the spectacle.

The horse whinnies and bucks again, and this time Eston flies clear, landing face down on the gravel street. Ruby rears and cavorts, bucking repeatedly.

The horse gallops away down the riverfront road, snorting and bucking every few yards. Bruised and dazed, Eston tries to sit up, but the fall has knocked the wind out of him. The hotel spins in front of his eyes, on its porch a gathering of gawking spectators, concerned and cowardly. They're afraid to confront the wild horse.

He sits up and spits dirt and blood out of his mouth, along with a tooth.

A man comes over. "Sheriff, you all right?"

Eston looks up, hating the man for asking the question right in front of everyone, hating the hazy day, the horse peddler, the horse herself. As Ruby bucks and pitches her way down the road past the hotel, he awkwardly picks himself up and limps back to the office, where Cotton is sitting at the desk taking the last praline from a plate that some lady dropped off earlier today.

He hates Vidalia, too.

Louis Maercru walks slowly down Main Street in Natchez, a bent figure in a gray slouch coat. When he catches his reflection in a shop window he hardly recognizes himself. He is greatly aged, he knows. The town seems so familiar to him, even if his own visage doesn't. Has it really been more than four years since he lived here, back when he was pastor at Saint Vigilius church?

When he comes to the corner where the church once stood, he stops and stares. Saint Vigilius was an ash-black ruin when he last saw it, not a single section of the wall still standing after the fire. Now he's standing on the brick walk that ran in front of the church; the grass is growing across the walk and by next summer the sidewalk itself will be buried under that spreading green carpet.

He's still surprised to find himself back in Natchez. It's strange he's been summoned here for the second time. The first time was when he was sent to be pastor at Saint Vigilius, a post he held for nearly twenty years. This time it's to assist at St. Mary's Church. Maybe it was just a kindness of the priests here to summon him; they would have remembered how his church burned; or maybe they really were without enough priests for a vigorous schedule of masses. Either way, he's on this street because he needs to make himself known to them.

Staring at the overgrown lot where Saint Vigilius once stood, he remembers his nephew Adrien, who came from France back in 1841. His brother Marcel sent the boy to him. The truth was, Louis felt himself sinking even before Adrien came here, and then for a few weeks that spring the boy propped him up. A waft of France was with Adrien in the way he talked, the way he dressed, and that refreshed Louis. But then the letter came from the police commissioner in New Orleans, saying Adrien was dead, killed in a New Orleans alley, and with no more information than that, Louis had been overwhelmed with hopelessness. Marcel would be bereft when he got the news, but Louis had to let him know, had to write the hard letter and tried not to picture the awful scene back in Lormont: the sound of crisp paper as the envelope was sliced open by the knife, and Marcel's pain and shock as he read the words that would change his life forever. Marcel has another son, and another wife; but Louis can't imagine that this new woman Isobel and baby Philippe could replace the memory of the slave woman Francine, who died ten years ago, and the boy Adrien, in his brother's life. He knows his brother well; as children they shared a bed until they were big boys, and where one was, the other was also. Marcel was softer than Louis, more likely to cry, more hurt by the thousand small cruelties boys are privy to. But they'd both grown up in the same household.

As the first-born son, Marcel was always more favored than Louis was. It's Marcel who should have gone into the Church, Louis has thought many a time. Marcel's temperament was more compassionate, more emotional, and that was why he couldn't leave Francine in Martinique, not after Adrien was born. And he brought them to France, to the village of Lormont. He brought Francine to her death, as it turned out. The unhealthy air found them. And then he sent Adrien to America, and another early death.

No: the beautiful Francine, the beautiful Adrien—they would not so easily be erased from his brother's heart.

After Saint Vigilius burned down, Louis fled and ended up in Saint Louis, which was a disappointment to him. The big river city was cold and inhospitable, and he lived on the fringes of the religious life there. An abbey took him in; the brothers there saw in an instant what he was, a ruined priest, deep in his cups. He found he couldn't get through a day, or half a day, without the whiskey and wine he treasured. And the brothers brought him his bottles every day, thinking a man of his age could turn to whatever comfort he needed, for the pains that were in his life. Sometimes a man needs time for healing.

Death tracks us everywhere, Louis thinks as he trudges along. Up ahead he sees the red brick building that is Saint Mary's, so much finer than Saint Vigilius. Mass has ended and the door opens. The parishioners spill out. No one looks at him. He's not expecting them to, doesn't want them to. He's an old man in a black cape shuffling along. He doesn't even look like a priest any more. He's hardly what he was.

But maybe he can find his way here, at Saint Mary's. Some of the old parishioners might remember him, back when he was younger, his hair not fully white like it is now. His best days, he thinks, were the first ten years he spent at Saint Vigilius.

He crosses the street and walks up the brick walk to Saint Mary's Church. He needs to make himself known to the priests here, to report, as it were, for duty. But first he feels a need to see what Saint Mary's Church is. Inside it's dark, and he slips into a back pew, crossing himself. He can pray.

August, unseen, ascends the attic stairs. He notices how quiet the attic is on a winter day, just the usual rising and descending of ephemeral forms in the angled light of the morning sun. The shadows linger among the clutter—trunks, old pictures, a candelabra missing an arm—all of it rising in dust. Outside the dormer window are the sounds of morning life:

horses nickering, kids chattering, laundry thumping on the clothesline. And voices: Thomas, Coella, Esther, Bo. And then softer voices: Cornelius and Phony, whispering together in their bedroom.

But the attic is so quiet. Not a sound slips from one end of the raftered room to the other. What the ghosts say is unheard by any but themselves, and not really heard by them either, since they lack ears. For that matter, they lack tongues too. They sense each other, as cats do.

August moves among the dust motes and flits between the bony knees of Josephine Coqterre. She rarely speaks; she always sits in her old-fashioned lace-trimmed cap, her eyes downcast, an example of ladylike modesty. But she was pretty once; August can see it.

Today her form rises as August goes by, and her jaw chatters. He can't ignore it; it's such an unusual sight.

"Because—" she says when she sees him looking at her. It's the middle of a thought, a half-finished sentence, and she's answering a question he's raised.

"That's my portrait," she says, pointing, and August floats away, apologizing because he's brushed against the painting in its ornate gilded frame. Since she's of an older generation, he's a little self-conscious.

"Yes, my portrait," she says.

He looks where she points. Even in the dim light he can make out the painted image: the young face with dark eyes, the lace-edged cap covering her dark hair, her rosy complexion, her inscrutable expression.

She died on the Natchez Trace, she says; it's a rare occasion when words float from her mouth. "The year was 1825. I was driving myself up to Washington, Mississippi, to show my poor babe to my mother there. He was a twisted little babe, poor thing. But I never got to Washington. It was just an eight-mile trip, and the axletree broke. Can you believe it?" Her teeth clattered, but it was hard to tell if they were clattering any more than usual.

"When we tipped over into the ditch, and the baby—Arnaud was his name—fell out onto the ground, I gathered him up and we sat. We waited."

At the back of the attic, lying over a chest, Emile Coqterre chatters and rises, his eyesockets flashing. "Enough, woman!"

"I will tell it, Emile!" she hisses, and August wouldn't have thought the mild-faced woman could speak so harshly. Emile jabbers himself back down to the floor, shaking his bony arms out in front of him. After he settles, Josephine continues, "Oh, the two men that rode up and saw me sitting by the flipped-over buggy, they said they were helpers. And by the time I realized they weren't, it was too late. Oh!" She puts her bony hands out in front of her and shudders.

Emile quivers and folds his bony limbs in on himself as he sinks. "I cannot bear to hear you tell it!"

Josephine rises and points at him. "You were a coward, Emile! And reckless at the same time. You should have known not to send a woman alone on the road with a tiny infant."

"Only eight miles, Josephine! And all the slaves were sick, and you were determined to go!"

Josephine says, "And I waited til dark." Her head nods and then it falls down onto her chest.

She's told this story before. August remembers as best a ghost can remember, since the chiming of a clock means nothing to them.

Now Josephine crouches before her portrait, her knees bent up. "Look how pretty I was," she says.

Emile, at the back of the attic, rattles.

Josephine goes on, "Now Euphonia's taken me down, when I hung over the parlor fireplace for twenty years. No, she swooped in and brought my portrait up the attic stairs so quick, as soon as she got here. And she replaced me with—a landscape!"

"It's a nice scene," Littleton offers, although August doesn't know why his brother chimed in. "I've always loved a beautiful landscape."

"I don't want to be forgotten!" Josephine says. "No one will know my face, thanks to her."

"Such a pretty face," Emile says.

"Euphonia's not worthy of Cornelius," Josephine jabbers, shaking her head. "And look at her now, making eyes at John Landerson, when her own husband is right there, so weak and needing help. Her heart has flown to John. She's an untrue wife, which I never was."

"You had two husbands, remember?" Emile says. "Husband number one, killed by Indians."

"Husband number two, right there." August points at Emile, who nods.

"I'll fix her," Josephine chatters, ignoring them. "I'll think of a way."

"Don't do anything rash," Emile says.

"I'll take care of it," August says. "You just settle down, Miss Josephine."

And Josephine sinks to the floor, her anger gone as the motes in the shaft of light shift and jump. Then all is silent in the attic.

CHAPTER TWENTY

Spring 1846

EUPHONIA PUSHES THE WINDOW OPEN to bring in the spring air.
Cornelius, sitting up in bed, says, "Thank you."

He's improving day by day, or at least week by week, and Euphonia
is both glad and uncertain about that. He should improve, certainly;
but malaria is a strange train of a journey. One person may recover so
quickly, the next may take months, years, if they ever get better. Day after
day she studies Cornelius, encouraging him with every inch of improve-
ment she sees. And every evening she waits on the gallery behind the
big crepe myrtle for John Landerson to ride up. Ostensibly he comes here
to see about Cornelius, but he's really coming to see her, she knows. She
blushes at the thought. *What am I doing?* But she's never had this desperate attraction for a man before, and she knows John feels the same
pull for her; they are magnets together.

One day Mal and Elliot Badeau heft Cornelius down the stairs and
help him to the chair in the parlor, and an hour later John comes to the
house as always.

Euphonia is waiting for him on the gallery. "You should come into
the parlor and see Cornelius," she says when he rides up, and she notes

the surprise on his face. This won't be an evening like the others.

"I'm glad to see you're improving!" John says, coming into the parlor. "I wish I'd known you were out of bed, I'd have brought the latest drawings for the steamer. We need your input."

Cornelius puts out his hand, a weak stick, for John to shake. "Sick as I've been, I haven't given it a thought."

"We've made the boilers larger," John says. "The steamer's going to be so large, we felt they should be enhanced. The salon itself will be sixty feet long."

"Would it be better to use that space for staterooms?"

"We want the look of luxury from the moment the passengers step aboard." He brushes a fly away. "I envision vast luxury."

Euphonia smiles at John. His enthusiasm has brightened the room, and Cornelius simply stares at him, still too sickly to respond.

After he leaves Carefree, John rides down to the riverbank. It's already dark, and the streets are quiet. He pulls his horse to a stop at the top of the bluff and stares at the river, a silver highway that seems alive, pulsing silently below Natchez. It won't be long now, and the steamer will come down the river like a white ghost, manned by a skeleton crew. What a magnificent sight she'll be in the moonlight. All down the river, people in the big cities and small river towns will gather on the bank to watch the still-unnamed white vessel float past, a queen of the river. He can hardly wait.

Two weeks later Cornelius is strong enough to sit up all day, and then not long after that, he's able to walk around the house with a cane. Euphonia is surprised one day when she walks into the office and finds him sitting there. Ever since May disappeared, the women of the household have become vigilant in keeping track of everyone, not just the children. They all know, although they never mention it, that May was able to vanish out of the big house because everyone thought the girl was with someone else, out in the kitchen or in some other room of the house. The guilt they feel for letting her slip away keeps their eyes glued to Thomas all day, and to little Henry and George, and even, out of habit, to Cornelius.

Cornelius is thinner, but the sick look in his eyes is beginning to vanish. One morning he even rode Chico, mounting from the gallery so the step wasn't too high for him. Mal helped him onto the horse and then Mal mounted Eagle, so Cornelius would have a riding companion.

That night, after John leaves, Euphonia lies down with Cornelius for the first time since his illness. His arm under her head, he looks up at the ceiling.

"I have some concerns about the steamer," he says in his raspy voice.

"What?"

"I want to get a good look at the boilers. You know, on a steamer that's a common cause for explosions, when the boilers blow."

"I didn't know that."

"I'm sure John knows it."

"You'll have to remind him."

"I don't think he'll want my advice."

"Well, he might not, but you have a responsibility to tell him, surely. You can't let him build it with a design flaw."

"He's hired some experienced builders, so I guess he'll get the right advice."

"I don't know," Euphonia says.

He rolls over her and she reaches up for him. She thinks this will help him. They all must put thoughts of May out of their heads. May was here, and now she's gone. A steamboat's being built. Someday the house will have to return to normal.

An hour later, Euphonia listens to his long slow breathing, and she thinks about the steamer. Cornelius is too ill to make a strong point of it with John, but John needs to hear this word of caution. The house can't take any more disasters. They may never recover from May's disappearance, and she's begun to see things in the house that trouble her. Yesterday, a painted china cup sitting on the mantel in the parlor flipped off and shattered on the floor. Well, Dancy probably didn't set it back far enough after she dusted the mantel. And then in the afternoon the spinning wheel in the back bedroom began to whir, its wheel turning slowly, as if a ghost were spinning invisible yarn. But the wind was picking up outside; that probably turned the wheel.

A tickle runs down her neck. *Are the ghosts rising?*

And John Landerson comes up to Carefree every day now, and it always lightens her heart when she sees his black horse coming up the road. The pull she feels for him is something she couldn't have foreseen, when she lived out in the Cocodrie.

It's strange, she thinks, that a woman of her age, forty-five her last birthday, would experience something she'd never foreseen, an unfaithful heart.

Three months later the steamer arrives, docking at the mouth of Saint Catherine Creek, just south of Natchez. John, barely able to conceal his glee, rides up to Carefree to tell Cornelius the news. The next evening Cornelius asks Daniel to drive him down to Saint Catherine Creek. When they get there he slowly lowers himself from the buggy and leans on his cane as he makes his way down the bank to the silent boat. The workday is done and only a couple of workers still remain, painting the last of the white wooden railing along the upper deck. They nod at Cornelius as he taps his way up the gangplank and goes inside. After he glances around the immense salon, he goes down the steps to the boiler room, where the hulking black boiler sits cold. He opens the door and peers inside. When he closes it, he notices the lighter welds on one side of the fire box. *This is a repair.*

He mentions this the next afternoon when John comes up to the house. Cornelius meets him in his office with the plans spread out on his desk.

Cornelius taps his pencil on the paper. "Look at this," he says. "The relative size. Think of the wood requirements. The boiler will fire awfully hot. And why do the welds appear lighter in some sections than in others?"

John has his answers ready, which makes Cornelius think that Phony has told him of her husband's concerns. "In Pittsburgh they hired a replacement crew to build the engine," he says. "The first crew kept showing up hungover. And I imagine they had to repair some of the work the first crew did. But the boiler's big enough. The boat's been designed for speed. Passengers will want to get to New Orleans in an hour's less time than it takes now, and we can charge a higher fare."

Cornelius taps his pencil again. "But I just can't help but think the welds are a problem. I looked at how they were put together, and they don't look as strong as the original ironwork."

"I trust McCann," John says. "The boilerman will have to keep an eye on it, that's all."

He turns around to speak to Euphonia, who's come in to stand next to him and look over his shoulder at the chart that covers the desk.

"We're getting the details worked out," John says to her. Phony nods and smiles.

On a warm evening two weeks later, when the boat's interior is near completion, Cornelius again drives down to the shipyard where the boat lies like an apparition, waiting for its finishing touches. John, seeing him standing near the dock, walks over to him.

"Next week at the latest," John says. "The boat'll be ready to launch by the first of May."

"Well, it's your design, not mine," Cornelius says, fiddling for a cigarette. "I've told you my concerns. Last week the *Gazette* carried a story about the *John Jay*. It blew up south of Memphis. A total loss."

"I read about that," John says. "But I'm confident in my crew. This boat has years to run the river. We can work out whatever changes we need once we get her up and running."

"It's not the overall design I'm concerned about," Cornelius says. "It's the welds on the boiler. I know the boilers have to be big to carry the boat, especially if you consider the passengers will have wardrobes and trunks with them." They stand for a few minutes watching workmen stacking paint cans at the foot of the gangplank. Cornelius looks over to the mouth of the sleepy bayou where the Mississippi River cascades past.

"The river's up," he says.

"It's been up since last month," John says. He grins as he points to the boat. "Are we calling her the *Euphonia*?"

Cornelius shrugs. "Phony doesn't know it yet, but I guess we are. That's what we agreed to."

The next day John comes up to Carefree in search of Euphonia. All last night he'd lain awake, thinking about her. All night the wind blew, and the Elenora house creaked with tree branches brushing against the windows.

He seldom thinks about his children these days, because the *Euphonia's* taken all his thoughts. He knows the kids are well cared for; the people who have them are well fitted with slaves who can tend them. Well, as long as children have playmates and grownups to see to their needs, he can't see what else he could provide for them. He does wonder about Cyrus, who'd been his favorite. It seems so long ago that Cyrus was here, teething and wailing, and Delphine was trying her best to soothe him. One night she went to get a piece of ice from the ice house, he remembers now, and she wrapped it in a piece of towel so he could hold it to the boy's gums, and the baby quieted. But Cyrus would be a big boy now, almost four years old. He wonders whether Cyrus favors him, or Elenora. And he wonders if Dolly favors Lissy, her one big sister. Lissy would be—he calculates—about seven by now, and Dolly two. Well, his sister-in-law Dinah is a fierce woman, a mother hen. Dolly was a newborn then, but what was he to do? He couldn't shepherd so many children and run that infernal law practice too. And the slaves couldn't be left without supervision.

He knows he needs to go see the kids. If only they weren't so far away; as time has passed they've become dimmer in his mind. But between his ever increasing load of work every day at the office, and now with the steamer project, his days are full. And every evening he goes up to Carefree to see how Cornelius is doing. And to see Euphonia.

Earlier today a letter came, addressed in a child's block letters, to Mister John Landerson, Natchez, Mississippi. He opened it, startled to see a childish letter enclosed, one page, and signed, "Lissy."

June 5, 1846

Dearest Papa,

Aunt Dinah says I should write a letter to you so you would know how I am and how Freddy is too. It would show you how I know how to write. She helped me write a little bit, because I'm not good at it yet. I am seven now, and Freddy is almost thirteen. All is well. I play with Julia every day and Freddy plays with cousin Alfred. We have a swing made of rope in the back of the house. Uncle Jeremy takes us fishing sometimes, down at the river, but we don't usually catch anything.

How are you? I hope you will write to me sometimes and do not forget me and Freddy.

Lissy

All his children's childhoods are slipping away from him, he thinks. Hadn't he better go see them? But he knows he has no intention of reclaiming them, and surely they're settled in where they are. He pictures how it would be: he'd show up and Dinah would welcome him, invite him into the parlor of that big house where they live, and then Lissy would come into the room, a big girl, looking at him with curious eyes. And what could he say to her?

No, it would be better to go see the littlest ones, who couldn't fault him for sending them away since they knew no other life. But in the meantime, there's Euphonia. She's in his thoughts all the time.

When he goes to Carefree the next evening, Cornelius is sitting on the gallery. He waves as John rides up.

Cornelius is still gaunt from his illness, but he no longer needs a cane to balance himself. Tonight he looks like any grandee in his white suit, John thinks. The man's face is handsome still, but narrow, his cheeks more sunken. Rosabel and Henry are crouching on the step, trying to catch a toad. The sight of them reminds him again of his own absent children, but it's a fleeting thought.

"The boat's ready," John says.

"I thought as much, when I was down there earlier today," Cornelius says. "Mister Oates gave me a tour."

"I think we should take it out on a test run," John says.

"I still don't like the look of the welds. I want to get an experienced boilerman here to look at them. I'll find one, but it may take a few days."

John paces the gallery. "Cornelius, when do you plan to launch this boat? It's already summertime. We don't want to miss the season."

"Tomorrow I'll go talk to some machinists I know. Let's not rush things," Cornelius says. "I want to make sure of the welds, and then we need to christen it. Let Euphonia swing a bottle of wine at the prow, and get a band to play. After that we can give her a test run. Her maiden voyage."

John paces the gallery. "After all these months, it's finished," he says, punching his fist into the palm of his other hand. His coat-tails swing as he walks.

CHAPTER TWENTY-ONE

THE RECTORY OF SAINT MARY'S CHURCH is a long red brick building extending down the block behind the church. Jenny holds Rosabel's hand as they walk down the sidewalk past the church and onto the next block, curious to see the place where Saint Vigilius once stood. She stands at the grassy empty lot on the corner and stares for a long time, remembering Adrien.

The sidewalk is familiar to her; it's odd, she thinks how it's the sidewalks that stick in our minds, even though at the time we paid so little attention to them. Here the bricks are arrayed at an angle to each other, and there's the low place where the water runs across when it rains. And some bricks stick up above the others, where tree roots have pushed them up—she remembers those. An old lady stumbled on them once, and Adrien helped her up.

And now all the bricks are speckled with green moss. The wide concrete steps that led into the church are still there, but they lead nowhere. Anyone would know a building once stood here. Saint Vigilius was a world of its own back then, but now it's just a grassy patch on the street corner. At the back of the lot there's a pile of burnt bricks almost hidden in the high weeds; those bricks might have been part of the foundation.

She walks along the side of the lot to the alley, which is familiar to her. Here's the same board fence she remembers. One high window of the rectory stares over the fence; Adrien said that was his window. Here's the place where he first kissed her, and here's what remains of Walker's old shack, reduced to rubble, where they made love. This is Rosabel's beginning place, although she won't ever know it.

She wonders where she'd find Father Maercru. She wants to let him meet Rosabel, who's his great niece, if she's figuring right. She takes Rosabel by the hand and they walk back down the sidewalk and go up to the plain front door of the rectory.

She knocks and when no one answers, she eases the door open. Inside is a large square room. The hallways extending to right and left must lead to the rooms where the priests live, she thinks. A few chairs are lined up along the green walls, and a crucifix hangs on one wall. A side door opens and a young man comes in; he must be a new priest, she thinks; he hardly looks like he's out of his teens.

He looks surprised to see her. "May I help?"

"I need to see Father Maercru."

He hesitates a moment, then says, "I'll see if he's available," and he disappears down the hallway.

Jenny stands near the door, feeling she's intruded into this religious world. A nun comes in carrying a platter of dishes, the aroma of breakfast coming in with her. She looks surprised when she sees Jenny, but she says nothing. She goes out the back door.

Rosabel buries her face in the front of Jenny's skirt. Jenny pats her on the back.

On a table against the far wall is a silver candlestick Jenny remembers from when she used to go to mass with Adrien; the base is a hammered bouquet of lilies. A pair of those candlesticks used to stand on the altar at Saint Vigilius, she remembers. Apparently only one of the pair survived the fire.

A few moments later the side door opens and Louis Maercru comes out. Jenny stares at him. The priest, whom she recalls as a kindly middle-aged man, has grown much older since she saw him last; the lines in his face are deeper, and his gray hair is nearly gone from the top of his head. His eyes have a heavy look. He doesn't look much like the genial priest who presided over mass at Saint Vigilius.

"Hello, Father," she says.

He studies her face for a moment. "Are you Jenny?"

She nods.

"How long has it been since you were here with Adrien?"

"Five years. It was before we went to New Orleans."

He stares at her, and then folds his hands, monklike, over his paunch. "Let's go outside and sit on the bench there," he says. "There's a garden for reflection out there."

She follows him out the back door, noticing that he looks at Rosabel curiously. Rosabel is glad to be outside again, and she prances ahead of them down the well-kept brick path. They come to a secluded place where there's a fountain shaded by tall trees. A statue of the Virgin is nestled in the center of some boxwood. Father Maercru motions Jenny to sit on the bench, and he sits beside her. Rosabel goes over to the fountain and hoists herself up over the edge of the stone wall, dabbling in the water.

"Are you back in Natchez now, my dear?"

"I am." She looks at the old man, thinking, what is it he would like to hear? Is it all right to talk about Adrien? It will make him sad, but surely he'll want to know what happened to his nephew. "I came to tell you about Adrien. About the way he died in New Orleans."

"I know a little about what happened," he says. The lines of his face sag even deeper.

She hesitates. On this beautiful morning, should she tell him every detail of Adrien's death? She knows so little about it, really. But in all of America there are only two people who loved Adrien. Who else will ever speak his name?

"He was killed in a card game," she says in a low voice.

"I thought it must be something like that," he says. He shakes his head. "I was crushed when I got the letter from the police."

"I don't think they knew many of the details, and I don't either," she says.

"The police commissioner wrote to me—" He stops, looks away, gathers himself—"and said Adrien had a note in his pocket with the name of Saint Vigilius, and that's how they knew to contact me. I hope the church meant something to him." He looks over at Rosabel, who's splashing herself wet. "I always wondered—why did you go to New Orleans?"

She hesitates. She can't say, 'Because Adrien didn't want to be a janitor in the church anymore'. So she says, "Because Rosabel was coming and he felt we couldn't stay. He wanted us to be man and wife, and be a proper family. Adrien was kind, really. That's why he didn't tell you himself; he didn't want you to feel disgraced."

Maercru stares at Rosabel, who seems in danger of tipping over the stone wall into the water. "I wouldn't have felt disgraced."

"I saw a candlestick inside that I recognized from the church. I guess it was saved from the fire," Jenny says.

"Yes, only the one. I imagine someone swiped the other one before the ashes were cold." He smiles. "It's probably gracing someone's mantlepiece." He looks up at the blue sky. "I wrote my brother in France, to let him know what happened to Adrien. I heard back from him just recently. It's been years since he wrote me."

Jenny watches Rosabel as the girl climbs up on the stone wall circling the fountain and teeters around it, her arms out for balance. The front of her pinafore is soaked.

"Look, Mama!" she says.

Maercru stares into the distance, and then looks at Rosabel. "So that's his child," he says. "Rosabel."

"Yes sir. She's four."

"So —" His eyes brighten, giving his face something like the genial look she remembers. "I thought I was alone in the new world. Now I find there's a small girl who is of the Maercru family also."

"Jean-Pierre is the name she'll go by," Jenny says. "She has Adrien's name."

"As he carried his mother's name. Do you take that name, also?"

"No sir. I'm Cornelius. It's the name Master Cornelius gave me, and it's still the name I use."

Rosabel jumps down from the wall and Jenny motions her to come over. Louis stares at her. "I see Adrien's features in this child."

Rosabel climbs up onto her lap. "Rosabel, can you say hello to Father Maercru?"

Rosabel leans against Jenny's chest and stares at him. He takes her hand and gives it a gentle shake. "Hello, Rosabel. Bon jour, Mademoiselle Jean-Pierre."

Rosabel presses her face into her mother's chest.

Father Maercru smiles. "You know, I haven't had much joy since the fire. I help at the Mass here, of course, and that's familiar. It's a beautiful church. Have you been inside?"

Jenny shakes her head.

"Oh, when you get a chance you must go in. It's truly lovely, all white and gold. It reminds me of the glory of the heavens. But now this child— well, she's a joy, I must say. And so like Adrien."

"She's headstrong like him, too," Jenny says.

Later Jenny walks down the shady path back toward the street. Father Maercru has met his great-niece Rosabel, and that was her mission in coming here. But she had another mission too: she wanted to right what had always seemed to her like a small injustice, the way she and Adrien had left so abruptly, and without a decent goodbye. *We skimmed past people too easily,* she thinks now, but Adrien was impatient. She was too.

As they pass the rectory, Jenny glances through the picketed fence. The nun she saw earlier is sitting on a bench beside a large camellia bush, her prayerbook closed in her hand. She looks up when Jenny walks past, and her lips curve into a small smile.

What is she thinking? Jenny wonders, slowing her stride. *What is her life like?* But she thinks the nun's experiences and her own must be an ocean apart.

Father Maercru watches Jenny and Rosabel walk away down the street. They'll head back up to Carefree, but they'll probably get a ride from a passing buggy, because a pretty woman with a child usually won't have to walk too far. She's a free woman, like all the ones at Carefree; he wonders why that place seems so cursed, since the owner obviously is a man of principles and every person living there is free.

He walks back to his room, which is much smaller than the room he had before in this same rectory, when Adrien was here. Instead of his commodious room with the fireplace, which Father Terrence now has, he has the room at the end, where Adrien once lived. He sleeps in the narrow bed where Adrien slept, and he folds his clothes into the same plain chest Adrien used. He even found Adrien's French school books stacked in the corner. The old yellow cat still hangs around, mewing, and Louis sometimes sets a dish of cream out beside his door for the animal; but he doesn't invite him inside.

He sits at the little scarred desk in the corner and sharpens his quill pen. He unfolds the letter he received from his brother last week, and he smooths the edges down as he rereads it.

Mon cher frere Louis:

I could not write before now. Death is all around. You have told me my beloved Adrien is gone, and it took me many months before I could accept that it was true. Finally I did accept that Adrien is dead, and—oh Louis—I can hardly bear to write this news! So are Isobel and little Philippe! A plague swept through this village and took them. The Angel of Death was hovering and we didn't know it. Now they both lie in the graveyard behind the church, and Philippe so young. I am truly accursed. I go to the church to pray for them every day. And where Adrien lies, in what cemetery in la Nouvelle Orleans, I know not. Can my prayers reach him there?

The anguish flew back and forth across the Atlantic Ocean on sheets of fragile paper, which might as well be the wings of an avenging angel, Louis thinks. And heartbreak multiplied with every passage.

But now he has a message he knows will soothe Marcel's burning heart. Marcel is not alone; there is a child, and he, Louis, will tell his brother. Won't Marcel's heart spring up with joy at this unexpected news?

He thinks about Rosabel dabbling in the water in the fountain as the birds sang overhead. Perhaps he can make Marcel see the scene in his mind: the bright morning, the young woman Jenny and her child, the sparkling fountain, the birds twittering. Life's joys may yet heal both their hearts, he thinks, his and Marcel's. He picks up his quill.

A few minutes later, because he's written everything he needs to write, and because the cat's at the door mewing, he signs the letter, *Je t'aime frere, Louis.*

In the nighttime Jenny sleeps curled up against Rosabel, whose small form is warm in the summer night. Her mind is filled with thoughts of Father Maercru in the hidden grotto behind the rectory, a kindly old man. Rosabel looked elfin, tiptoeing around the fountain in her wet pinafore. Suddenly Jenny feels overwhelmed; can she raise this half-French child, and help her know her dead Papa? Can she teach Rosabel to know herself, a child of Africa and a free person? Is she up to the task? Because now someone else here claims a part of Rosabel; up until now, the child was hers and hers alone. But the blood that flows in Louis Maercru flows in Rosabel too. Was it a mistake to introduce him to the innocent child?

She can't answer that, so, unhappy, she turns over and sleeps.

The dream continues.

The forest path is dappled with sunlight, and the path winds over roots as big as her legs. Alone, Esi stumbles and then picks herself up again. Night will come and the forest will scream even louder than it is now. The smell of smoke follows her down the trail, and after a couple of hours she can't smell it anymore. She should be afraid, she thinks, being out in the forest alone, without a weapon, but she will go. She regrets not going years ago, but now nothing holds her. Not the village where she was born, not the old man. Her time has come to find her children.

When she gets to Accra the ocean opens like a blue blanket stretched out before her. Some buildings are scattered up to the shore. She's in a strange city, and she speaks only the language of the upriver country. What language do they speak here?

The ships are bobbing gently in the harbor.

She stumbles on, to get as close as she can to the shore. Beside a small white building is a mahogany tree with a twisted trunk, and she sinks down beside it. The summer heat makes the harbor shimmer. She's never seen the ocean before, but she knows that's where the children were taken. In the village it's said that the captives are always taken to the shore and put on large ships, for a voyage on a lake so wide it has no other side.

She's had no food for the past two days.

The mahogany tree gives a little shade, and she sits there, a dark form against the dark tree-trunk. She hears a rumble of noises, chains clanking, men's deep angry voices. She closes her eyes and then opens them again when the sounds get louder. She pulls her legs up to one side and tries to make herself unseen in the shadows.

A coffle of slaves, men, women and children chained together stumble around the side of a building. Men on horseback ride alongside them. As the prisoners are marched past her toward the buildings at the shore, Esi sees the fear in their faces.

Woe to those who come from upriver. Woe to those who speak only the language of the backcountry.

Some of the women collapse but the men hit them with whips, so they have no choice but to stand again and stumble forward. The ships with white sails are waiting.

In the village it was said that the captives are put onto ships for a voyage so long, they will be eaten before they reach another shore.

Her world goes black.

CHAPTER TWENTY-TWO

AT NOON THE NEXT DAY Sheriff Jim Williams rides up to Carefree. Cornelius, sitting at his desk, is surprised when Dancy ushers him in. He stands up and extends his hand.

Cornelius hasn't seen much of the sheriff since the weeks after May disappeared, but during that trying time he appreciated the man's determination to find the missing child, even though every avenue they pursued was a failure. But Jim Williams is a father of several daughters himself, Cornelius knows, and he showed a dedication to the task of finding the lost child even after others who volunteered to search had drifted away, discouraged. The matter of the old crime in Vidalia seems to have vanished too.

Today the sheriff looks downcast. He closes the office door and sits down in the chair opposite the desk, staring intently at Cornelius.

"I think we may have found her," he says in a low voice.

Cornelius is startled.

The sheriff shifts in his chair. "Up at Washington, they've found an unidentified body in some woods. A young girl." He clears his throat. "Apparently she's been dead a day or two, but the sheriff there thinks it could be May. The deputy rode down here and told me this morning."

Cornelius stands up, shocked. "I've never really considered that she wouldn't be found alive. I hope it's not her."

"So do I, but the description seems to fit."

Cornelius walks to the window and looks out. "'It's been three years. She'd be bigger by now."

The sheriff nods. "This body seems to be a girl about eleven. Light brown hair. What I need is for you to go with me up there this afternoon to identify her."

"Can we get there and back in daylight?"

"Probably not. But it's a clear night, and the almanac says there'll be a moon."

Cornelius puts his hand up to his forehead and squeezes his eyes shut. "Lord, I hope you're wrong. This whole house has been mired in misery, not knowing what happened to her."

"I know. Can you go now?"

"I don't see why not. Let me tell Euphonia about this. On second thought—maybe I won't tell her why I'm going. In case it's a mistake. There's no sense upsetting everyone until we know for sure it's her. I'll tell her I'm going out on—some other business."

The sheriff nods, and Cornelius goes out into the hall. He turns toward the back bedroom where Euphonia is sitting on the bed surrounded by squares of embroidered birds, laying them out in a pattern to form a quilt top. She looks up wondering at his expression.

Later that afternoon Phony appears at the doorway to the bedroom where Jenny is going through May's old clothes. She's dressed for some occasion, Jenny thinks, in a shimmery blue dress and a velvet bonnet with tiny silk roses tucked under the brim; perhaps she's going to visit with her women friends, although such visits are rare since Elenora Landerson died.

"Jenny, I'm going out this evenin'," she says. "Keep an eye on Thomas, if you will. Cornelius isn't here. Coella's downstairs but you never know."

"Yes ma'am." Jenny stares at her. Phony looks tired all the time now, even though Cornelius has mostly recovered, and Thomas is a big boy of five and doesn't need much mothering. But Phony is at the age when a woman's looks start to change.

Phony snaps her purse closed as she turns away. "I might be late getting back. I'm going down to see this steamboat we've all heard so much about."

The sad relic of a body wasn't May. Cornelius saw that at once. The body lying on a table in the back room of the sheriff's office in Washington was a farm girl from some surrounding community, no doubt, tall and poker-thin and wearing a worn-out house dress and no shoes. With his handkerchief clasped to his face, Cornelius studied the girl's long fingers and her careworn hands, and he knew at once these hands couldn't ever have belonged to May. And the face with its long nose and deep-set eyes; no, that face looked nothing like the girl he remembered, even accounting for the distortions of death.

As Cornelius and Sheriff Williams rode back to Natchez side by side, the two men said little, each lost in his own thoughts. The ruined body of the girl was a shocking sight. Cornelius tried to understand how a young girl could come to die in a thicket of woods, and lie unclaimed and unidentified, her sunbonnet still tied around her head.

But he knew he wouldn't figure out the puzzle on the road back to Carefree. And when he got home, exhaustion pressed down on him and put him into a deep sleep.

The road into Natchez is turning blue in the twilight as Euphonia drives the buggy down Main Street. Daniel would've driven her, he even volunteered, but she wanted to go alone. It's not that far, she thinks; it won't even be full dark when she gets there.

A fleeting thought crosses her mind: that must be what Josephine Coqterre thought as she headed out toward Washington on that fateful day so many years ago: *It's not far.* The thought passes and she thinks instead of a moonlit ride on the river, with John. Yesterday, when he came to see Cornelius, she walked with John out to his horse and what he whispered in her ear has stayed in her mind all day. He invited her to come see the steamer tonight.

She holds the reins tightly as she drives through Natchez. Main Street isn't busy at this time of day. As she passes Miss Dolores's Shoppe of Finery, she runs her hand down across her thighs to smooth the crisp fabric of her skirt. Miss Dolores made this dress of robins'-egg blue taffeta for her last month, and it's different from the fabrics she normally orders. The skirt has a lustrous rustle, and the fabric is a summer pale, the color of the summer sky on a clear day. Most of her other dresses are dark and conservative, but just in the past few weeks she's felt the need to brighten up her wardrobe, to wear colors that reflect the season. It's a way to put everything the house has been through behind her. When Miss Dolores suggested the bolt of shimmery silk, Euphonia knew in a heartbeat that her next dress would be fashioned of this material. Tonight she's tied a rose-colored scarf around her shoulders to match the silk rosettes of her hat, and at the last minute she fastened her favorite string of pearls around her neck, so they lie against her white throat. Driving through town, she feels attractive in this dress, and that's a feeling she's not felt for a long time. Since May's been gone, Euphonia's been spending all her time at home. It's seemed the house has been holding its breath; but like any living creature, it can't hold its breath too long, or it will die.

But Carefree won't die, Euphonia's decided, no matter what stunt that crazy May decided to pull in the dead of night. They'll probably never know where she went, or why.

So they might as well face the future as a healthy household. Cornelius is getting well; he walks with a slight limp, but his cane can compensate for that. He's still the handsome man he was before the illness, although he's more gaunt and looks a bit older. But he's only thirty-eight, a man with a long future ahead of him. And she's a little older than he is, but she feels she's on a train that's pulling her to an ever-brightening horizon. John's a big part of the change in her feelings. Even so, there are moments when this strange attraction for John has caused her to stop and steady herself when she's waiting for him in the parlor or on the gallery. But she doesn't hesitate for long.

She thinks the surprise John has in mind for her is that he's named the boat for her.

The shops along Main Street are closing up for the night. The grocer watches her drive past as he rolls his vegetable tables back inside the store, but the lamplighter walking along with his light on a pole doesn't even glance her way. She turns onto a side-road and drives south down a narrow road with woods encroaching on both sides of the path. Then the road stops at the place where Saint Catherine Creek empties into the Mississippi, and there the steamer sits, its three stories of filigreed balconies rising like the tiers of a wedding cake.

CHAPTER TWENTY-THREE

IT'S A SPLENDID WHITE BOAT. No name is lettered on the side. A couple of workers are there, carrying provisions up the gangplank. They look around as Euphonia drives up.

When she gets off the buggy and ties the horse, she stands for a moment taking in the sight. John is right; it's a beautiful boat, and very large. It's graceful, nothing like the steamers that pull in at Natchez, which often seem saggy and in need of a coat of paint. Even tied to the shore, the *Euphonia*—she already thinks of it as that—is magnificent.

As she stands at the top of the wooden walkway that leads down the boat, John comes up behind her. She turns to him.

"It's beautiful," she breathes. "I had no idea."

"I knew you'd think so," he says, taking her arm.

He guides her down the plank and onto the boat. "I've asked the Captain to give us a moonlight ride," he says. "We'll be the first to try it."

"She won't sink, will she?"

"Not a chance."

She smiles at him. John's a handsome man, with his chiselled chin and his searching, understanding eyes. So different from Cornelius, who's cool and sometimes a little distant. John turns away from her and walks over to the front of the boat to speak to the workers. They set their hammers down and unfasten their work belts.

"Luckily there's a full moon tonight, so we don't have to worry about snaggers and sawyers. The river's a bright highway," John says when he returns.

"It is." They walk to the front railing and look out at the river, where a steamer called *Saint Joe* is ploughing upstream. A couple of flatboats pole past, and the boatmen gawk as they look over at the huge steamboat that's tethered just up the creek.

"Those boys are probably fresh out from Under-the-Hill," John says. He touches her arm. "Did you notice that space on the side of the upper deck there," he says, pointing. "That's where the name goes."

"I won't ask what the name is," she giggles.

"Ready, Cap'n?" one of the deckhands calls.

"Fire 'er up!" John calls back.

The boilers begin with a deep rumble, and the boatmen raise the gangplank. The shore workers knock the holding pins loose and the boat tilts and rolls as she moves into the creek. The captain nudges her into the river's strong current and then out to the middle of the river. The men on shore are still hollering and clapping, but Euphonia can't hear them anymore. The river banks are lines of dark trees on either side. She and John look out at the broad river.

"Let's go watch the sternwheel do its job," John says, and they walk to the back of the boat and stand at the railing as the wheel churns the blue-gray water into a train of white lace behind the boat.

He stands close to her. "Aren't we lucky?" he says. "I bet you've never had a boat all to yourself before. Well, almost to yourself. We've got a captain and the boilerman and those deckhands. But it's a skeleton crew. And us."

She leans against him as they study the river. "I've only been on a steamer once, when we went to get Kofi. And it wasn't a long trip. I've been on the Vidalia ferry, but I really haven't had the pleasure of travelling like most people have."

"You should have that pleasure," he says, his arm around her shoulder. He fiddles with the flowers on her hat. "Tonight you almost have the boat to yourself. How many women ever have that privilege?"

She smiles. "None that I know of," she says.

He puts his hand under his chin and tips her face up and kisses her on the lips. "Let's go inside and see the rest of it."

When they walk into the main salon, she stands in the doorway and stares. The salon is lined with tables and large, comfortable-looking red velvet chairs. The cream-colored walls are interspersed with mirrors that reflect tall tapered candles in crystal candlesticks. French tables line the walls.

"It's truly beautiful," she breathes.

"Can you picture how grand it'll be with passengers in here?" he asks.

"I can almost smell the cigar smoke," she laughs.

He takes her arm and leads her to the curving staircase at the far end of the salon. "The staterooms are all on the upper decks," he says. "The second deck and the third. And on top, there's a viewing platform for guests who want to enjoy a peaceful evening with their wine and brandy, and watch the world go by."

"Sometimes I wish it could go by," she murmurs.

They climb up three flights of stairs to the highest vantage point and stand at the railing. Above them, the fanstacks stream into the evening air.

"Isn't this grand?" he breathes. "We've had our share of troubles, you and I," he says. He kisses her neck. "But now I think only happiness lies ahead."

How can that be? she wonders.

The moon rises, a bright smear behind a string of silver-rimmed clouds. The breeze is cool, and she unpins her hat and shakes her head to let the wind dry her hair where perspiration has dampened it. John moves closer to her and lifts her hair away from her neck and kisses her there.

"Let me show you the staterooms," he says.

They go down the staircase to the second deck and he takes a lamp from a table by the wall. When he lights it, the panelling seems to jump toward them, gleaming yellow.

"These are the premier cabins," John says. "Every cabin has a name." She looks down the hall. Fastened beside every closed door is a small bronze plaque announcing a name: The Magnolia, The Holly, the Camellia.

He leads her halfway down the hall and opens a door. "This is the Natchez," he says. "The most luxurious suite on the boat." He walks in and lights the candle on the nightstand.

Phony walks in and looks around. It's obvious that great care has been taken with the furnishings; the walnut chests are burnished and gleaming, and the lamp light flickers across the lustrous silk of the counterpane. Silk curtains the color of whiskey puddle on the patterned red rug.

He puts his arms around her and they share a long kiss. They move toward the bed, and he kisses her again. She puts her arms around him, feeling his strong, lean torso.

"We'll muss the counterpane," she murmurs.

"I hope so."

As they move together on the bed, she arches herself away from him for a moment and looks up through the window behind the bed. The moon, shaken free of its tattered clouds, is sailing on a sliver of black sky.

She knows that if she were standing at the window, the moon's reflection would be a puddle of butter melting on the swift-flowing river.

There's an awkwardness to their lovemaking, which she didn't anticipate. He's stronger than Cornelius, and more insistent than Cornelius had ever been. Cornelius is a more patient man. She wonders, is this the way Elenora experienced John, night after night, in that big house? Did he pull at her clothes in this rough way, so careless about her fine dress, her petticoats, her fragile pearls? But even so, there's a desperation in the way she reaches for him. She thinks, *John, I need to tell you how my life's become a broken shell, with a husband so sick and a child who vanished. How you are my only hope.*

But his mouth is hard on hers. And then she lies in his arms, listening to the solid deep rumble of the engines far below.

An hour later she gets up and smooths down her petticoats.

"Don't go," he says, pulling her back to him.

"Won't I need to be home?" she says.

"You are home," he says, pulling her down to himself again, with that roughness she's getting used to. "And so am I."

She thinks, *I'll be sore tomorrow.*

The rumble of the engines becomes louder. "We're turning," he says later as he rolls away from her. "I told the captain to take us downstream a good distance."

They stand up and she reaches for her petticoat, his kisses drying on her throat. Her legs are wet from him. She takes a towel from the dresser and dries herself. Then, suddenly embarrassed that he's looking at her, she goes over to a folding screen and dresses behind it. Looking at herself in the mirror there, she brushes her hands over her flushed cheeks. Then she pins up her hair and fastens her pearls again. When she comes out, John is dressed and pulling on his high boots. He kisses her again and then they walk down the curving staircase to the main salon. He leads her out to the front deck. The river coming at them looks like a wrinkled highway carved of stone, flat in the silver light. He stands close to her and slips his arm around her waist. Flatboats float alongside them silently and a steamer headed upriver comes toward them as it rounds the bend in the river.

"We have —" John starts to say.

The explosion comes to Phony as a blast of water and steam, an animal-like sound like none she's ever heard, a crack so loud it reverberates from one shore to the other, followed an instant later by the sound of wooden framing wrenching apart amid a bellow of steam and exploding water. She sees John flying upward, a marionette of flailing limbs, his back twisted in a way no living body could withstand, as he rises above the hiss and roar of the explosion. Then he vanishes before her eyes. Her head is thrown backward and she too flies up; she glimpses the *Euphonia* breaking into two parts that crash together on the silver river, the curtains flying outward from the windows like women's skirts blown up in a storm. In the instant before the wreck is gulped by the ceaseless current, Euphonia feels the strangeness of the open air, her shoes gone, her pearls snapping free of her neck and snaking away to disappear in the dark air.

Rising toward the night sky, she thinks she can ascend like a heron and see every plantation house along the shores, every cabin, every cotton row. But an instant later she slams down into the black water, her skirt and petticoats rising around her until they pull her down, down, toward that unseen kingdom where catfish big as farm wagons crawl along the riverbed.

Then her face smashes into something hard and wet; a cotton bale is tumbling in the roil of the water. It spins and bounces in the current, and Euphonia claws for the rope that ties the bale; but it's far too taut for her to grasp. So she digs her fingernails into the wet cotton and lurches to the top of the bale where she sprawls, pulling precious black air into her lungs. The bale teeters and spins back down the river the way the boat has just come, and she thinks as she floats that the soaked cotton smells like Bayou Cocodrie used to smell after a summer rain. Blood from a gash on her face flows into the cotton like a river of its own.

Then a hand reaches down for her; a flatboatman seizes her arm and won't turn loose. As he hoists her up onto the flatboat, she looks down at herself; her dress isn't blue any longer. She lies on the top of the flatboat, staring into the astonished eyes of young men she doesn't know. Stars are above, catfish below.

She thinks, *What was I thinking, to wear a summer color?*

But then the moonlight goes from blue to black.

CHAPTER TWENTY-FOUR

ON A COLD SUNDAY MORNING in March 1847, Father Maercru sits at his desk and puts his head down in his hands. His morning's work has shaken him.

Mass was over an hour ago, but he'd already slipped out the side door before it ended, which was odd, because he almost never studied the people in the pews, preferring to focus as he should on the prayers and responses, the homily, the procession of worshippers to the communion rail. But today there'd been a sudden brightness in the church as the sun hit the stained glass windows—that happens sometimes, he's noticed—and it flashed on the blond hair of a woman kneeling halfway back. It was Cecilia. Even under her black lace mantilla he recognized her; he knew her face, the pretty features and smooth complexion that now have the mature look of a woman in her fifties. He'd kissed those full lips, brushed that hair back from her neck, felt those plump arms around himself. It was more than fifteen years ago, the only time he broke his vows. But long ago he put the affair out of his mind, thinking he'd go mad if he continued to dwell in that howling place between desire and desperate yearning to keep his vows. It was sin, for him and for her. So he'd told her to go, and she disappeared from his life. Sometime later he heard that she moved to New Orleans.

He rubs his eyes. Well, he won't let himself revisit that spring of 1831. It's still winter; a raw wind scratches at the high window of his room. He needs to go down to see Father Terrence about a replacement for the broken window pane. For now he's stuffed some old socks into the crack that appeared after a hailstorm last month, and he needs to put on his coat. A humid climate can be cold as anything; he feels it in his bones. Father Terrance has the room with the fireplace, which Louis imagines is roaring right about now. Sister Angela will see to it that the slaves keep the logs piled high.

Shivering, he watches his breath form in the air. When has Natchez been this cold? Normally, a mildness hangs over the town even in winter, something he didn't see in France or in Saint Louis. That same humid desultoriness usually hangs over the whole south like a soft blanket, and in summer it becomes a baking steambath. But in winter the air is normally as mild as a custard.

He blows into his hands and gets up to take his coat from the chiffarobe. Then, wrapped warmly, he sits on the side of the bed. Catching his image in the mirror on the wall, he sees that he's become an old man. Saint Louis aged him, or he aged himself there, not knowing why the bottom fell out of his life in his fifty-fifth year.

In the middle of my life's journey, I stepped off the narrow path and found myself in a deep wood.

It's a scrap of a line from Dante's *Inferno*, remembered from his days at the Latin School in Lormont. Maybe that old Florentine Dante knew a thing or two about a life's journey, Louis thinks, even though the young brother who was his teacher seemed unsure what the lesson might be.

He knows Father Terrance likes him; of all the priests here, it's Louis who prays most often, and most fervently. His prayers keep him upright in the darkest of times; he learned that at the abbey, after he got off the drink. His fervor took away the pull of the whiskey. Now he's afraid to turn that fervor loose, lest he spiral down into that drink-soused place where he was before.

He fingers an unopened letter that came today. When he came back to the room from Mass he found it wedged in the crack between his door and the doorframe; the slave Quincy must have put it there. The letter is postmarked Lormont, and for a few moments Louis is afraid to open it. The last letter from Marcel was a cry of such anguish it haunted Louis for weeks.

He opens the envelope, putting his gnarled finger under the flap to ease the envelope open. Yes, it's from Marcel; and mercifully, it's not tear-spotted. He holds the paper up to his face, breathing in the air of his childhood.

Then he reads. The letter begins hesitantly, and then Marcel's penmanship becomes more insistent, a forward-leaning slant on the page. He's writing in haste, Louis thinks. He pictures his brother sitting at the ornate desk that once belonged to their father, in the library at Lormont. From the window, Papa would look out over the knot garden and out to the green fields and forests beyond. But at this time of year the vista wouldn't be green. It's only green in Louis's memory.

Mon frere cher:

We have had a terrible year. So much suffering and death, and now in the cold of winter with its leaden skies, it all seems so much more tragic. The plague has swept through Lormont, and carried off so many: the mayor, the schoolmaster, the parish priest. How can anyone survive in this vale of tears?

And all this coming long after I received your letter bearing your own tragic news, of Adrien's death. Oh, my son! It was months before I could speak of it to anyone, even to my dear wife Isobel. And then, as I wrote you, another tragedy befell me: the plague swept into my house. It must have come in on the wind even though we were keeping the doors blocked, with cloths wedged beneath them. And day after day I walked these halls wringing my hands, but I suppose not really fearing enough. I guess you would say not praying enough.

Because the plague found Isobel and claimed her, and a week later, little Philippe in his innocence was taken. I found him in his crib, the sweet boy not yet a year old. Louis, both my wives and both my sons are lost!

But then, on a day as dark as any day can be, I received your letter. Your wonderful letter! I held it to my chest and read it again and again. How you told of your meeting with the woman Jenny, and her sweet child Rosabel Jean-Pierre. Adrien's own child! And so resembling him, you said. I picture the girl in my mind, a precious relic of Adrien himself.

So I said to myself, I must write to you. Bring the child to France. She and her mother can live here on the estate. I will rear her, my granddaughter, as a gift come from America. A beautiful jewel from across the sea.

Bring her here! And bring Jenny the mother, because a girl will always need her mother. Everything I have, in this silent house, will be theirs. The child will be educated by the finest teachers, and will want for nothing. Neither will the mother.

Brother, you may think this is the rambling of a deranged man, but I assure you I am seeing this with the clarity that only a harsh lesson in life's losses can give. Write to me, and let me know when you can arrive with her.

Affectueusement
Marcel

Louis lets the letter rest in his hands for a long time. He hears a scratching sound, and the mouse he calls Daricke comes out on his fleet feet and runs along the wall. Louis brushes a breadcrumb off the desk so the mouse can find it.

"Daricke, I protect you, but I have a cat I protect too," he says to the mouse. "It won't do for the two of you to meet. But you don't need to worry. I keep the cat outside now."

He leans back in his chair and thinks about Jenny, who lives at Carefree in that nest of free people set up by Cornelius Carson, a man who walks with a cane. Whose wife is a socialite here in Natchez. What will he do with Marcel's request? It sounds so urgent; he knows his brother well enough to know that what Marcel wrote springs from his heart. And Marcel was always soft-hearted about Adrien, and surely he loved Isobel and little Philippe, although Louis never saw the second wife or baby boy. Marcel inherited the estate, but he really didn't have the hard-nosed attitude a successful aristocrat had to have.

I should have been the first son, Louis thinks, and Marcel could have gone into the church. It would be Marcel, the tenderhearted one, who'd pray at bedsides and burials, not Louis, whose heart was harder. Louis may save a cat and a mouse, but Marcel would save the town, if he could.

CHAPTER TWENTY-FIVE

WINTER STILL SCRATCHES AT THE WINDOWS and all the fireplaces are roaring on a Saturday morning a week later when Dancy ushers Louis Maercru into Cornelius's office.

He's aged, Cornelius thinks, motioning the older man in and standing to shake his hand. Father Maercru is a man he's never known well, but he'd heard the priest had returned to Natchez a few years back. In spite of the white hair the face is still familiar.

Louis sits in the leather chair opposite the desk. Dancy, standing in the doorway, says, "Would you care for a cup of coffee, sir?" and Louis nods, blowing his nose into his handkerchief. He coughs.

After she leaves, the priest says, "I've received a letter relating to Jenny."

"Our Jenny?"

"Yes. Well. You recall —"

Dancy returns with a silver tray which she places on the desk in front of the priest. He pours himself a demitasse cup. "It's quite cold out today," he says, and Cornelius nods. "Well, you remember that Jenny and my nephew Adrien Jean-Pierre went to New Orleans a few years ago, and Adrien died there. And there is a child —"

"Rosabel," Cornelius says.

"Yes. The image of Adrien. I wrote to my brother Marcel, in France, to tell him of the little girl, because after all she's his granddaughter. And now Marcel has written to me, asking me to send Jenny and the child to him in France, so he can raise the little girl. Marcel is alone in the world —" he clears his throat—"because his wife and son were carried off by a plague. He wants to bring up Rosabel and care for Jenny, too. He inherited our father's estate, being the eldest son. I assure you the estate is vast, the home palatial and historic. They would want for nothing."

Cornelius frowns and leans back in his chair. "That's a big move."

"It is. And I wasn't at all sure you'd be receptive to the idea, but I knew I had to discuss it with you."

Louis opens his coat and takes a small picture in a gilded frame from his inside coat pocket. He hands it across the desk. Cornelius studies it; it's a finely detailed painting of a turreted chateau nestled under a gently rising hill. A road lined with poplars leads to the front gate.

Cornelius hands the picture back to Louis. "Rosabel's still a young child," he says. "Her life is settled here, with her mama."

Louis nods and sips his coffee. He sets the cup down on the tray. "Yes, but as a Creole child in Mississippi—she may have a hard life."

"I'll see to it she doesn't," Cornelius says shortly, and Maercru thinks again, *What kind of man is Cornelius Carson? What drives him?*

He hands Cornelius the letter. Cornelius glances at the unfamiliar French script and folds the letter and places it on the desk.

"This may be an opportunity for her that won't come again," Louis says. "If Jenny doesn't go, Marcel may find himself a new wife," Louis says. "And he may have another child, another heir."

"He may do that even if she chooses to go to France," Cornelius says. "And then where would that leave Rosabel? Or Jenny?"

Louis shrugs. "He may. But of course, with the child—." A clock sounds a soft chime somewhere in the house, and another moment ticks away. When Cornelius doesn't say anything else, Louis knows he's lost his argument. He stands up. "Of course, I will leave the decision up to you."

"Let me get her in here," Cornelius says. "All I can say is I'll present the proposal to her. After that, it's her choice."

"Of course," Louis says.

Cornelius walks to the doorway. "Dancy, tell Jenny I need to see her."

Jenny comes downstairs, wiping her hands on a towel. When she walks into the office, her face registers her surprise at seeing Father Maercru.

Maercru suddenly feels as if he's intruding into a world that's not his own. "I shall leave the discussion with you," he says to Cornelius. Then he nods to Jenny. "Au revoir, Madame Jean-Pierre." He walks out the door, buttoning his coat.

"I will not go," Jenny says without hesitation after Cornelius presents Father Maercru's proposal to her. Cornelius stares at her. He's made his case, the same one Maercru laid out to him, but Jenny is firm.

She knows he wants an explanation, but the look on his face is one of relief.

For Jenny, there's no question: *If I go to France, I will lose my child.* Rosabel would be swallowed up in some French life Jenny can't even foresee. As Rosabel grows up, she'll have a hard time, as Adrien did. His mother was a slave in Martinique, and Marcel Maercru took her and Adrien to France. But after his mother died, how was Adrien supposed to survive in France, a child whose face and accent were those of Martinique?

Rosabel is a child of America, but this French grandfather would claim her as his own, and it would be the easiest thing in the world for him to push Jenny into the background. At the slave auction Jenny vowed that whatever she had to face in slave-land, she'd face it with her child. And there was no way some French nobleman was ever going to change that.

Walking back to the rectory, Louis is troubled. The young woman won't agree to go, he's certain. Carson will see to that. And that means that he, Louis, won't have welcome news for Marcel. He was foolish to think he could be a hero to his brother. A second son can never be a hero; every second son in France knows that.

It's not in his nature to intervene in his brother's affairs, but at least he'll get to watch Adrien's child grow up in Natchez. He can write to Marcel from time to time and report on the girl's welfare. Marcel will never lay eyes on this American child, unless he takes it into his head to visit Natchez, which isn't an impossibility.

A sadness washes over him. His own life will lead nowhere, he thinks. When he was a young man he thought he'd rise in the church, but given his age now, he knows he won't. His life can return to what it's become: the church, the rectory, the tower from which he views the town. And the people, ranked into levels of society in this scrabbling place: all the follies humankind can dream up are on display here. Every sin, every nobility. Fate has assigned him a place from which to view it all, to be a watcher, not a participant. To rescue a Creole child was beyond his reach. She'll grow up in this slave-holding world, protected by Carson and a free mother. Her life will have its dangers, though, when she marries.

He walks up the steps to Saint Mary's and opens the door. The church is dark inside, candles flickering along the walls. After the bright sunlight, his eyes take a moment to adjust, and he blinks.

He slips into the last pew, as he usually does when he comes in solitarily to pray. Saint Mary's is familiar to him now, and it comforts him to be here. Only a couple of parishioners are in the church, dark rounded shapes kneeling here and there.

Pray, he commands himself, but the visit to Carefree has been a rend in the fabric of the day. The girl Jenny—he can see why Adrien loved her, even though she was an awkward teenager then. Today, he saw the easy beauty in her inky-black face.

He kneels and closes his eyes. After a moment he hears a rustling sound as someone slips into the pew in front of him. He opens his eyes. The woman hasn't settled herself yet. She looks to one side and her black mantilla frames what he can see of her profile. She glances around at him and then looks away.

He sits back in the pew, his prayers forgotten. Seeing her sweeps him back twenty years to his younger self, to the man he was with her. Over the years Cecilia's become like a ghost to him, a memory wrapped in gauze. But here she is, the curve of her neck the same as he remembers, and the way she clasps her hands together so delicately—he remembers that.

His heart races, and he smiles. He can't help himself. The sun may shine on his old face yet. An old sin, remembered, is beckoning. And he thinks, surely as a priest this isn't the thing that should brighten his life. But here she is, not five feet from him, and look how she kneels so quietly, so gracefully.

Surely he mustn't reawaken the joys of his youth. But the joys rise before him now, because perhaps he can be more than a man with a quiet future. Cecilia is here, not a ghost at all, but a solid form in this quiet, darkened church.

And after all, doesn't the Lord move in a mysterious way?

CHAPTER TWENTY-SIX

A YEAR LATER EUPHONIA HAS RECOVERED ENOUGH to sit on the gallery for an hour or two each day. She can't yet walk well, and her attempts at using Cornelius's cane have been awkward because it's so heavy, so she's taken to using Jane's old walking stick, which Jenny pulled out from under the bed in the Dependency.

For a long time after the accident, Euphonia would turn her face away from Cornelius, not wanting him to look at her; but in recent months she's begun to face him squarely, not concerned about the scars that snake across her face from her eyebrow to her upper lip. They never speak directly of the accident, but the last time he sat with her on the gallery she turned to him and said, "Did you know that a cotton bale is hard as concrete when it's wet?" But he didn't answer.

Most days Jenny goes upstairs to help Phony brush her hair and button the pretty dresses the woman likes to wear, even on these days when she sees no one outside the household. Phony sometimes brushes her own hair, but she usually can't catch all the loose strands in the tortoiseshell combs she pins it up with, and she's always grateful for Jenny's help. Since the accident left her helpless and convalescing, Phony's turned meek.

Jenny's taken pity on Euphonia, and helps her when she can. And

Rosabel is a spark of brightness. Often the child walks along with Euphonia, holding her hand as Euphonia's cane taps across the floor. When the three of them sit on the gallery, Phony folds her hands quietly in her lap like an old woman would, and Rosabel plays with the half-grown kittens that some stray abandoned under the steps. Jenny usually brings her sewing. Phony can't see well enough to sew, but the two women talk about Jenny's sewing projects. They have a companionship based on the fabrics and threads they're both knowledgeable about, as country women.

Today Phony fans herself with her folding fan and watches Jenny stitch a hem. "Is it something for Rosabel you're making?" she asks.

"Yes ma'am." Jenny holds up the partially-hemmed dress so Phony can see it. "I bought this fabric in the store yesterday. Ain't it pretty?"

"It is pretty." Phony reaches for the dress and holds it close to her eyes, fingering the fabric. "Did Rosabel help you pick it out?"

"Well, I picked it out, but she likes it."

"How'd you learn to sew?" Phony asks.

"Esther taught me. I came here to stay when I was twelve years old, after Miss Stephanie died. I don't think Esther figured I could learn anything else, so she taught me how to sew, and I got good at it. I used to make dresses for Helene and Theresa."

"I always wanted a little girl," Phony says, handing the dress back to her.

"I didn't know that."

"I did. 'Course when we got married we already had Thomas, but he ain't my child, not really. He's Hattie's child. You knew Hattie, didn't you?"

"Yes ma'am. I knew her when we was livin' in the Cocodrie. Thomas favors his mammy."

"He does. But I never expected to have any child of my own, boy or girl," Phony says.

"You never know, do you?" Jenny says.

"You think you might ever have another one?"

"I don't hardly think so. Since Walker's gone." Jenny ties a knot in the thread, winding the red thread over her finger and pulling it to tie a knot. "They don't just drop down out of the clouds, you know."

A moment later the door opens and Bo comes out, carrying a small infant wrapped in a white crocheted shawl. She lays him in Phony's arms.

"He's fed," Bo whispers. "And he's about to go to sleep, too."

Euphonia folds back the shawl so Jenny can see the infant's face.

"Ain't this one right pretty?" she says to Jenny.

"He is. Mighty pretty."

"He's a miracle, really. To think I'd have my own child, at my age."

"And Thomas has a little brother."

"He does. And Cornelius a second son."

"Yes ma'am."

"With my eyesight, I can't really make him out as good as I wish I could. Everybody tells me he's pretty."

"He makes me happy every time I look at him," Jenny says. "He has a good name, too: John Landerson Carson. It sounds like he'll grow up to be a man of importance."

"It does."

"Even though everybody's already callin' him Jack," Jenny says. "I think it's gonna stick."

Later, after Bo's taken the baby back inside, Jenny helps Phony back upstairs. Then she walks out to the kitchen to find Rosabel, who's gone to the kitchen to visit Dancy. When Jenny comes into the kitchen, Rosabel smiles, her upper lip covered by a cream mustache.

"When I was your age, they didn't give me coffee," Jenny says, reaching for a towel to wipe the girl's mouth.

"That's 'cause they didn't have coffee where you come from," Dancy says. "You bein' an African child."

"I was." She touches Rosabel's dark hair, and the girl pulls away from her. "I been sittin' with Miss Phony."

"How's Phony feelin' today?" Dancy asks.

"Not much different from any other day," Jenny says. "Bo brung out little Jack."

"If Phony ain't careful, Jack's gonna think Bo's his mammy, 'cause of the milk tie."

"Phony's a good mammy, much as she can be," Jenny says. "I guess it was good Bo had little Alice last winter. That baby was a surprise too, weren't she? I was surprised."

"We was all surprised. Elliot is sure proud of that young'un," Dancy says, "So yes, I think it was a good thing. And now Master Cornelius has got two boys, and neither one of 'em looks a thing like their daddy." She grins. "Well, I take that back. Little Jack does look like his daddy." She leans close to Jenny and whispers, " 'cause there ain't no way his daddy's Cornelius Carson. That babe's the spittin' image of John Landerson. 'Course, we ain't gonna say it to anybody out loud."

Jenny shrugs. "I expect Cornelius knows it."

When Jack is a year old he learns to walk by lurching himself across the gallery from one set of welcoming arms to another, and Cornelius asks Elliott to build a railing there to keep the boy from tumbling off. All day, the men—Elliott, Daniel, and Kofi—measure and saw and hammer, and then in mid-afternoon Kofi brings out the big can of white paint. By dark the project is finished.

"We'll need to let the paint set up for a few days, Miss Phony," Elliott says, coming into the parlor. "Y'all need to keep all the children out back. You don't want 'em to get themselves all messed up with paint."

"No, we don't," Phony says.

A week later, Jenny thinks the porch is ready, and she opens the front door so Thomas, Jack, and Rosabel can go out there. The older kids step out onto the porch and then run back and forth the length of the railing, squealing with laughter, while Jack toddles over to the railing and steps up on the bottom rail to hang his head and arms over the edge. Even at a year old, Jack has a handsome face with a strong jaw. It's not hard to see the man he'll grow into. He already has a sober, determined look and bright hazel eyes.

"Just like his daddy," Esther whispers to Jenny later, as they stand in the foyer and watch through the open door as Rosabel rolls a ball down the gallery toward the little boy. Cornelius, wearing his white suit, comes down the stairs with Euphonia and guides her out to the gallery. She sits on the settee and he sits on the wicker chair beside her.

"The new railing looks good," he says to Phony. Jack toddles over and Cornelius lifts him to his knee.

Esther comes out and reaches down to take the boy. "He might get fussy before long," she says. "Do you want me to get Bo to feed him so he'll sleep?"

"Oh, let him stay out here with us a while," Cornelius says. "I'll bring him in later." He sits the boy up on his knee and pulls a piece of soft divinity candy from his pocket. He unwraps the waxed paper wrapping and pops the candy in the boy's mouth.

CHAPTER TWENTY-SEVEN

New Orleans
1849

IN JULY THE AIR SHIMMERS WITH HEAT from dawn till sunset every day. Clouds stand around the edges of the sky, gray elephantine hulks rimmed in white; but no rain comes. The city is experiencing a slowly rising putrefaction, and holding its breath. Nothing washes it clean. All over town cisterns grow emptier as mosquitoes wriggle in the sinking darkness of each echoing cylinder.

On the last Sunday in July, May and Lulie walk down to the French Quarter. They usually only get to go out once a week, on Sunday, so it's always a special occasion.

"Don't we look fine today," Lulie giggles; she's put on her new straw bonnet and pushed her brown curls up under it. Both girls wear the same style of pale blue checked dress. Miss Parlenge wants the girls to dress alike, for some reason; she picked up that idea somewhere, that the girls working in her house should wear the same dresses, like uniforms. *We look like ridiculous twins*, May's thought many a time: same pale-checked dresses, same aprons that used to be white. But Lulie doesn't complain about their clothes.

But at least May's checked dress fits her well enough; she's outgrown both of the dresses she brought from Carefree five years ago. Her legs got so long the hems of her dresses were hanging halfway down her shanks, something Miss Parlenge would never stand for.

"It's not decent," she said after May'd been wearing the same two dresses for a year. "I think I'll get you girls some new dresses." Thinking of getting new clothes made May and Lulie giggle with excitement; but then Miss Parlenge said they'd be dressing alike, which they both thought was stupid, although they could only say so to each other.

May looks over at Lulie. Lulie's a thick-built girl and she kind of lumbers when she walks. May's noticed how clumsily Lulie handles the china when she sets the table for Miss Parlenge's dinner, and how sturdily she moves when she sweeps the front walk. But she likes the way Lulie lets her take charge. It's May who decides where they'll go every Sunday, and they've seen so much that New Orleans has to offer— they've even been to Congo Square, tiptoeing along behind the bushes and watching the slaves do their African dances, the men leaping with sharp hoots as the women sway in their red and yellow dresses.

Today, as they walk toward the Vieux Carre, the air changes: it's older air, May thinks, the kind that smells of the river and the French Market. Shops are open, and the girls wander in and out, looking at hats and cookware and antiques, handling everything unless the shopkeepers tell them not to.

"This place is sure noisy today," Lulie says as they walk along the dock. "I never heard so much racket."

About that time a seagoing ship, the *Christine*, noses up to the dock at the foot of Canal Street with a creaking and clanging sound that May remembers. The girls stop and watch as sailors throw the ropes to the dock. Then the passengers stumble down the gangplank, and they look like skeletons, May thinks: skinny men in bent-over stove-top hats, and bony women in patched dresses and holey knitted shawls. Up on the deck the sailors scramble around like monkeys.

The girls stroll down to the French Market, which doesn't interest them much. Mrs. Parlenge has the cook buy the food there, and she usually brings Lulie or May along to help, so the girls have seen the place many times.

They turn up St. Ann Street, with no particular destination in mind. The houses here are built close together and open right onto the sidewalk. When they reach Burgundy Street, May looks as she always does for the yellow house where she stayed with Jenny, way back when she was just a little kid right off the boat. And there it is, and it still looks like no one's living there. She wonders if Margot is still living on the patio behind Madame Devrot's house, and she thinks sometime she should go see Margot, just slip in through the gate and say "Hi." Wouldn't Margot be surprised? But she never does. Today she points down Burgundy Street and they walk right past the yellow house.

Lulie looks around. "May, where are you takin' us? I never been in this part of town."

"I used to stay in that yella house over there," May says.

"This ain't even a real street. You think this is a shortcut back to Miz Lacey's? This don't look so good."

"No, it don't."

The street becomes an alley, a dark passageway of buildings with doors closed on both sides. Up ahead is a window with a net curtain, and a blond haired woman is sitting on a windowsill looking out into the alley. The girls walk past her, not looking at her, and then May glances back. She stops and stares.

"Celestina, is that you?"

The woman, picking at the edge of her shawl, looks up at the two girls. Then she slips off the sill and disappears into the dark room.

May runs over and puts her hands on the high windowsill, standing on tiptoe so she can peer over it.

"Celestina? Don't you remember me? I'm May, the girl in Natchez. 'Course, I was littler then. You told me I could sing on the showboat."

The yellow-haired woman is just a dim form in the darkness until she walks back to the window, where the girls can see her. She stares at May. "Oh, yeah, I remember you. You that girl with the big voice. You was just a young child then. You look all grown up now."

"I'm fourteen."

Celestina looks up and down the alley. "What y'all doin' in this part of town?"

"We just out for a walk," May says. "You still got the showboat? I looked for it when I come to New Orleans, but I couldn't find it."

"I ain't got it no more. We had to sell it for timber when we got here. So we broke it up and sold it board by board."

"Didn't you want to put on a show here?"

Celestina fiddles with a little silver tin. She opens it and dabs red color on her lips, which May's never seen anyone do.

"We tried to put on a show a couple of times, Henry and me, but we couldn't raise a crowd," Celestine says. "People gettin' off the boat, they ain't wantin' to stop and see a show, they just want t' get on into the city. So our money run out pretty quick, and Henry decided we had t' sell the boat."

"Is Henry someplace 'round here too?"

"Yep, he is." Celestina looks back over her shoulder into the room.

"What'd y'all do with Evie?" When Celestina doesn't answer, May turns to Lulie. "Evie was the biggest snake you ever saw." She turns back to Celestina. "Tell Lulie what kinda snake it was."

Celestina shrugs. "I ain't real sure."

"What happened to her?"

For a moment she thinks Celestina didn't hear the question, because the woman pats her yellow hair into place and tugs her gossamer dressing gown up under her armpits. Then Celestina looks at Lulie and grins. "We were keepin' 'er in a cage down below, but when we was stopped for the night at Saint Francisville, somebody musta forgot to lock the cage. 'Cause Anton —" she stops and looks around. "I don't know, but that night Anton went down there to sleep like he always did, and Evie got loose. The next mornin' we fount him dead in his bunk with that snake coiled right around him. I'm the one who fount him. His face was plumb purple."

May stares at her, picturing the scene. Lulie stands with her mouth open.

Celestina takes a deep breath. "So that was the end of that."

May wonders if she means Anton or Evie. "What happened to Evie?" she asks.

"She's gone. Henry and me turned her loose in the swamp. There wasn't nothin' we could do about Anton bein' dead, so we just pitched him right off the side of the boat into the river with Evie still wrapped around him like a rope. He sunk, and Evie just unwrapped herself so quick and slithered on off. I reckon she's likin' livin' out in the swamp."

May pictures it, the snake cage with the lock hanging broken, and the sleeping Anton. She looks at the woman's slender arms; there'd been purple bruises up and down her arms back then.

"So what you doin' livin' in this alley?" May asks.

Celestine shakes her head. "Henry says I gotta work. What y'all doin' down here? This ain't no street for girls like you."

Lulie pulls at May's arm, but May ignores her. "We just out for a walk. We work for Miss Parlenge over that way."

"What you do for her?"

"Cleanin' and laundry. And she pays us. When I got to New Orleans I looked for your boat every Sunday I had off. I walked up and down the dock lookin' at the flatboats, but I never saw no *Merry Belle*."

"You the orphan girl, ain't ya? What was your name again?"

"May Carson. This is Lulie."

Celestina looks at Lulie, and then says, "Say, y'all gonna be here awhile? Lemme get dressed; I'll come visit with ya."

She ducks back into the dark room. May and Lulie sit down on the steps leading up to the closed door. Lulie wrinkles up her nose.

"This alley smells like puke," she says.

When Celestina comes out a few minutes later she's wearing a regular gray dress with a white collar and puffed sleeves. The three of them walk down the alley and out into the street. Celestina points to the left and they turn to where the street forks in two and there's a bench and some bushes in the triangle. They sit on the bench, wriggling together to make room, looking up and down the street, May and Lulie on either side of Celestina in her puffed-sleeve dress.

Margot strides down Burgundy Street, gripping her purse. Her heels click on the brick sidewalk. She's come from a hard delivery that took all night, before a girl named Yvette—too young to be birthing a baby and with a narrow build to boot—gave birth to a wailing boy. Which was a relief, because for several hours Margot thought the babe would never make it out; but he did.

The houses along here are mostly empty, and she hardly ever walks this way. It's kind of a spooky street, she thinks, because the people who used to live here were just squatters and then one day they were all sold back into slavery. They had no business living in these shanty houses in the first place.

At the corner she stops. Three young women are sitting on a bench near the corner. They're an odd sight: two girls, one large, one small, in matching checked dresses, and one of them wearing a straw hat like a farmhand. The other girl has a long unpretty face. A blond-haired woman sits between them.

Margot stops and stares at the smaller girl. *Is that May?* She looks so much older than Margot remembers, but then it's been a long time since May showed up unexpectedly on her patio, wanting Margot to take her in. Well, that wasn't gonna happen, especially now that Margot's finally got her business built back up. And it'll stay built up.

The three girls get up and saunter off down the street. Margot watches them until they turn at the corner. Then she hurries down the street toward her patio home. She doesn't need to pick up trouble.

"I can't go too far away," Celestina says, looking over her shoulder. "Henry'll come lookin' for me."

"Why's he carin' where you go?" May asks.

"He thinks I work for him," Celestina says.

They're sitting on the curb in front of a saloon on Toulouse Street, their knees pulled up under their skirts. A rag picker driving a cart down the street grins at them.

"You like working for Henry?" May asks Celestina.

"Hell no, I don't," Celestina says.

"Why you doin' it then?"

Celestina shrugs. "It's the only way I can get money."

"You ever think you might get back on a showboat?" May asks.

"Shoo, I'd like to. That was fun." She wriggles a little and picks at her puffed sleeves to fluff them up. "Except for Anton. He wasn't fun. But he's dead now."

"When you was on the showboat, wasn't you scared when he shot at that apple on your head? I woulda been terrified."

"Girl, I was so scared. But I figured he wasn't gonna kill me, since I was the main attraction. So I just kept smilin'." She smiles a wide false smile to show her teeth.

"I saw how bruised you was. Your arms," May says.

Celestina pushes up her sleeves to expose her white arms. "They all healed up now. The kinda work I'm doin' now, I gotta look good."

"What kinda work you doin' now?" May asks. When Celestina doesn't answer, she says, "Me, I'd like to be on a showboat."

Lulie looks over at her, the whites of her eyes big. "What's a showboat?"

"It's a boat with a stage and ever'thing," May says. She stands up and looks up and down the street. The French Quarter is in motion: horses clop down the street, rough-faced stevedores head over to the dock, dark women with baskets on their heads saunter along the sidewalk, their wide hips swinging.

"Okay. Here's what," May says. She points at Celestina. "You don't like workin' for Henry?"

"I told you I don't."

"And I don't like workin' for Miss Parlenge. And neither does Lulie here."

Lulie grins bashfully, her full face dimpling.

"Well, us three—we got some money, ain't we? I got ten dollars I saved up myself," May says.

"I got twelve dollars in my coat pocket back at the house," Lulie says. "I'm good at savin'."

A donkey cart goes by, the driver looking at them curiously. Celestina glances around and then says in a low voice, "I got twenty-seven dollars sewed in my mattress that Henry don't know about."

May walks back and forth along the curb. "Listen, y'all, why don't we take our money and get us a steamboat ticket and head up to Natchez. We don't have to tell Lacey Parlenge one thing. Lulie and me can get our money, and Celestina, you get your money outta your mattress and sneak away from Henry. We all got enough money for a ticket."

"Why would we want to go to Natchez?" Celestina and Lulie ask at the same time.

" 'Cause I know where we can get us a showboat," May says, and all three of the girls squeal with happiness.

CHAPTER TWENTY-EIGHT

ESTHER LOOKS THROUGH THE KITCHEN WINDOW as three young women she doesn't know walk up the path that leads to the back gallery. She stares, thinking at first it must be some farm women selling peas, but she doesn't need any today. Or they might be handing out religious tracts, like the Presbyterians sometimes do, but she doesn't need any of those either. Or they might be friends of someone who lives here. Harriett's made friends around town, and nobody at Carefree seems to know much about them. But Harriet's a talkative happy girl, devoted to Kofi; and Kofi's friendly to everyone, too.

As they walk closer, the girls stop where the path forks, one way leading to the big house and the other way to the Dependency, and they seem to be discussing which direction to take. Esther folds her dishtowel and lays it on the table. She walks to the door so she can watch them more closely. In moments like this she misses Walker Jackson. He used to intercept any unwanted visitors down at the drive. It's not that Carefree is a house of hermits, but it's comfortable to keep the town at bay.

The girls walk up the brick walk toward the big house. Esther stares at the girl who's walking ahead of the others. Her light brown hair hangs to her shoulders, and she's wearing an odd get-up, some kind of white shimmery skirt that's too short. When the girl looks back toward the kitchen, Esther sees that her eyes are big as a raccoon's eyes, with rings around them painted blue.

Esther turns back to the fried chicken that's sizzling in the skillet over the fire. Moving the skillet off the fire, she suddenly realizes who it is, and she sits down at the table, hard.

"Oh my lands."

She hurries up the path behind them and runs into the house. The girls are standing in the back hall looking around as if they've never seen the inside of a house before.

"Mister Cornelius and Miss Phony ain't here right now," she stammers. It's all she can think to say.

May sits on the velvet chair in the parlor. Esther's given her a cup of coffee, piled high with cream and sweet with sugar the way she used to like it, and for the past hour May's felt like a circus exhibit with a stream of watchers staring at her. The other girls are sitting outside on the back step.

Dancy comes in after Esther, wiping her hands on her apron and staring.

"You're so much bigger," Dancy says.

"I'm fourteen," May says.

"We all thought you was just a runt when you was here before."

"So I grew."

"What's that get-up you wearin'?"

May runs her hands over her crinoline skirt. "This is what I wear when I sing on the showboat. Celestina gave it to me."

"Girl, didn't none of us here ever know you sung a note," Dancy says.

"I bet Miss Coella could tell you I did."

Dancy shrugs. "Well, you are a sight for sore eyes, girl."

Then Coella herself comes back to the house from taking Thomas to the creek, and when she walks down the hall with the barefoot boy, she glances into the parlor and then walks in.

"May?" she says, as if her eyes are conjuring up a ghost.

May stands up.

Coella walks over. "Is that you?"

"It's me."

"How'd you get so big?"

"I grew."

Coella looks up and down at May's clothes. "Why you dressed like that?"

"It's what I'm gonna wear for singin' on the boat."

"What?"

A buggy rumbles up to the front gallery. A moment later Cornelius and Phony come into the house. Cornelius walks down the hall, glancing into the parlor, and keeps going. A moment later he stands in the doorway staring at the girl sitting there. There's a long silence. Then he says, "Is it really you?"

Jenny stands up. "Yes sir. It's me. I'm just bigger now, like everybody says. I'm fourteen."

"How long have you been gone?"

"Well, I was nine, so I guess it's five years."

Euphonia appears in the doorway. Cornelius helps her to the sofa. After she's settled, he bends down to her and says, "Look, Phony, May's come back."

Phony squints at the girl, who sits with her too-short crinoline skirt spread out around her, her ankles crossed.

"I never knew why she left," Phony says.

"Why *did* you leave?" Cornelius asks.

May says, "I figured I oughter bring the spelling book back. It weren't mine. Look." She reaches into her sack and takes out the battered brown book that says *Byerly's New American Speller* on the front. "I wrote my name inside it, right below Miss Stephanie's name. I figured y'all might need it for some other child. Maybe Thomas."

They all nod in unison, which makes May giggle.

"Where did you go?" Cornelius asks.

"Why'd you come back?" Phony asks.

Everyone on the place comes in to stare at May. After a few minutes Cornelius invites Lulie and Celestina into the parlor, and the three girls sit side by side on the sofa in their too-short skirts, their ankles crossed primly, and their eyes outlined in paint.

Later, when Euphonia goes upstairs with Cornelius, she sits on the side of the bed and faces him squarely.

"I can hardly believe —" she begins. "And did you see her friends? My word, Cornelius, we can't have those girls staying in the house."

"Phony, May's come back. After all these years. Surely we can accommodate —"

"Oh, but can't you see what they are? In those get-ups and with that paint on their faces? Especially Celestina. What will people think —"

"I don't imagine they'll think much at all, since we have so few visitors. The girls can stay here, and things will sort themselves out. What harm can it do?"

Euphonia frowns and gets up to look out the window. "I felt so sad when May disappeared. I felt I hadn't been warm enough toward her, and that plagued me after she left. But Esther had taken her on, and I thought, if she needed a mother, Esther filled that spot better than I ever could."

"Don't torment yourself. You did the best you could. And we did give the girl an education."

"But now she's back, with these friends, and you can see what they are."

"All I see are three young ladies who're starting out in life. May's only fourteen, but Celestina and Lulie can't be past twenty. They're just kids, really."

"I'd sure like to know where Celestina comes from. And who can tell anything about Lulie." Euphonia's face is bitter. "And you know people will talk."

Well, I do know that, he thinks.

An hour later the afternoon light is beginning to fall through the blinds in Cornelius's study. May sits in the leather chair.

"You need *how much*?" he asks.

"Maybe a few hundred dollars to get started, if you could spare 'em. Mostly we need a boat. So we can put on the show up and down the river. It'll have to be a steamer, but it don't have to be big. A little one'll do."

He looks out the window, where the hickory tree leaves form a canopy of green. "May, when you left, it practically destroyed us here. I want you to know that. Now you're back, and we're all glad, but you can't do that ever again. You can't disappear again."

"No sir, I wouldn't."

He stares at her, trying to see the child he remembers in the mature young woman in front of him. He's glad to finally have May back here, but Euphonia's already made it clear that she doesn't want May's two odd sidekicks remaining in the house for one minute longer than necessary. Euphonia always has one eye on what townspeople might think.

"Now, what about your friends?"

"So, us three'll be in the show, and we'll run the boat too. Lulie's strong; she can be the pilot good as a man. And Celestina knows the acts. I'll sing, too. I'm a good singer."

"It takes more than three women to run a steamboat."

"Yes sir, but if we had a man to help Lulie, and one more act, we'd be set. I think I'll see if Jenny would like to be an act, too."

"I've never seen Jenny do any act. And I don't know that she'd be interested." *She didn't want to go to France,* he thinks. He remembers how quickly she rejected that idea when the priest came to present his brother's proposal.

"I bet she might want to do an act," May repeats.

"And she has Rosabel to see to. You couldn't take Rosabel on the boat."

May leans forward, her hand under her chin. "No sir, couldn't do that. Showboat's no place for a young child." She looks out the window, her brow furrowing.

"Well, I can probably find you a boat," Cornelius says. "If you're determined." He shuffles the papers on his desk. "Lately I've been getting all these advertisements in the mail, and they're for boats of all kinds. Some are for steamboats. People who own boats always want to sell them sooner or later, provided they don't sink in the meantime."

"We're very determined." She stands up. "Thank you." She puts her hand out. Surprised, he stands up and shakes her hand.

"You need more than four people to run a steamboat. I'd say five or six anyway, even for a little boat."

"Yes sir."

"Well, you and your friends can stay in the house here 'til I locate a boat. But I warn you, everybody here's gonna want to keep tight tabs on you. We'll lock the doors and hide the keys. Give me some time to see what I can find. Then we can go look at a couple of boats," he says, shuffling the papers on his desk. "Only because I'm so glad you're back, and I'm so relieved you're all right. Even if I think your plan is crazy."

"No sir. It ain't crazy. You ain't heard me sing."

"No, I ain't."

May grins at him and goes out the back door, where Celestina and Lulie are sitting on the steps, waiting.

"Ladies, we're gonna get a boat!" she squeals.

"See, this is what I don't like," Josephine says as Lucy Ida crowds up against her, their bones rattling in the chilly air. The whole attic's been restless for a week, or a month, since ghosts have no sense of time. But those who complain tend to keep doing it, and those who wear big grins showing their teeth are the same as they were in life. It's only Littleton and August who have happy outlooks; they were so young when they died, their outlooks didn't have time to harden, and today they've left the attic to head into town. But Carefree's never been a happy place, they all know that, so they're used to giving in to whatever sourness or meanness they feel.

"What's that, Miss Josephine?" Lucy Ida asks, trying to pull the old quilt off Stephanie, who's lying below the one window examining her fingernails like a teenager. She protests when Lucy Ida succeeds in getting the quilt, a sound like the branch of the hickory tree scraping across the roof over their heads. But Lucy doesn't give it back.

"The way August and Littleton are always flyin' off into Natchez. Those boys oughter stay home. They got no business bein' out there in town. They're gonna cause trouble," Stephanie says.

"They always say Cornelius needs help," Lucy Ida chatters. "So I say let 'em go. Where was it they was goin' today, anyway?"

"Down into town. Canal Street," Emile says. "I'd go too, if I could."

"I think you better stay here," Josephine says. "You ain't got good sense goin' out in town. You remember how you sent me to Washington."

"I said bury it, woman," he jabbers, holding his bones up in front of this face.

"August says he's gotta see a man about a boat," Stephanie says.

"Cornelius makin' a trip?" Emile asks.

"We ain't never had a boat at Carefree," Josephine says. "This is the most landlubbin' place in all of Mississippi."

"Cornelius ain't a sailor. But I did hear him say he had a job on a boat one time," Stephanie says.

"We know how that turned out," Lucy Ida hisses. "That boat's at the bottom of the river."

"Man gets in trouble if he don't stick to what he knows. Look at that boat he built. It nearly cost him his wife," Emile says.

"He coulda married so much better," Lucy Ida says, "fine lookin' man like him. I don't know what he seen in that Euphonia."

They ignore this. It's the same thing they all say from time to time.

"He's got even less to see in her now," Josephine says, meanly. "Her face is a scarred up mess."

"Y'all hush," says Emile. "There ain't no causes to be pokin' at a woman who's down."

They all go quiet, but they know there'll be more to say when the wind quits howling outside, because ghosts have no basic kindness in their bones; and they like to complain about changes in the weather.

CHAPTER TWENTY-NINE

"THAT'S THE PRETTIEST BOAT I EVER SEEN!" May says two weeks later as she stands on the bank of Saint Catherine Creek with Cornelius, staring at the little steamer listing in the brown water.

"It'll serve your purpose," Cornelius says.

"What's her name?" Jenny asks.

Cornelius points. "Well, it says *General Lafayette* right there. It's faded."

Lulie snorts. "This puny boat can't be no *General Lafayette*."

"Well, that used to be its name. You can name it whatever you want."

"It's pretty, so it oughter have a lady's name," Lulie says.

"Well, call it *Martha Washington* then," Cornelius says.

"You think Martha Washington would ever ride on a tiny boat like this?" May asks.

Cornelius shrugs. "Probably not."

May glances at Cornelius, not sure if he really wants to change the name. "It'd make a showboat, wouldn't it? It's got room to have passengers sit inside. We can't do one of them shore shows, because none of us can talk loud enough. We need to be inside. I guess we could do the apple-shootin' inside too, if there's room enough. And if we're sure the shot goes out the door."

"You'd better be sure there's nobody out on the shore who's in the way."

"No sir. We'd always aim out at the river," May says.

"Try not to shoot any boys on a flatboat."

May studies the boat. It's three stories high, although the top is just the captain's roost. And it's painted bright white, which makes it stand out here on the creek bank. A jaunty red stripe is painted around the decks, so it looks like a giant layer cake. It's a sternwheeler, and the paddle wheel is painted red too.

"A man had it up at Memphis," Cornelius says. "But he wanted something bigger. I figure you could sit twenty or thirty people in there. Y'all could sleep above decks. I think six of you could handle it."

"If we can get that many," May says. "I'm havin' trouble persuadin' Kofi, with Harriet about to drop her young'un. So far, we've got me, Lulie, Celestina. Maybe Jenny, like I said. Maybe Kofi, maybe not. I'm thinkin' Daniel might join up too, and he'd be handy to have. Him and Lulie could handle the wood."

"Remember, when you're out on the Mississippi, it's serious business. You've got to know how to navigate, and you'll have steamers and flatboats all around."

"Oh, we can figure it out. It can't be that hard. I seen those flatboats, and you know those flatboatmen don't know a thing about running the river."

"Well, that's true enough," Cornelius says. "Who's gonna be the captain?"

"That'll be either me or Lulie," she says. "And I don't want to call this pretty boat the Lady Lafayette. I'd say let's call her the *Merry May*. 'Cause it's a happy name, and it's gonna be a happy boat."

"You're namin' it after yourself?"

"Sure. Why not? And we're workin' up a good show. Give the people their money's worth."

"How much you gonna charge?"

"Five cents."

"That's not enough. Charge ten cents, since you're bringing 'em onboard."

"Okay."

"And for my investment, I'll need ten percent of the ticket sales."

She frowns. "I thought you were givin' us this boat."

"I'm loaning it to you. This boat's in my name. You might get tired of bein' a show, and then I want the *Merry May* back in good condition."

"Okay. But we are gonna *love* doin' a show. It's the best thing in the world."

It's raining, and the ghosts are huddling against the dampness, as if they feel the chill, but they don't.

"I feel the cold," Josephine says. "I always did."

"You ain't really feelin' it now, Miss Josephine," Littleton says. "It's just somethin' you're used to, wrappin' yourself in a shawl even though it's still summer. It ain't because it's cold up here."

"How do you know what I'm feelin'?" she snaps. "These old bones—"

"That's what I mean," he mutters and then sinks back rattling into the spot he's claimed for himself, between the rafters.

"We gettin' too crowded up here anyway," Josephine says.

"Miss Josephine, just let it go," August says. "You ain't got no reason to complain."

"Too crowded," she says again, hooking her thumb back toward the far end of the attic; in the dusty motes under the eaves, a new form has appeared. It sits half-hidden behind some boxes of Miss Stephanie's old china that she left here when she took herself off to the Bayou Cocodrie with Mister Cornelius.

August rises, dust flying up from the attic floor and hovering around him like a cloud, the motes dancing. "Well, I'm not sure I've met this new person."

"It ain't a person," Lucy Ida says. "You know that."

"Who then?" August asks her.

She shrugs.

"I'll go see." August shakes his bones and floats toward the far side of the attic, where all of Miss Stephanie's childhood things are strewn— boxes of baby clothes, a trunk of crocheted blankets, even a two-story playhouse. Under the slanted rafters a small round window lets a little light in, and he sees her. He didn't need the light.

"You new here," he says.

She looks up at him but says nothing.

He shakes his bones. "Just come on in. I think Lucy Ida saw you floatin' right through that lattice. And with all this rain. It ain't right you had to travel on such a stormy day." Then he smiles, because whether the day is stormy or not doesn't matter to shades.

"I reckon you come a long way, ain't ya, Auntie?"

Still silence. Then she rises, shaking her own bones, and the scrap of red cloth around her skull turns loose, exposing the round white orb.

He sits down on an old washtub that's turned upside down. "Well, now, it's mighty good of you to come visit us, or ain't you plannin' to stay from here on out?"

She chatters, he can sense it, but no words come that he can understand. He picks up the scrap of red cloth that's lying on the attic floor.

"This here's your tignon," he says, holding it out to her. She extends her hand and takes it.

"Now that's an interesting pattern. That ain't somethin' I've seen around Natchez," he says. "The way them diamond designs are put on there together. I'm thinking you come a long way to be here. So whose bones are you?"

Her head falls down on her chest.

He thinks. "Well, you ain't one of this household. Are you sure you s'posed to be here? You got the right address?"

She raises her head and rises halfway, then settles again.

"You ain't from around here, that's for sure," he says.

At the other end of the attic, Lucy Ida hisses at Josephine, who's moved over to her space and spread herself out. "What's that foolish August sayin' to that shade?" she harps, but the only sound in the attic is the pounding rain outside and a *thunk* on the roof as a branch falls on the roof. "We got so many now, and we know who we are. We all belong to Carefree, and Mister Cornelius. We don't need no newcomers crowdin' us out."

Littleton chatters, "You hush that talk now, Aunt Lucy. Look at August; he's over there just bein' polite, like our mammy taught us to be. Didn't your mammy teach you your manners?"

"Shoo, I dunno. I ain't seen her since I was in Caroline, more than sixty years ago. I don't know what she might'a taught me. But I tell you what, if we take on a newcomer, I don't want it to be James Foster."

"Who's that?"

"My old master's boy, back in Caroline. The ugliest man for a white man you ever saw."

"Well, he won't be comin' here."

"He better not be. If he did, I'd pick up that ole skillet over there and hit him over the head with it. I'd kill 'im."

269

"Too late for that, Miss Lucy," Littleton says. "He's already dead." He looks over at the dim eave where August is sitting with the newcomer. Then August floats up, holding the newcomer's hand.

They reach the place where the other shades sit, bones all. The others look up and study the small woman who's holding August's hand.

"This here's Jenny's ma," he says. "She come from Africa."

There's a sound like an owl hooting that sounds among them, while the rain lashes the roof just over their skulls.

"And she don't talk like we do."

"We don't talk at all," Josephine says.

"Well, you know what that means," Emile says. They all turn to look at him; he speaks so seldom.

"She come a long way. I hope Jenny ain't still lookin' for her," Josephine says.

Littleton reaches up and pulls the bony form down to sit or crumple beside him. "You come stay by me, Mamma," he says. "Here's a nice rug you can have. And don't mind these others. We got plenty a room."

"I just don't think—" Lucy Ida begins, but then there's a sound like a whoosh of the wind through the little window, and Lucy Ida knows she's being shushed. So she settles deeper down into the pile she already is.

CHAPTER THIRTY

CORNELIUS STANDS ON THE BANK OF SAINT CATHERINE CREEK staring at the little steamer that sits listing at the side of the muddy creek. The *Merry May* has a jaunty look. She's rather pretty, he thinks, and perfect for the women's enterprise, if they can get their acts organized. They're still short at least one crew member. As of yesterday only four—May, Lulie, Celestina, and Daniel—had signed on, and he knew they needed another strong-backed man for the undertaking.

But it's coming together. This morning Felisa clumped into the house and knocked at his office door.

He stared at her. Of all the women he brought back to Carefree from Bayou Boeuf, Felisa is the one he knows the least. She's childless, and husbandless, as far as he knows; she drove the wagonload of slaves all the way back from Rapides Parish, and that couldn't have been an easy task. She sat before him wearing a plain calico dress, and he noticed for the first time her big shoulders. That strength carried twelve people, if you counted Daniel and George and Henry and their mothers, clear across the state of Louisiana. And she never once showed the slightest fatigue, or complained.

"Sir, I'd like to go on the boat with May and them others," she said.

"Do you know anything about steamboats?"

"No sir, but I'm strong, and I can learn. I reckon I know as much as Daniel—"

Cornelius chuckled.

"And I want to do it."

"Well, you don't need to ask my permission, you know."

"Yes sir, but I thought I should ask anyway. If I go, I won't be here to help Esther or Dancy with the cookin' and the washin' up. So I want to know if it's all right if I just go off. I been down there and looked at the steamboat, and I think I understand what they'll need. We got to have a captain though. A boat that's got no captain is gonna end up sunk right off."

"There won't be one experienced person on that boat."

"Yessir, but it ain't all that big."

"It's one thing to run up and down the bayous, or a little lake, but the Mississippi river's something else altogether."

"Yes sir."

He looked at her broad dark face. "Will you be in the show?"

She shook her head. "Oh no, sir. I ain't gettin' on no stage. I'm more the mechanical type."

"Why would you want to be part of this cockamamy scheme?"

"Well, I heard Celestina and May talkin' about it, and I got to thinkin', I ain't never been anywhere much. And ridin' on that steamboat, I'd get to see all kinds o' things. And places I never seen before. Places I always wondered about."

"Well, if you're wantin' to undertake the risk, I have no objection."

She stood up, a mountain of dignity, and extended her hand. "Thank you, sir."

"Well, that's a crew of five," he thought as the door closed behind her.

The next week, with rehearsals well underway, and the women talking and giggling together at all hours in the upstairs bedrooms, Cornelius begins to think the *Merry May* enterprise will be setting sail soon. He's still unsure about the crew, although from what he's heard through the bedroom doors he's pretty sure the show will be a hoot. But he's hoping Celestina doesn't embarrass the household with a raunchy show. Who knows what show's she's put on in New Orleans? Meanwhile, Euphonia's face shows her impatience more and more every day, as the noisy girls seem to have taken over the once-quiet house.

The next day a man on a powerful white horse rides up to the front gallery and dismounts. Mal sees him coming and walks through the center hall to greet him.

He sees a handsome young man, very tall, and well-dressed, with high leather boots and a well-tailored jacket. The visitor comes up the steps, taking two steps at a time.

"May I help you, sir?" Mal asks; the visitor is more a boy than a man, not out of his teens, even though his square jaw and blue eyes make him look mature.

Before the boy can answer, Cornelius comes out of his office and stands beside Mal, staring at the visitor. Then Cornelius says, "You're Freddy Landerson."

Mal steps back, frowning. "Who is this?"

Cornelius steps forward and shakes the stranger's hand. "I'm Cornelius Carson. I haven't seen you since you were about nine years old, but I still recognize you. You look a lot like your papa."

"Yes sir. I've been in Tupelo since Papa sent us to live with my aunt and uncle, me and my sister Lissy."

Cornelius escorts him into the parlor and they sit in the chairs near the fireplace while Dancy continues polishing the silver candlesticks that sit on the side table. Cornelius asks, "Is Lissy well?"

"She is."

"And what brings you to Natchez?"

"I told Uncle I can hardly remember Mama and Papa, and I didn't know where Mamma's buried, either, so I ought to come here to see the house where they lived. I thought it would make them real to me."

"Did you find the Elenora House?"

"Yes sir. I knocked on the door, but no one was home. But it looks like it's being lived in. It's a distinctive house, with that cupola on top. I remembered that. My uncle told me that Dad was proud of that house. I can see why."

"It's a local landmark. And how'd you find us here at Carefree?"

"My uncle gave me your name. He told me you were Papa's business partner."

"I was. It was tragic in the end, though."

Freddy nods. Then Euphonia comes into the room, carrying Jack, and Freddy stands up. Euphonia looks at the visitor curiously and hands the baby to Cornelius, who holds him on his knee.

"This is our younger son, Jack," Cornelius says. "Phony, this is Freddy Landerson. John Landerson's oldest boy."

Euphonia stares, her mouth open. "Oh, you are the very image of John," she says.

"Well, I guess we got somethin' else to talk about," Dancy says in a low voice as she scrapes the remains of breakfast out of the skillet into a bowl for the cats.

"I ain't talkin' about it, and you ain't neither," Esther says. "You just hush up."

"That boy's the spittin' image of his little brother," Dancy whispers, "and they both the spittin' image of Mister John Landerson, much as I can remember him."

"That man's been dead nigh unto three years, so I expect you ain't rememberin' him too clear," Esther says. "You let bygones be bygones. And you ain't thinkin' nothin' but what Mister Cornelius already knows, so just let it be. He's fond o' both his boys."

"What I think we got to talk about is how we gonna do all this work here, with everybody leavin' on that showboat. Daniel's goin', and Felisa is too. You better watch out, Helene'll decide she wants to go too."

"Helene says she ain't gettin' within a mile of that showboat," Esther says. "She's scared of water, so she don't want t' have *nothin'* to do with it. There won't be anybody here but Cornelius and Euphonia and the two boys. 'Course, Harriet and Kofi'll be here, but they take care of themselves. Coella can take care of the kids, and you and me and Helene can handle the housework and cookin'. And we won't have t' be cleanin' up after the mess Celestina and May and Lulie make. Them girls ain't never heard of hangin' up their clothes when they through with them, or doin' one lick of housecleanin'.'"

Riding up the hill to Carefree a week later, Cornelius pulls Eagle to a stop at the turn in the road and stares at his house. The morning's business has left him with an odd feeling; his business enterprises still need to be attended to, and even after the seasons of calamity his house has been through, there's still the ordinary affairs of life that take his attention. Before today he paid little attention to the townspeople and their gossip. Going to the bank and the post office are commonplace activities, but today for some reason he was aware of the stares and whispered comments that seem to follow him. Ever since the steamboat accident, he's felt like an outsider. He knows he's been a subject of talk. His wife and his business partner were together when the boat exploded, and that's set tongues wagging all over town.

He still feels the loss of John Landerson; his body had never been found.

And Euphonia's injuries were so severe, the doctor wasn't sure she could recover. She did, but with a scar that disfigured her pretty face. He thinks she won't ever be in the circle of women she was in before, because her disfigurement will forever advertise the accident, and the whispers will never end. It's a story that will be retold a thousand times, of Euphonia Carson and John Landerson, together on a doomed steamer.

Why did Euphonia decide to go down to see the steamer on the very night he had to go out of town? Had he been home, he would have told her to wait until he re-checked the welds. But he has no answer for his own question. It was just fate, he thinks. Such things usually are.

Staring at the big house, the white columns standing out starkly against the red bricks, Cornelius senses that a kind of darkness has settled over his house, even though it's a bright afternoon. For the past few months he's felt dusk settling on his spirit. Too much calamity can bring a house down as it brings a person down. A spirit can only take so much, before it twists into something altered from its true form. Even little Jack, a pretty, lively child, can't brighten his spirit. Euphonia had named the child for John, and Cornelius didn't object, knowing none of John's own children were named for him. But now he wonders if the boy should have been named something else. John Landerson Carson is a name with grace and balance, but Jack himself will always be a living memento of the ill-fated project, because of his name.

He rides up onto the lawn behind the house and ties Eagle by the back gallery. Going inside, he sees Euphonia coming down the stairs holding Jack's hand, and Jenny walking behind her carrying Phony's shawl. Jenny looks up at him, and something about her catches his attention. Her face has begun to set into a mask of sadness, too. She's too young to live her life as a widow, he thinks. He remembers her bright flashing eyes when she was a kid, working with him in the cotton fields; now she seems defeated and her eyes are dull.

Is she kidding herself that Walker Jackson will ever come back? He was sold into slavery and taken to Texas; can he get free and return to her? Should she spend her life hoping for something that can't happen? Isn't that just slavery of a different sort?

Later that day he summons her into the parlor.

"Yes sir?"

He motions her to sit down. Where did she get the idea that she had to stand in his presence? From her slavery days, he knows. Those days have taken away her sparkle, which should be hers by right.

"Jenny, I think you should go on the showboat."

She looks astonished. "No sir, I couldn't do that."

"They need another crewmember. They've only got five. They need at least six."

"It ain't that big a boat."

"You need to go."

"But what about Rosabel?"

"She can go too."

She looks at him, shaking her head.

"Why do you think I oughter go?"

"Because as long as you're here, you're taking on too much of the house, and too much of Euphonia and little Jack. You're starting to think they're your obligations. But you're young, and your life's spread out ahead of you. You need to grab your own gold ring."

She shakes her head. "I'm pretty sure May and the others won't want an old lady like me, with a small child, on the steamboat. And I don't have an act to do. Wouldn't I just be in the way?"

"No, you wouldn't," he says. "I'll talk to May. Plan on it."

Just before dark Jenny comes back into Cornelius's office. She sits down opposite him, frowning.

"Well, did May tell you about what they have planned?" he asks.

"Yes sir. And I'm gonna try it."

"I'm glad to hear that. Have you developed an act, or will you be just a deckhand?"

"I'll do an act. But since there's only five of us counting Daniel, I guess we'll all be deckhands when we need to be. There's just one or two things I need to ask you."

"Fire away."

"Rosabel can't go. I don't feel right takin' her on the boat. Somethin' might happen, and I'd never forgive myself. She'll have to stay here with Esther, and she'll be all right. Esther'll baby her just like I would. Rosabel's out at the kitchen all the time like it is."

"I don't doubt she'll be fine. You don't know how long this show's going to run anyway. I'm guessing y'all won't make too many trips, and then y'all might get tired of it all."

"Or I might get to missin' my baby so bad, and then I'd have to come back."

"Right."

"But here's the thing. While I'm gone, I want you to teach Rosabel to read. She shouldn't have to go around like me, not able to read a lick. When she grows up, she's got to know how to do it. Can Coella teach her along with Thomas? He's older so he's probably a little ahead, but Rosabel's almost eight, and she's smart. She'll catch up quick."

"I've noticed she's smart."

"But the thing is, if Coella's leaves like she's always threatenin' to, you'll have to teach her yourself."

He throws up his hands in mock horror. "Oh, no! I'd never make a teacher." The room's getting dark, and he reaches over to turn up the lamp.

"You could do it," Jenny says. "Somebody musta taught you."

He stares at her face, a dark oval. "'My mammy taught me, when I was just a little chap, since there wasn't no school around. Every morning we'd sit and study for an hour. She'd been to school herself, back in Charleston, before she married my daddy."

"You've got the spelling book. May brought it back. That way, when I come back off the boat, Rosabel can show me how she can read. I think it would make her real proud."

"It would make you proud too," he says.

"Oh yes! And you too!"

"Well, let's hope Coella sticks around," he says. "Have you got some act worked out for the showboat? Nothing to embarrass us all, I hope."

"Oh, no sir!" She puts her hand up to cover her mouth as she laughs.

"I only mention it because I've been to New Orleans," he says. "I know what those shows are like."

"That wouldn't be me," she says, giggling. "That'd be Celestina." When he rolls his eyes, she says, "Is Miss Euphonia around? I need to find some of my old clothes. I think they were in a trunk. Probably up in the attic."

"Why would you need your old clothes?"

" 'Cause I've got to make a costume if I'm gonna be in the show," she says, as if it should be obvious.

CHAPTER THIRTY-ONE

ON A SUNNY AFTERNOON TWO WEEKS LATER Cornelius and Euphonia drive down to look at the *Merry May* one more time. They go into the large room on the main deck where chairs are set up in front of a stage. Daniel and Freddy are busy hanging a curtain on a rope across the stage. May is supervising. When she sees them she walks over.

"Well, this is it," she says. "We'll have one more rehearsal tomorrow, and then we'll be ready to sail."

"Where will you start out?" Cornelius asks.

"I think we ought t' head up to Natchez first," she says. "There's been some people already comin' out to see what's goin' on here, so I think they'll be ready to see a show."

"Is Freddy going on the boat?" Euphonia asks.

"Yes'm, he says he wants to go," May says. "That gives us a crew of seven. We'll make it fine with that many."

"His aunt might not be so happy about that," Cornelius says. "But what she doesn't know —." He pauses in mid sentence. "And then you're headed upriver?"

"Yes sir. I think we'll just go on up at least as far as Cincinnati. Maybe all the way to Pittsburgh. There ain't gonna be no showboats on the river as good as this one."

"How will you summon your audience?" Cornelius asks.

"That there horn," May says, pointing to a French horn standing up in the corner. "I fount it up in the attic, and I didn't think you'd care if I took it."

"I don't care."

"We'll blow it loud when we get to a town, and people will come down to the shore to see the show."

"What acts have you cooked up?"

"I can sing," May says. "I've learnt a couple of good songs. And I can sing loud as anything. Then Celestina will sing. She knows all kinds of pretty songs. And Freddy says he's a crack shot; his uncle used to take him out hunting all the time, plus he's been practicing his marksmanship. But we ain't gonna take a chance on him hittin' an apple off Celestina's head. He might not be as good a shot as he thinks he is. We just gonna let him shoot a bullseye on a board. And Lulie can tell some of them strange stories she knows. I don't know where she got 'em from."

"And Jenny?"

May hesitates. "Well, she's got some stories to tell too."

"Daniel?"

"He won't be in the show. He's the woodsman and he'll watch the boiler. Lulie too. So I think we're ready. We been practicin', and if we find we need some different acts, we can work 'em up as we go."

"How long will this trip be?" Phony asks.

"If we get clear to Pittsburgh, I'd say three months, up there and back."

"It might be cold up there," Euphonia says. "Take your coats."

"I ain't sure Celestina's got a coat," May says. "You got one she can borrow?"

Celestina coughs behind her hand, looking at Cornelius.

"It'll be a grand adventure for all of you," Cornelius says, turning away and stifling a laugh.

May makes her hands into fists. "I can hardly wait," she says.

The following Wednesday, Elliott Badeau drives Cornelius, Euphonia, and Helene down to the river in Natchez. He turns the buggy onto the grassy slope next to Silver Street and parks it under a tree, where they can see the vista of the Mississippi.

"I'm not sure about this whole thing," Phony says. "Them goin' off this way."

"You wanted the girls out of the house," Cornelius reminds her. "They're young, Phony. Let them have some fun. With seven of them, they can look out for each other," Cornelius says.

"I'm not sure they will, the way they gossip and fuss."

"I went off on a big adventure when I was young," he says. "That's how I got to Louisiana. I came over here after my mammy died. I got a job on a steamboat, the *Abigail*, and I tell you, it was a whole lot sorrier than the *Merry May*."

"I thought you came here to be a farmer."

"Well, not at first. After the *Abigail* sank I took what money I had and bought that place on Bayou Cocodrie."

"I never was much for adventure," Phony says. "Too much can happen."

"It can," he says, reaching over to cover her hand with his own.

"I'm surprised Jenny wanted to go," Euphonia says.

"I talked her into it," he says.

She looks over at him, astonished. "Why?"

"Because she needs it. She just stays home at Carefree all the time, helping you and tending Rosabel. She needs to get out a little."

"This is kind of a big way to get out."

"It is."

"I'd rather she stayed. She's a lot of help to me."

"You'll get by."

After a few minutes they see the *Merry May* coming up the river like a little river princess, white smoke streaming prettily from her fanstacks and her sternwheel thrashing the water.

"Here they come," Cornelius says.

They get down from the buggy, Phony leaning on her cane, and walk down to the riverbank. As the boat gets closer, Cornelius sees Lulie in the captain's perch. She navigates the boat past three flatboats and a steamer called *Regulation* that's pulling out from Natchez. The *Merry May* noses close to the riverbank. Lulie cuts the engine and Freddy comes out and lowers the plank. He goes back inside and comes out a moment later with the French horn. He blows it with a loud "Whaaa", the sound reverberating up the slope. Travelers on Silver Street stop and gape.

Euphonia says, "You'll have to tell me what's going on. I can't see that well."

Daniel comes out, grinning when he sees them. He hangs a long banner on the side of the steamer: "Show today; ten cents. Three o'clock."

Cornelius is glad to see somebody on the crew knows how to spell; the bold red letters stand out against the white background.

Then Daniel and Freddy lower the gangplank, and Freddy positions himself at the bottom behind a small table with a sign that says "Tickets."

Cornelius buys three tickets, and then he takes Euphonia's arm as Helene follows behind. They walk up the gangplank and then step down onto the deck. The show will be in a large interior room that takes up most of the lower deck. Cornelius guides Euphonia and Helene to the third row of chairs, where they'll be close enough to see but not so close as to make the players self-conscious. In a few minutes the room is filling up. Freddy comes in again and looks around, counting the empty seats, and then goes back out.

There's a sound of cymbals clanging, and then the door is closed. The afternoon sun shines through the open windows, and a little breeze circulates. Freddy comes out and lights the oil lamps on the edge of the stage.

The audience grows quiet.

May comes out wearing a green glittery dress—that must be the one Jenny was working on, Cornelius thinks—and she says in a loud voice, "Friends, welcome. I'd like to sing you a song." When she sings "Sla-a-ck your rope, Hangman," her loud voice echoes from one side of the hall to the other. At the final verse, she wails,

True love have you brought me hope
Or have you paid my fee?
Or have you come to see me hangin'
Hangin' from a galla's tree?
Yes, I have brought you hope
And I have paid your fee
For I've not come to see you hangin'
Hangin' from a galla's tree.

The audience claps enthusiastically.

Next Freddy comes out and stands on the stage grinning bashfully and fiddling with his hat like a frontiersman. In his aw-shucks twang, he tells a ghost story about a man stranded in the mountains in a snowstorm. Then he pulls a wooden calf from behind the curtain and swings a rope, lassoing the wooden animal. The rope makes a whooshing sound as it seems to hover in the air, making odd shapes, until it lands with a "thunk" around the neck of the carved animal. The audience applauds again.

Celestina comes out, wearing her short white crinoline skirt. Cornelius squeezes Euphonia's hand. Celestina swings her hips from side to side before she starts to sing a sad ballad, "My Bonny My Lass." Women in the audience wipe their eyes as she warbles through all the verses. Then everyone applauds.

Then she says, "Now I'd like to sing you another song. If you don't want to hear it, if you're the bishop, the preacher, the old maid who ain't never had a lover, you best cover your ears."

Cornelius whispers, "Oh no." He looks around and sees the leering grins on the faces of men around him. Celestina's dress is too low over her bosom, and she pulls off her gossamer shawl to expose her bare shoulders.

With her voice high as a squeak, she launches into a version of "A Sailor's Lament," which Cornelius thinks must be the mildest of the songs sung in New Orleans by drunken sailors too long at sea. In the song a woman named Salty Sal finds love among the sailors on the dock at New Orleans; and then finds more and more love. To his great relief, Celestina leaves off the raunchy last verse which as he remembers is about Sal finding love with an entire fleet. The rest of it was innuendo. He's relieved when she curtsies, giggling, to the audience and disappears behind the red curtain, the audience—the men at least—laughing and clapping enthusiastically. The women titter with their handkerchiefs pressed to their lips.

"Well, maybe no one will guess I sponsored the show," he whispers to Phony.

Jenny comes out from behind the curtain, an inky-black vision in the yellow dress Cornelius remembers. It was Stephanie's wedding dress;

she wore a pink ribbon around her waist, he recalls, on the day she stood beside him at a Methodist camp meeting and a preacher pronounced them man and wife.

It's the same dress Jenny wore when he put her on a steamer headed for free soil, back in 1841, after he rescued her from the jail in Vidalia. Against her skin, the soft yellow fabric looks almost white. She walks slowly to the center of the stage, the audience watching her raptly.

After a moment of silence, Jenny speaks.

"My name was once Abena. I was born —" she pauses—"an African child. Free-born in a far-off land."

Cornelius looks around. How will the people of Natchez take this message?

"And I am still a free woman now." She reaches into her bodice and takes out her freeing paper and holds it up for the audience to see, walking slowly from one side of the stage to the other. Then she carefully folds it and slips it back into her bodice.

"There was a day when my brother Kofi and I were playin' in the forest, makin' a town out of the sand along a little creek bank there. This was in Dahomey, where the king has an army of women warriors, and there are witch-women who cast spells and hexes. If any of you ladies need a hex on your mother-in-law, or your friend who gossips behind your back, or your husband who cats around, you need to go to Dahomey and find one o' them witch-women." The audience titters.

And then she tells her dream, how a woman named Esi looked for her children until she couldn't look any more. Until her dream went black. As she speaks, Jenny reaches into the satchel she has set on the stage and takes out a wide strip of green cloth. She wraps it around her head, covering her hair. Then she takes out a long length of red fabric and slowly turns, wrapping herself in it, as she speaks. She wraps it under her armpits. The limp fabric of her yellow dress flattens as she encases herself, and when she turns again, she is transformed into an African woman, her dark face a perfect oval above the red African dress.

The audience is silent. After a moment she smiles at them, her teeth wide and white, as she bows. When the applause begins, the sound rolls down the rows in loud thundery waves.

CHAPTER THIRTY-TWO

Summer 1850

THE MAN WHO GETS OFF THE STEAMER *Star of Ohio* at Natchez-Under-The-Hill on a steamy morning in July 1850 looks around curiously as a middle-aged woman waves frantically at him.

"Walker! Walker Jackson! Yoo-hoo over here!!"

He walks over to where she's waiting in line to board the same steamer for its downriver voyage.

"Miz Crawford," he says. He nods at the tall young man standing next to her. "It's mighty nice to see you."

"Well, Walker!" she says. "Where have you been? I haven't seen you around town for the longest!"

"I been gone a few years, ma'am," he says.

"You remember my boy Michael," she says, indicating the sullen young man standing next to her. "We're headed down to Baton Rouge to see my sister Lorene and her family."

"I do remember you mentionin' her. And are all your family well?"

"They are. Walker, you are still wearin' that coat I gave you when Michael was just a boy."

Walker grins. "This coat's always been my favorite, ma'am, and it's so well made. I've took real good care of all them clothes you gave me. I'm mighty appreciative. Mighty appreciative."

"You gonna be back here in Natchez from now on?" she asks.

"I might be. I ain't sure what my plans are exactly."

"Oh, I remember how proud you was when you got your freein' paper from Alcie Blanchard. It was good of Miss Alcie to let Walker buy himself out, wasn't it, Michael?"

Michael mumbles, "Yes'm," shuffling his feet around and looking at the ground.

"We're sending Michael to the University of Louisiana next year," Mrs. Crawford says. "He's gonna study to be a lawyer."

"That's mighty nice, Missus. I know he'll do very well. Very well."

The line starts to move and she says, "Well, I can't help you with any more clothes. You see how tall Michael's got."

Walker smiles. "Yes'm. But I'm still very appreciative for the ones you gave me."

As the line for the steamer begins to move, Mrs. Crawford flutters her handkerchief at him while Michael mumbles something under his breath. Walker stands for a moment watching them go. Yes, he remembers Mrs. Crawford cleaning out her boy's closet; dressing sharp in Michael's clothes helped him become the Mayor of Natchez. She still seems like a decent old woman, but Michael looks like trouble. He'll probably make a good lawyer, though.

Walking up Silver Street, he thinks about the encounter. He didn't mind Mrs. Crawford, even though it grated him a little to act so thankful for a twelve-year-old's castoff outgrown clothes. *You have to act grateful*, he thinks, *because you're back in slave-land. You knew that before you came back.*

He whistles a little under his breath, thinking it sure would be nice if somebody would offer him a lift up to Carefree, or at least part of the way. He sticks out his thumb.

On Main Street several buggies with plenty of space rumble past him without stopping. Then one does stop.

"Where goin'?" a man in a black suit asks.

"Carefree," he says

The man motions him to jump on the back, and he does. Then Walker calls over his shoulder, "Sir, ain't you Father Maercru?"

"I am."

"I'm Walker Jackson," he says. "I used to know Adrien, used to see him around town and such like. I was sure sorry when I heard he got kilt."

The priest looks around at him, surprised. Then he nods and shakes the reins and the buggy rumbles up toward the Woodville Road.

Jenny walks into the kitchen as Walker finishes eating the fricassee Dancy cooked. He stands up and wipes his mouth on a towel.

She stares at him.

"Hello, Jenny," he says.

She walks over slowly to him, holding out her hand. "Walker? Is that you?"

"Yes, it's me. I'm back."

"Let me touch you. I always knew you'd come back. I had a feeling. But seein' you now—it's like seein' a ghost."

He gazes at her. "You lookin' older, Jenny. How old are you now?"

"I'm twenty-seven. I can hardly believe it's you."

"You ain't married, are you?"

"No, 'course I ain't. I figured I was married to you."

"Well, I'm glad to hear that. So you knew I'd come back one day, didn't you?"

"I thought you would, if you could. How'd you get out of slavery?"

"Oh—it took me a while, but I did it. You got time to hear a long story, I'll tell you."

She holds both his hands in hers. "I got time."

They sit together at the table. Walker shoves his plate to one side and Dancy takes it. "Jenny, I am so happy to see you." He leans over and kisses her.

"I'm goin' out," Dancy says. "Y'all got a lot to say to each other." She goes out into the bright day.

Walker puts his arm around her shoulder. "Jenny, after I got sold off in Vicksburg—"

She puts her finger up to his lips. "Walker, don't talk about that. I vowed I never would speak of it again in my whole life."

He nods. "Okay. So I went to Texas, but I wasn't much good in the cane fields. Then I got sold to a man in New Orleans who was needin' a valet. And I was glad t' be sold to him, 'cause I sure didn't like that cane field, and I figured takin' care of a man's pants and his top hat was right down my alley. He was Duke Paul, from Germany, just travellin' around the country, he said; he wanted to see the sights. So after we stayed in New Orleans a while, me pressin' his pants and brushin' his beaver hat and layin' out his cufflinks, the Duke got tired of New Orleans society—they was always some lady tryin' to marry 'im off to her daughter or her niece—but I could tell the Duke weren't the marryin' kind. So we headed out west. It'd take all day to tell you about the things we seen out there in Indian land. You wouldn't hardly believe it. We rode a steamboat clear up the Missouri River as far as we could take it. And every night the Duke would write down in his diary what we seen that day. It was somethin'."

"Walker, I can hardly believe you're here."

"I told you I'd be back."

She nods. "You did, but I didn't think you could come back. I was afraid you was lost in some canefield, sweatin' dawn to night."

"Well, there was times I was sweatin' all right, 'cause New Orleans can get pretty hot. But what about you? Where'd you end up?"

She swallows. "Well, a man named Milton Crum bought me and took me to be a housemaid right there in Vicksburg, only about a mile from your mammy's house. I used t' go see her every Sunday on my half-day off. Have you seen Minnie? Is she all right?"

"She died, Jenny. Just last year. It hurt my heart so much that I missed her."

"Walker, she was good to me. The things she told me was what made me think I had to get out of slavery. And I had to get Rosabel out too."

"Where is Rosabel?"

"She's in the house with Coella. She's learnin' how to read and write. You'll be surprised how big she is. She's almost nine years old."

"I can't hardly believe that."

"When I was at the Crums's, I knew Milton Crum was a bad man, the way he kept lookin' at me all the time. So I got Cooper to bring me down here. We just snuck off, and then Cooper went back. I tried to tell him he ought t' stay here, that Mister Cornelius would get him his freein' paper, but he wouldn't do it. How is Cooper? Is he all right?"

"He's all right. He's got hisself a wife and a baby boy."

"Oh, that's good. How'd you get out of slavery?"

"Oh, well, the Duke and me, we ended up in California. It's free soil. Jenny, there's things goin' on out there you wouldn't believe. Here, I'll show you." He opens his satchel and brings out a small bag. He opens it, and a handful of shiny little rocks tumble out into his palm.

"Jenny," he whispers, "this here's gold. Real gold, not fools' gold. And it's worth a fortune. The Duke and me, we panned a little, just for fun, to see if we could do it, and I panned out this much. The Duke got some too."

"Then the Duke said he figured he might as well let me go, since there wasn't no place for slaves out there. The other prospectors didn't want slaves helpin' their masters get rich, so they took one look at my brown face and didn't like what they saw. But I want t' go back, Jenny. You, me, and Rosabel, let's go to California. It's free soil."

The steamer *Martha* is waiting at dawn the next morning as Cornelius drives Jenny and Walker down to Natchez-Under-The-Hill. Rosabel sits between them with her feet propped on her satchel, which is stuffed with all her possessions, and her spelling book. Jenny's satchel is in the back.

Euphonia stood on the gallery and watched them go. Jenny looked back and waved, thinking how pretty Phony looked from this distance. Maybe her looks are coming back, with the way her scars are fading. And since she's had Jack, her features have softened, and she looks rounder; all her dresses are pulling a little tight.

This really is goodbye, Cornelius thinks as he lifts Rosabel down and stands her on her feet. He stands near the gangplank and watches them get on. Jenny reclaimed herself by going on the *Merry May*; her youth returned, something she was entitled to. Whatever future she might find in California belongs to her, and slavery won't be part of it.

He watches them until they go to the front deck and stand at the railing. In his pocket some gold pieces jingle.

"I know you don't need these, sir," Walker had said as they prepared to leave Carefree. "But I'd be pleased if I could leave you some."

"You're right, I don't need them," Cornelius said, as the shiny gold bits rested in his palm.

"But you might need them on the trip."

"I've got plenty," Walker said. "You get out to Californy way, you come see Jenny and me."

"I'll do that."

"We'll get Rosabel to write to you and give you our address. We're gonna get her to teach us to write, too."

Headed back up to Carefree after the steamer has pulled out, Cornelius looks up at the rising sun, a smudge of light behind a string of gray clouds. Jenny's gone for good this time, he thinks. Once again his household will be a changed place. Maybe he'll run for the legislature next year. He's been toying with the idea. He knew John Landerson considered it. Cornelius could pick up the mantle. Natchez needs a good representative, and the state could use the ministrations of a quiet abolitionist. It would be good for people to see that abolitionists don't have horns.

Yes, he'll consider that. Because he knows a person has to seize the moment, and not wait for whatever else may be out there in the ether, about to happen, that you can't foresee. The Mississippi legislature may be his future. Will the party bosses support him? They might. He's well-known in Natchez, after all, the proprietor of Carefree, a man with a handsome wife and two sons; and no slaves. None at all.

Considering his future, Cornelius drives his empty buggy up Silver Street and then east toward Carefree. Phony will be waiting for him in the dining room, wearing one of her pretty dresses, and if he's lucky, Thomas and Jack will be there too, little boys with sweet faces and tousled hair, and when he comes in they'll look up at him with shining eyes.

Euphonia is halfway up the stairs in the late afternoon when she sees the ghosts. She's always known they're hovering in the house somewhere, but silent as they are, and evasive, they're always gone before she's been able to give them a form. But before her on the stairs stand two women she recognizes: Josephine Coqterre and her daughter Stephanie, both of them dressed in shimmery taffeta dresses from Miss Dolores's Shoppe of Finery. Her own pearl necklace—didn't that go to the bottom of the river?—is around Josephine's neck, and her gold earrings dangle from Stephanie's ears. They scent each other like cats do, and then float away into the air of the upstairs hallway.

Phony stares into the shaft of sunlight falling into the hall. She's always known ghosts are thieves, and show-offs too, if they get a chance to be. Will they always be here, in the closets, or up by the ceiling in the parlor? Who knows how many there are? She turns around and goes back downstairs; doesn't she feel a warmth in the air, where they passed through?

In the parlor Cornelius is sitting on the sofa reading the *Gazette,* catching up on the political news, no doubt. He'll run for the legislature and get himself elected, and her place will be here in Natchez, running a big house.

He doesn't believe in ghosts. Well, she knows something he doesn't. And since she started up the stairs a few moments ago, she's thought of something she can do while he's off in Jackson, politicking. There's no role for a wife over there in Jackson. But on the other side of Natchez, her former friend Deedee Roxwood owns a house called Camellia Run, and she rents out bedrooms to tourists and charges a pretty penny, because according to Deedee there's a ghost who comes down the stairs every night at two in the morning. Oh, her guests can hardly wait to open their wallets and pay so they can peep out of the bedroom door in their nighties and underpants to catch a glimpse of the shade that's floating down the stairs.

Deedee used to be in the circle of wives who came to Carefree, to gossip in the parlor while Euphonia made sure the petit-fours were iced and the coffee steaming hot. After May disappeared, the circle of wives did too. Euphonia has former friends now.

Well, she has shades, and after seeing Josephine and Stephanie she knows they don't mind showing themselves. She could rent out the upstairs bedrooms, and the added surprise will be that the guests won't know which shade they're going to get, because Phony suspects there are several. She'll have to caution the guests to hide their jewelry and keep their suitcases locked, but that will just add to the thrill. And the money she takes in will be something she can keep for herself.

It suddenly seems so obvious that this is what she should do. A woman needs her own income, no matter how generously her husband opens his wallet. She'll have her own wallet now.

Cornelius has grown even more handsome as he's gotten older. That will help him in politics. When she comes into the parlor, he looks up and starts to say something, but when he sees the expression on her face he folds the newspaper and sets it on the table.

THE END